Long Road Home

JoAnn Ross

1

FREEDOM. FOR THE first time in too many years, Sawyer Murphy was doing things his own way. In his own time. In this wild, western land he loved. *This home.*

When summer arrived, fishermen would stand in Black Bear River's rapids, casting for rainbow trout. Come fall, as colorful leaves scattered over rocks and water, bright pink salmon—which provided a buffet for the bears the river was named for—would swim upstream to their annual spawning grounds. In winter, it would become a ribbon of blue ice framed by a blanket of glistening snow.

This time of year, as the land stirred from its deep winter's sleep, the tips of ponderosa pines shone a bright Kelly green from new needle growth, while trees whose limbs had spent the past months bare and cold were sporting coats of spring leaves. The river was running fast, fed by snowmelt flowing from Modoc Mountain, one of the peaks in the Cascade Volcanic Arc. There'd been a time, long ago during the Ice Age, when the ice and snow on the mountain had been up to three hundred feet deep.

Now, as it rushed down through wildflower-brightened meadows and evergreen forests, the water refreshed. Renewed. In the same way being back in this beautiful wilderness land he loved had always renewed Sawyer.

But not today.

A flash of sunlight hit the water, triggering a rapid-fire series of flaming images that flung him back to another mountain, thousands of miles away. As fast as it had struck, the flashback dissolved, and he was back on the Oregon riverbank.

Sawyer shook his head to clear it. Pressed his fingers into his eyes. When he took them away, he saw a woman headed toward him. Seemingly at one with her horse, Austin Merrill rode as if she'd been born in the saddle, which she'd almost been. Her father had stuck her on the back of a gentle trail mare before she'd been old enough to walk.

She stopped at the boundary between their two families' ranches. When they came together, as they had so many times over so many years, past and present collided.

Austin's family had owned Green Springs Ranch as long as his had settled the Bar M. Not only a neighbor, she'd also been, aside from his brothers, his best friend.

When they'd been children, they'd run free through meadows and woods, swung from a rope tied to a tree limb over the river swimming hole, screeching like banshees as they plunged into the icy water. They'd gone out with flashlights, patrolling dampened grass for night crawlers to use to catch the rainbow trout Sawyer's mother would fry to a golden brown in an old iron skillet.

They'd both begun having success on the local rodeo circuit at a young age, and although he'd watched her practice racing those barrels, by the summer after they'd graduated middle school, things had begun to shift. The wild-child tomboy who'd been as close as his brothers had, seemingly overnight, turned into a girl with shiny hair the color of winter wheat and eyes as blue as the wide western sky. She'd grown taller, and how had he never noticed that her legs, tanned to gold dust by the sun, were so coltishly long and smooth?

One day, while they were picking wild blackberries, a strap had slipped off her shoulder onto her arm. As he'd stared at that delicate white strap against her sun-gilded skin, Sawyer became all too aware that, beneath her sleeveless blue-and-white gingham blouse, Austin Merrill had breasts.

By the time school started up again, her body was showing slender curves that tormented both his waking and sleeping hours.

He wasn't the only one who'd noticed the change. When she'd walked down the hall of Eaglecrest High School, heads would turn and hungry eyes would follow. Since his hormones had revved up by then, Sawyer knew exactly what those other guys were thinking. And hated every one of them. Especially since, as a lowly freshman who still hadn't grown into what would become his six feet, two inches of height, he was definitely outgunned by those upperclassmen who'd put on sinew and muscle and had perfected their slick, woman-seducing moves.

If his first year of high school had been a time of agony, their sophomore year became even worse because Austin had dipped one of her pink-tipped toes (that new, shiny polish being another thing that had driven him crazy) into Eaglecrest's dating pool. Just the sight of her, sitting next to Brody Ames as his pickup passed the school bus Sawyer had been riding, was nearly enough to make his head explode.

Although time had passed at a glacial speed in those days, finally Sawyer's sixteenth birthday had arrived. After leaving the DMV with his driver's license, he'd driven over to Green Springs Ranch to pick Austin up for the party his father and grandparents were throwing for him.

She'd seemed puzzled at why she couldn't just ride her horse over to the Bar M, as she'd been doing for years, but apparently sensing it was important to him, she'd flashed her sunny Austin smile and agreed. Unfortunately, as she climbed up into the front seat, the white shorts revealed a hint of panty line that had given him a boner even harder than the one inspired by the Miss August centerfold from the *Playboy* he'd stolen from Ryan's stash. A situation that wasn't helped when she casually put her boots up on the dashboard, making it impossible to ignore those long tanned legs. With the scent of her soap or shampoo or whatever it was that had her smelling like peaches causing his head to spin, Sawyer was relieved when he managed to pull off the short drive without running off the road.

His master plan, carefully thought out over the past months, had been to ask her to a movie at the Roundup Drive-In, where, maybe, in the privacy of a darkened car, he'd get lucky and she'd let him touch those breasts he'd been thinking of for what was beginning to feel like his entire life. All evening the words he'd rehearsed in front of the bathroom mirror ran in a continuous loop in his mind. So much so that he'd found it hard to concentrate on anyone or anything else going on around him.

And then, after the marble sheet cake with his name written over it surrounded by sixteen candles had been eaten, and the remnants of chocolate fudge ice cream were melting in the churn, he'd chickened out.

Fortunately, she'd been so merrily chatting away about the party, she didn't seem to notice that he'd gone mute as a stone on the drive back to Green Springs. He'd have to try again. The Roundup didn't close for the season until after the Labor Day showing. There was still time.

The problem was, back whenever they'd talk about their future, Austin always wondered why anyone would ever want to leave River's Bend. She had no desire to chase rainbows when her pot of gold could be found right here. Working on Green Springs, getting married, having babies she'd watch grow up beneath the wide Oregon sky.

Which was why, every time he'd gotten the nerve to make his move, Sawyer's logical mind would override his body, and later, he'd realize, his heart, and bring up all the reasons the odds of a serious relationship surviving were about even with winning Powerball. Even if they could stay together until graduation, he still had four years of college, and after that, military service ahead of him. At least that's what he'd kept telling himself.

But the simple truth was that he'd been a coward. What if she hadn't felt the same? Not wanting to risk the humiliation of her shooting him down, which could threaten their lifelong friendship, he'd kept his mouth shut.

He *had* kissed her. Once. It had been two years ago, outside the hospital where his father had been flown for urgent bypass surgery. Forgetting where they were, and letting his little head do the thinking for his big head, he'd pulled her tight against him and taken her mouth.

Hot. Freaking. Damn. It had been as if a dam had burst. Austin had definitely kissed him back, digging her fingers into his shoulders, clinging to him, pressing against him, with an eager enthusiasm that had included some hot tangling of tongues.

He'd wanted her. Then and there, and damn the consequences. With his head spinning and his knee between her thighs, pressing against her *there*, Sawyer's lust-filled brain had scrambled to strategically war plan the mission logistics like the Marine Special Operations officer he was.

Where to go to get some privacy? How to get there since he didn't have wheels due to his brother Cooper picking him up from the airport? And why the hell hadn't he thought to buy a damn pack of condoms somewhere on the way from the airport to the hospital?

The intrusive scream of an ambulance racing down the street toward the ER had broken them apart and sent Sawyer crashing down to earth like he'd just done a HALO jump without a parachute.

It hadn't been the place. And, once again, he'd told himself that it damn well hadn't been the right time. Having witnessed too many wartime deaths, Sawyer wasn't about to ask her to sit around and wait for him to return to River's Bend safe and, please, God, in one piece.

As he'd flown back to Afghanistan, he'd assured himself that apologizing for what he'd called a momentary lapse was the right—the only possible—decision.

Which hadn't kept his heart from feeling bull stomped when, three weeks later, she'd emailed him with the news that she'd married some rodeo cowboy she'd met in Las Vegas while she and her dad had been there as stock contractors to the National Finals Rodeo.

Their correspondence had dropped off after that, during which time Sawyer had tried, and failed, to put her out of his mind. Then one day his brother, Cooper, had mentioned in one of his daily emails that Buck Merrill had come down with post-polio syndrome and was selling off his rodeo stock. Which meant, he'd suggested, that Austin's dad might be willing to lease some pastureland. If Sawyer was interested.

As sorry as he was to hear about Buck, Sawyer damn well was interested in the land. Then the good news/bad news got even better when his brother had tacked on the little bulletin that Austin had finally wised up and dumped her blacktop cowboy husband.

Stuck on a mountaintop in the Afghan Kush, he'd tested the waters by sending her what he hoped sounded like a casual Happy New Year email. He did not mention the husband.

She'd emailed right back, thanking him for thinking of her father. After two days of back-and-forth, while she'd only brushed over her divorce—which told him that she wasn't exactly weeping tears into her pillow over the breakup—she'd brought up the idea of him leasing the pasture that Merrill cattle had grazed for decades.

Sawyer had jumped at the opportunity, raising the offer she'd suggested. From what Cooper had said, money was tight around Green Springs Ranch, and even after he bought some stock from his own father, he had more saved up than he'd need.

Sitting on his helmet out in the middle of nowhere, for the first time in longer than he could remember, Sawyer was looking forward to the future.

Then he'd gotten called out on that clusterfuck of a mission that had changed everything.

2

"I'M SORRY I missed your party last night," she said as she pulled Blue, her blue roan mare, up beside his buckskin gelding he'd named Duke. For John Wayne, not any English royalty.

"No problem." Sawyer rubbed the back of his neck as he felt the damn walls closing in again. "We wouldn't have had that much time to talk, anyway."

His family's welcome home dinner at the Murphy's Bar M ranch had been a noisy, enthusiastic gathering of friends and family. Toby Keith, George Strait, and Dierks Bentley had belted out honky-tonk from hidden outdoor speakers, adding a country-western soundtrack to thick steaks sizzling on the grill and myriad conversations tumbling over each other like the river's water crashing over rocks during spring thaw. While he'd appreciated the turnout, Sawyer had found trying to keep up more exhausting than a day humping his gear over miles of Afghan goat trails.

His dad was a typical rancher, never using two words when one would do, so his official welcome home speech was short and to the point, but Dan Murphy's husky tone, and momentary brain fart when he'd lost his train of thought, revealed to everyone how relieved he was to have all three of his sons safely back from war.

Which was all it had taken to cause another shitload of guilt to come crashing down on Sawyer's head. What the hell had he done to deserve steak, music, beer with moisture dripping down the side of the bottle pulled from an old metal tub, and all those well-meaning folks who just wanted to talk? And talk. And effing talk. By the end of the evening, he'd decided that if one more person came up and thanked him for his service, he was going to tie cement blocks to his ankles and throw himself in the river.

"Still, I wanted to be there," she said. "I heard from Heather that you got a big turnout."

Heather was her best friend, whose husband had been like Sawyer's third brother back in the day. But that was then. And this was now, and sometime between Keith's "Courtesy of the Red, White, and Blue" and Aaron Tippin's "Where the Stars and Stripes and the Eagle Fly," Sawyer had decided that, in many ways, his life was proving to have been easier, and certainly less complicated, in Afghanistan than back here in the real world.

"Have you ever been to Grand Central Station at rush hour?" he asked.

Lips he'd tasted too many times in his dreams turned down. "You know I've never been east of Las Vegas."

Yeah. He knew that. If only the damn rodeo championships had been held in a state where it took more than a nanosecond to get legally married, he might have been able to stop her from getting herself hitched to the totally wrong guy.

The problem was, after how he'd treated her, there would have been a better chance of the Cascades morphing into the Big Rock Candy Mountains and Modoc Mountain erupting and sending streams of Jack Daniels trickling over the rocks than of her listening to why she shouldn't get married to anyone but him.

"I've never been to New York, either. But I'll bet last night's dinner came close. Seemed like nearly everyone in the basin showed up. Guess they couldn't pass up the Bar M's grass-finished rib eyes."

Her gaze swept over him. Then her generous lips curved. "Your dad could've served hot dogs, or no food at all, and the turnout would've been the same. You're a hometown hero, Sawyer. That's a big deal. Especially around these parts."

"I'm not a hero." The actions that had won him that silver star had not been born from heroism but from red-hot anger at having seen one too many men in his Marine Ranger unit killed by IEDs and ambushes. Just having it brought up again caused the hole inside Sawyer to grow larger.

"Well, you won't find many who agree with that, but I'm not going to ruin a lovely spring day by arguing." She flipped a blond braid over her shoulder. "Let's go look at the pastureland."

She leaned down and spoke a word into her horse's perked ear. An instant later, it took off like a shot, leaving Sawyer to follow.

Even caught off guard as he'd been, Sawyer quickly caught up. Together they galloped side by side along the river, then streaking along the dirt trail through the woods, their horses hitting their powerful stride as they raced across the rolling fields of breeze-bent meadow grass.

Five minutes later, they'd reached the pasture nestled up against the mountain lowlands. Austin might have edged him out by a nose. Or maybe he'd beat her. It was too close to tell. But for that brief time, Sawyer had felt . . . maybe not quite alive. But not exactly dead, either.

They reined in, slowing the horses before bringing them to a stop.

The grass was still winter short but greening up. The paddocks were empty, stretching out to the boundary line that separated their families' properties. Sawyer envisioned cattle—his cattle—grazing on rich green grass dotted with balls of sweet white clover and experienced something that vaguely felt like anticipation. Which came as a surprise after so many mornings waking up dreading the day. And the next. And the next.

"You've been away a long time," she reminded him unnecessarily. Like he hadn't had a countdown separation day calendar in his head for months? Especially since getting that email about her divorce, which meant he wasn't going to have to deal with living up close and personal with her husband. Watching some lucky bastard living the life he'd once hoped would be his.

But before he'd returned home, he'd had one last mission to fulfill. Promises to keep. Which he had, even if the past three months had felt like one long, unending act of contrition.

"Does it look the same as you remember?" she asked, breaking into memories of suffering too many pots of coffee, photo albums, and tearful hugs.

"Even better." After all the years spent in a dusty, barren landscape, the green pastures, foothills, and the glistening white mountain with its cap of snow were a bright, much welcome sight.

He glanced over at her and saw the concern in her eyes.

Was she worried he wouldn't lease it? Or worse yet, that he would? While leasing wasn't as bad as selling out, it had to sting to have someone else's herd grazing on pasture that had been in her family since both their four-times great-grandfathers had arrived at the river originally seeking gold.

"Are you sure you're okay with this?" Sawyer didn't have a plan B if she decided to back out of the deal, but felt he had to ask.

It was her turn to shrug. "It's not like it's being used. We sold off all the stock except the horses and Desperado last fall."

Desperado was a huge Hereford-Brahma cross-mix who'd been born to buck. It wasn't that he was vicious, but despite his sixteen-hundred-pound muscular bulk, he could spin quicker than a rattlesnake's strike. He was also smart enough to somehow sense a rider's moves, then pull a swift and effective counterattack to unseat him.

Many cowboys over the years had tried to ride Desperado. Only Sawyer had managed to last the full eight seconds, and while he'd enjoyed hearing the cheers of fans rock the rafters of the grandstand, he'd mostly credited his success to knowing the bull so well. And the bull knowing him. What most of those he'd sent flying into the air in under three seconds didn't realize was that, despite his name and reputation, the bull was docile as a newborn lamb when at home in Green Springs Ranch's pasture.

"Coop said you kept the wily old guy for breeding."

"That wily old guy just happens to be the gift that keeps on giving. He has prodigy throwing cowboys into the dirt from Canada, most U.S. states, through South America, to as far away as New Zealand."

"Green Springs was the best rodeo stock provider on

the circuit."

They'd always bred their rodeo horses and cattle with as much care as any Thoroughbred breeder aiming for a Triple Crown. Before his retirement, Desperado had been universally known as a class act. Not only did the bull not go after a downed rider, the way most tended to do, he actually appeared to try to avoid any fallen cowboy.

"Past tense being the definitive description," she said on a sigh. She tilted her hat a bit, shading her eyes from both the sun and his gaze. "One thing I've learned is that looking back into the rearview mirror doesn't do any good. Life moves on whether you're ready or not. As you undoubtedly know firsthand."

"Yeah. I do." He paused, giving a moment's thought to lost Marine Raider Battalion Spec Ops whose voices he could still hear in his head. Especially when he was lying in his rack, wide awake at zero-dark-thirty. "How's your dad doing today?"

The reason she'd given for not coming to the party was that her father had taken a fall. Sawyer's brother Ryan, River's Bend's sole doctor, had dropped by the ranch and checked the older man out before coming to the party. He'd reported that, while Buck Merrill was shaken, nothing was broken.

"Physically, he's okay. Though I do wish he'd let Ryan talk him into a wheelchair. Or at least a walker. He's so damn stubborn and prideful that he won't admit the cane just isn't working anymore."

"After battling off polio when he was a kid, it must suck for him to have it hit in what should be the prime of his life."

"It does. Especially since ranching is not only what he's

always done, it's *who* he's always been. And now that's being taken away from him." They'd been friends long enough that Sawyer heard what she wasn't saying and didn't need her to fill in the blanks.

"He's not happy about me leasing his land."

"It's not about you."

Her gaze moved out beyond the pasture, where shaggy evergreens climbed from the foothills up the snow-topped mountain rising majestically above them. Despite the slight bite in the air, the wedge of Canadian geese flying overhead on their way home was another sign of spring. Which wasn't any guarantee of warm weather, since snowfall in May, or even once flurries on the town's Fourth of July parade, wasn't unheard of in this part of the Cascades.

Being away had only reaffirmed Sawyer's belief that the best thing that had ever happened to his family was when Malachy Murphy discovered this homeplace while searching for gold in Black Bear River. And he knew Buck Merrill felt the same way. Gold dust might glitter and, if a guy was lucky, could bring riches. But that wealth was easily spent, too often quickly gone. While the real treasure, the land, was forever.

"If it were anyone else leasing the pasture, it'd be even harder on him," she said. "But you're practically family, and to be perfectly honest, we need the money. Still, I can't deny that he's having trouble dealing with the idea of *any* cattle grazing on it but our own. He's convinced that he'll be back on the circuit soon."

"You sure that's not possible?" As much as Sawyer wanted this prime piece of land, and had intentions of offering to buy it and the neighboring section if Buck Merrill ever was willing to sell, no way did he want it at the expense of hurting a man who'd always been like an uncle. The bond between the Merrill and Murphy families was as long and wide as the river, even including a scattering of marriages between second and third cousins over the generations.

"Anything's possible," Austin allowed, without sounding at all optimistic. "But I wouldn't bet the ranch on it. Literally."

She shook off the complex brew of emotions that had her eyes glistening in the spring sun. *Cowgirls don't cry.* Sawyer knew her father had drilled that edict into her from the cradle. Although at first glance, a man's attention might be captured by the silky blond hair she'd inherited from her Scandinavian mother, her blue eyes, lush pink lips, and slender-as-a-willow body, inside, Austin Merrill was as tough as any Marine Sawyer had ever served with. He also knew that inside that protective outer shell was a soft and closely guarded heart.

There'd been a time when he would have put his arms around her, held her tight, and assured her that everything would be all right. That he'd *make* it right. The same way he'd ached to unbreak her heart back when they were seven. Which, he'd belatedly come to realize, was when he'd lost his heart to the pretty blond cowgirl next door.

But hell, not only had *he* been the one to break her heart years later with the lame apology and lie about the kiss not really meaning anything, these days Sawyer was having enough trouble straightening out his own life.

He sure as hell didn't have any business messing with anyone else's. Especially hers.

"I've got some money set aside," he said. "It's yours if you need it."

She tossed up her chin in a gesture he'd seen countless times over the years. "We'll be okay." Knowing that her pride went deep to the bone, just as her dad's did, Sawyer wasn't surprised by her response. "Especially now that I'm no longer paying Jace's hefty travel expenses."

"I'm sorry the marriage didn't work out." Which was only partly true. Sawyer was sorry as hell that she'd had to go through a divorce. But he couldn't deny that he wasn't at all unhappy to have the guy out of the picture.

"It was a mistake from the beginning. I acted impulsively and paid the price." She squared her shoulders, and he watched the familiar glint of determination flash in her eyes. "But now I'm moving on, turning the page, starting a new chapter, whatever cliché you want to call it."

"Sounds as if we're both pretty much in the same situation," Sawyer said.

"And back together in the same place," she agreed.

Their eyes met. And held for just a moment too long. As the years spun back, his fingertips practically tingled with an urge to reach out and trace her face.

And then what?

And wasn't that the effing sixty-four-thousand-dollar question?

Her mare, apparently bored with standing still, began to impatiently sidestep. Seeming grateful for the interruption, Austin picked up the reins and began heading toward the cabin. "Are you sure you want to stay in here?"

"If you'd rather I throw my gear in the bunkhouse—"

"No." She shook her head. "I just thought you'd be staying with your family on the Bar M."

"With the honeymooners?" It had been a little weird to see his widowed dad acting like a besotted newlywed.

Weird but nice.

"I think they're sweet."

"And I'm happy for them, but I think it'd be better if we all have our own space." He'd come down to the kitchen last night for one last beer, only to find Mitzi seated on the kitchen counter, his dad standing in front of her, and although—thank you, God!—they were both still dressed, it looked as if clothes could start flying any moment.

"Good point. And of course you're welcome to the cabin. It's been empty since Jim, Janet, and the kids moved out six months ago."

"Coop told me that you found Jim a job at a cow-and-calf operation in Bozeman. That was nice of you."

"It was the least I could do. The Longs were like family, but there wasn't enough work here any longer to make the situation viable. He says they're happy in Montana, so that's something. Meanwhile, we've extra furniture in the main house you're welcome to have."

The Green Springs Ranch compound consisted of a main ranch house with dual wings to allow for multiple generations to enjoy breathing room while living beneath a single roof. The cabin she'd offered him had been built for the ranch foreman's family. There was also a bunkhouse that, during the ranch's heyday, had been home to three full-time hands and other seasonal ones. But that was now empty.

"Don't worry about it. I'll work something out. And it's not like I've got much gear to deal with."

After being screened by the command transition counselor and attending the mandatory separations brief and seminar, Sawyer had driven out of the main gate and headed straight to a Walmart, where he'd bought a cheap canvas duffle to replace the sea bag he'd been lugging around for years. He'd picked up the straw Stetson at the Boot Barn not far from Camp Pendleton. A Marine might be a Marine all of his life, but for now, Sawyer was past ready to wrangle cows instead of terrorists.

"I wouldn't have expected your dad to get into holistic ranching." He looked out at Austin's beloved horses contentedly grazing in other pastures. "Especially since he wasn't selling all that much stock for food consumption."

She laughed. "Why would you be at all surprised? Just because of all his complaining about tree huggers and having bitched when Rachel took down that old sign Johnny Mott had hung in the front window of the New Chance offering a spotted-owl breakfast special?"

"He might bitch about tree huggers," Sawyer said as their horses walked side by side through the grass. "But deep down he loves the land. If Merrills hadn't taken such good care of this place over the generations, it wouldn't have survived."

"Dad's always believed in leaving a light footprint. But you know as well as I do that ranching isn't the most secure way to make a living."

"The best way to make a small fortune in ranching is to start out with a big one."

"True." She smiled at the familiar axiom. "Green Springs has survived by running a tighter ship than most. Good breeding records allowed us to sell off the majority of steers and calves to other stockmen. Any that weren't rodeo quality went to conventional food markets. I'm probably not spilling any deep, dark secrets by admitting Dad initially scoffed when your father decided to go grass-fed, grass-finished organic."

"A lot of ranchers get stuck in tradition, running their spreads the way they've always been run." While earning his B.S. in range management from OSU, Sawyer had studied both the good and the bad.

"True. But your father was generous enough to share his profit ratios, and even a man as stubborn and set in his ways as Dad could see the benefit of not having to buy truckloads of feed every year by changing over to grass finishing.

"He also noticed that even without automatic immunizations, Bar M cattle weren't getting sick because the nutrients they get from the grass and legumes your dad grows boosts your cattle's natural immunity. Borrowing that idea offered us additional savings. Not to mention easing concerns of stock getting sick just when we were due to deliver a contracted number to a big rodeo."

"Green Springs has always had a sterling reputation."

"It has," she agreed with understandable pride. "But we always needed to keep a lot more extra steers on hand, just in case. After we switched over, on the rare occasion we did get a sick animal, we separated it from the herd, treated it until it was healthy again, then shipped it out for the general retail market.

"More and more folk are starting to take notice that not only is holistic good for the planet, it's good for the bottom line. Which, in turn, allows more families to stay on their ranches instead of selling out to big-city developers."

"Or movie stars," Sawyer said, thinking of an A-list action star who'd been buying up nearby land as if God wasn't making any more of it.

Which, oh, yeah. He wasn't.

"Oh, please don't even bring Hollywood wannabe cowboys up with Dad," she said. "Nothing gets his dander up more than people who can afford to offer millions for their own private paradise, never minding that they've no need to make a living off it. Which drives up property values and forces those struggling to live off their land to have to go to work in town."

"Which our families have avoided."

"So far," Austin qualified. "Not that the Bar M has any reason to worry."

"The ranch is doing well." And although Sawyer knew that he was the logical Murphy son to take over operations, he wasn't in any hurry. Not only did he want to prove himself capable of running his own spread, he was looking forward to his dad being in the cattle business for a very long time yet.

They'd reached the cabin.

Austin had never been much of a toucher. It was well known throughout the basin that just because his only child happened to have an extra X chromosome, that hadn't kept Buck Merrill from raising his daughter to be as tough as any boy. She'd never been coddled or pampered. Except, when Buck wasn't watching, by Winema Clinton, the brisk and busy housekeeper who ran the domestic side of the ranch.

But as they pulled up in front of the cabin, which, like the main house and bunkhouse, had been built with lumber grown and milled on the property, Austin reached between them and placed a slender hand on his thigh.

"I'm so glad you're home. I was worried sick. I don't think I ever prayed harder in my life."

There'd been a time, back during their teen years, when

Sawyer had teased her about finding a church on Sunday morning in whatever town she happened to be in while traveling the rodeo circuit. But that was before he'd discovered the old war axiom was true: there weren't that many atheists in foxholes. Or when you were dragging your butt over rocks out in the open in the Helmand Province, a perfect open target for some Taliban sniper's bullet.

"Believe me," he said as his leg tightened beneath her light touch, "you weren't alone."

Austin gave him a long, direct look. "You've changed."

Sawyer wasn't going to lie. Although his dad had expected all three of his sons to pull their weight on the Bar M, Sawyer had been the one with a wild streak.

"Life happens."

"Now there's a pithy observation," she said dryly as she took her hand back. "We'd better check the place out. Give you time to change your mind."

"Not going to happen."

It wasn't as if he didn't have other choices. He'd been invited to partner with his dad while staying in the big house, which, as he'd just told Austin, wasn't a choice his father, the new Mrs. Murphy, or Sawyer would've honestly wanted.

If he was going to settle back into River's Bend, he needed to make his own decisions and his own mistakes. And hopefully climb his way out of this deep, dark pit he'd landed in before he ended up becoming one more statistic.

Leasing these Green Springs pastures seemed like a good start.

3

"ARE YOU SURE you're going to be all right?" Austin asked her father. "With Winema away visiting her grandchildren?"

"I told you, I'm going to be fine," Buck Merrill grumbled from his saddle-brown leather recliner as he watched a rerun of an old bull riding competition. "I just had a little tumble. Nothing like falling off a horse. You don't have to treat me like I'm a damn toddler who needs a babysitter."

"That's not what I'm doing."

Grizzled brows dove over eyes framed by deep lines that came from years spent outdoors. "Aren't you?"

"I worry."

"Don't."

They'd had this argument too many times to count. And it never did any good, so Austin had no idea why she kept trying. Perhaps, she considered, because although her dad had forgotten more than most ranchers knew about raising cattle and quarter horses, he refused to read any of the PPS information Ryan Murphy had given her. Or the many articles she'd stayed up late into the night researching online. In this case, he was behaving exactly like a stubborn toddler, determined to have his own way come hell or high water.

"The lasagna's in the fridge. Just stick it in for an hour at three hundred fifty degrees. I'll be home by nine."

"And I'll be in the sack by then, so you might as well stay as long as you like." They might have sold off the stock, but Buck Merrill would probably keep rancher's hours until he took his last breath. Which Austin dearly hoped would be years and years from now.

Just the thought of losing this man, whose crusty exterior hid a warm and generous heart, had her eyes swimming. She leaned over the torn arm of the recliner and kissed his bristly cheek. "I love you, Dad."

"Have fun at your wine party." He might not say the *L* word, but the gravelly huskiness of his voice assured Austin that she was, indeed, well loved.

"It's a book club."

His chuckle, as rough as a mile of ungraded gravel road, was one she didn't hear all that often since his old polio nemesis, which had been lurking all these years inside him, had made an unexpected and unwelcome appearance. "Sure it is." The warmth in his eyes belied the gruffness of his tone. "You're a good girl, sweetheart. You deserve a night out. Even if you want to insist it's all about the book."

"It is," she said, even though they both knew that wasn't totally true. Ranch life could be a lonely life. Even lonelier for women. Austin valued her time with friends as much as she did whatever book the group would agree to read every month.

The drive to the Bar M was less than five minutes house to house. During the day, she might have walked or ridden Blue, her roan quarter horse, but tonight, with a new moon and rain on the horizon, she drove the ranch pickup that had turned over a hundred thousand miles long ago but was still running. That was the first cardinal rule of ranching: you either made do, did over, or did without. The Dodge Ram might look as banged-up as an old bull rider, but it got her where she needed to go, and that was all that mattered.

Although the meetings changed locations every month, most of the women who'd begun the group had remained, becoming close friends. Jenna Janzen ran the Chapter One Bookstore; Layla Longstreet was a nurse practitioner who also was in charge of Ryan Murphy's medical office; Rachel Hathaway was engaged to marry Cooper Murphy this summer; and real estate agent Mitzi Murphy had married Sawyer's father, Dan, this past Valentine's Day.

Rounding out the group was Heather Campbell, whose husband, Tom, was a large-animal vet, while she was an avid gardener who sold her flowers and vegetables at the local farmers' market. The past few years she'd begun to gain a reputation around the Northwest for her weaving, which, she'd told Austin, allowed her to have the best of two worlds: a career doing what she loved while being able to be a stay-at-home mom to her twelve-year-old daughter and seven-year-old son.

Heather had been Austin's best friend all their lives. And Tom, who'd grown up on a small, struggling ranch that his parents had sold a few years ago, could always be found hanging out with the Murphy boys. Sawyer in particular.

"Oh, yum!" Jenna said as she took the container and lifted the lid. "You brought brownies!"

"I'm trying out a new recipe." Along with breeding

Desperado and training and selling her horses, Austin picked up much-needed extra income baking for Chapter One and the New Chance Café. "They're dark fudge with a caramel sea salt frosting."

"I swear," Layla said, "you don't ever have to read any of the books we're supposed to be discussing as long as you show up with your unbelievable baked goods every month."

"I second that," Rachel said. "I can't wait to taste them. Your lemon meringue pie bars sell out like hotcakes. Actually, better than hotcakes," she amended. "Which is really saying something because the place is packed at breakfast."

For even longer than Austin had been alive, once local ranchers finished with early-morning chores, they'd driven into town for a hearty breakfast at the New Chance. Since Rachel had bought the café, they were not only getting the best food in all of Southern Oregon, they no longer had to risk food poisoning the way they had when the previous owner, Johnny Mott, had been in the kitchen.

"So," Heather said, "how did this afternoon with Sawyer go?"

"It was nice seeing him again," Austin said mildly, taking the glass of wine Rachel handed her. "Thanks."

Heather was not one to give up. "Just *nice?*"

"I think you'll like this Oregon rosé," Rachel said in a less-than-subtle attempt to rescue Austin. "It just said spring to me. It's complex, crisp, with flavors of peach, rhubarb, and the slightest edge of salinity."

"You read that off the bottle," Layla said. It was well known that while Rachel had aced her studies at New York's Culinary Institute of America before buying River's

Bend's New Chance Café, she'd flunked wine.

"I did not." Rachel laughed. "It's how Gabriel Lombardi described it when he came down from the Willamette Valley to sell me a case from his family's vineyards. I've learned to trust his advice. Although, to be honest, I would have bought it without the salesmanship because it's such a pretty pink color."

"It reminds me of spring apple blossoms," Jenna said.

"Speaking of spring," Heather pressed on, "we all know what men's fantasies turn toward during this time of year. So, I'm going to try again." She speared Austin with a look. "Well?"

"He's leasing the land."

Austin had mixed feelings about that. She didn't have any problem with a Murphy grazing cattle on Merrill land. But as much as they needed the money, she wasn't certain how she felt about Sawyer being so close after he'd already let her know, in no uncertain, heart-crushing terms, that the mind-blinding, toe-curling kiss they'd shared outside the hospital had merely been triggered by jetlag and stress about his dad's heart condition. And had had nothing to do with her. Really.

While she'd been wanting that kiss for as long as she'd been able to remember. Which had made his curt brush-off even more painful.

"So, he'll be living right there on the ranch with you."

"In the foreman's cabin," she clarified. "Which isn't exactly across the hall from my bedroom."

"More's the pity," Mitzi said, eyeing Austin over the rim of her glass. "How long has it been since you've had sex?"

"And solo doesn't count," Heather clarified.

"That's personal." Austin could feel the heat rising in her cheeks. No way was she going to admit that it had been so long she'd almost forgotten what it felt like. Though, being with Sawyer that afternoon had caused a lot of vivid sexual fantasies to come flooding back.

"I brought my copy of this month's book," she said, holding it up as a hopeful diversionary tactic. "With all the discussion question scenes highlighted. Who's ready to dive in?"

"Well, I think she just answered that sex question," Jenna drawled. "Obviously too long if you'd rather talk about fictional characters than a hottie like Sawyer Murphy."

"*These Three Words* is a wonderfully romantic book," Austin insisted.

While reading about the estranged couple who hadn't been able to say "I love you" to each other, although she knew it was impossible, she'd almost felt as if Holly Jacobs, the author, might have been writing about Sawyer and her. She'd gone through nearly an entire box of tissues before the hero and heroine finally got their happily-ever-after ending. Unlike hers and Sawyer's, which had gone up in flames, leaving behind a mess of cold ashes.

"It's a great emotional story about the need for couples to remind each other that they're loved," Mitzi said. "Dan, who, heaven knows, isn't the most talkative male God ever put down on this green earth, never turns off the light at night without telling me that he loves me. And I tell him the same thing.

"Of course," she added, "we were fortunate to have found each other later in life. After he'd loved and lost his first wife, and I'd certainly made my share of foolish romantic mistakes."

"I enjoyed the dynamics of the couple having moved their relationship from friendship to lovers, then marriage," Rachel said. "Which was totally different from Cooper and me. When we first met, I felt as if I'd been struck by lightning."

"Been there, done that, and have the divorce papers to show for it," Austin said dryly. "Not that it wasn't the right thing for you and Cooper," she said quickly, not wanting to throw cold water on what had turned out to be a true love match.

"It was obvious, when you had dinner at the Bar M your first night in town, that the chemistry between you and Cooper was off the charts," Mitzi told Rachel. "But the fire that gutted the New Chance's kitchen turned out to be a blessing in disguise, because while you were busy rebuilding, you had time to get to know each other before things got physical."

"True. There was also Scott to consider," Rachel said of her nine-year-old son. "Which kept me from jumping Cooper's bones every chance I got."

"Kids are the ultimate birth control," Heather agreed. "Which is why, thanks to you taking ours, Tom and I are going to be able to spend our anniversary in Ashland. Tom even surprised me with tickets to the Shakespearean Theater to see *Twelfth Night*."

"I'm happy to take the kids," Rachel said. "Scott's excited about the sleepover, and fortunately, since business has taken off, allowing me to hire both a sous chef and a manager last month, I'm finally able to take some evenings off." Her lips curved in a slow, secretive smile. "And maybe start working on making a baby brother or sister for

Scott."

And didn't that comment sidetrack everyone for the next ten minutes?

Finally, everyone settled down with their wine and brownies, which won unanimous approval. Then, contrary to what Austin's father had suggested, Jenna opened up the discussion of this month's book.

The conversation flowed easily as they shared insights and opinions about the fictional Gray and Addie's winding road to finding each other again.

"Do you think it's truly that easy?" Austin asked what she'd been asking herself for the past week since staying up way too late finishing the novel. "Would just saying, 'Here I am,' actually get a man to notice a woman? In that way?"

"Sweetie," Heather said, "if you're talking about Sawyer, he hasn't stopped noticing you since grade school, and from the way he kept watching the door all during the party, I'd bet nothing's changed."

Austin wasn't so sure Heather wasn't engaging in hopeful thinking. She certainly hadn't gotten that vibe from Sawyer when they'd checked out the pasture. In fact, he'd seemed more interested in Desperado than her. "I called to say we couldn't make it."

"That didn't seem to stop him from acting like a bird dog on the lookout for a covey of quail." Heather reached out and snagged a second brownie from the tray Rachel had set in the middle of the coffee table. "The problem, the way I see it, is neither one of you have ever actually done anything about what's obvious to everyone else in River's Bend."

Since not every woman in the room knew about the kiss, Austin chose not to share that debacle. "It's scary," she admitted.

"Hell, hon, love is always terrifying," Mitzi said. "Like I told Rachel when she and Cooper were doing their dance around the situation, I sure as hell wasn't looking to fall in love when I walked into the New Chance that day.

"But then I saw Dan and my heart went all pitty-pat"— she patted the front of a pearl-decorated peony-pink spring sweater—"and I knew I'd finally met my soul mate. Which didn't mean that things fell right into place. Oh, no." She wagged a finger lacquered in a shiny hot pink polish. "It took me a while, not to mention a lot of pillow talking, to convince him to take another ride on the marriage-go-round."

As one of the people who hadn't believed the citified blond real estate agent who'd come to town in search of ranch property for a wealthy client would ever stick around, Austin envied Mitzi's confidence. Especially since her own self-esteem had taken a major dent after her husband texted that he'd fallen in love with another woman.

One, it turned out, who could better support him in the style to which he'd like to become accustomed. Even knowing the morning after her impulsive, tacky Vegas chapel wedding ceremony that she'd made a mistake, even having suspected infidelity, she'd been hit hard by Jace's desertion.

Heather and Rachel had managed to convince her that her ex-husband's behavior had nothing to do with her and everything to do with him being nothing but a slick-talking player in a cowboy hat. Something anyone could buy at any western wear store in the country.

Real cowboys weren't playacting at being John Wayne.

They had ranching in their blood. They believed in what many these days might consider old-fashioned values of honesty, integrity, and character. And yes, those values could sometimes tend to be more black and white than shades of gray, and even the quietest among them had a capacity for rowdiness from time to time, but you always knew that you could count on them for standing by you. For having your back.

Like Sawyer had always been there for her. Unfortunately, Austin allowed, there was also the chance that she was romanticizing their relationship. He had, up until that kiss, always treated her more like a sister than a girl he was interested in. And it wasn't as if he'd been lacking for girlfriends back in high school.

Not that she'd stayed home and taken up knitting. While her dating life hadn't been as active as Sawyer's, she'd been kissed lots of times, and once, while parked on the bluff above the river, which had long been a popular make-out spot, she'd come close to letting Radley Biehn get to third base.

Later, she'd happily shed her virginity with a bass player in a motorhome at the Pendleton Roundup. She'd been there with stock while he'd been in a band that had opened for George Strait. The earth hadn't moved, and it had been awfully quick, but at least she hadn't had all of River's Bend watching to see what, if anything, would come from what turned out to be a four-day hookup.

Which had set the stage for other out-of-town affairs whenever she and some appealing-enough cowboy landed in the same town. Like that first time, the men were no more interested in a forever-after relationship than she was.

Which, whenever she thought about it, Austin found

ironic. When had she—the girl who'd grown up looking forward to settling down, becoming a wife and mother—become so averse to marriage?

It was only when she'd received that New Year's email from Sawyer that she'd realized the reason she hadn't wanted to settle down was because none of those other men were the one she wanted. The one she'd always wanted.

And wow, hadn't she gone and screwed that up?

"What if Sawyer's happy the way things are?" she asked. "What if he doesn't want to move out of the friend zone?"

"That's possible," Layla allowed. "But you can waste time wondering—"

"Not to mention giving him mixed messages," Rachel broke in. "Which I'll admit to having been guilty of with Cooper. I wanted him from the beginning. But I didn't *want* to want him."

"Most of us have been there," Layla agreed. "It's damn hard putting your heart on the line. But here's the thing. Guys are simple. They're not real big on nuances. Especially when it comes to relationships. So, my point is, you should simply cowgirl up and ask him."

"Or seduce him," Mitzi suggested. "That'd give him the idea real fast. And save on words because guys also aren't big on multitasking. Asking them to talk coherently when they're presented with the girls all dolled up in lacy bits is expecting a bit much."

"I wouldn't have a clue how to do that." Nor did she have any lacy bits for her girls, even if she'd had that much to present. Which, unfortunately, she didn't. Also unfortunately, she was probably too old for stuffing her bra with tissues to create the illusion of boobage. Which would set up another problem of what would happen if they ever got to the point of undressing.

Austin could burst into a rodeo arena at full speed, her horse leaning at nearly a forty-five-degree angle as she raced the hairpin turns around the barrels, finishing off with a no-holds-barred exit as easily as she could breathe. But having watched way too many buckle bunnies flutter their lashes, toss their big sprayed-to-a-rock hair, and swivel sprayed-on jean-clad hips in ways hers would never be capable of moving, she'd reluctantly decided that she'd been born without so much as a single flirting gene. Nor, if her debacle of a marriage was any indication, any talent for keeping a man in the saddle. So to speak.

"No problem," Jenna said. "Stop by the store tomorrow. I'll have a selection of hot romance novels waiting that will not only have you primed to jump Sawyer Murphy's bones, they'll also give you some creative seduction ideas."

"You know," Rachel suggested with a slow, sly smile, "there just happen to be other uses for a rope than lassoing a steer."

Austin sprayed out the wine she'd just sipped. "Rachel!" She could feel the heat flooding into her face.

"Just saying." Rachel topped off Austin's glass. "You might want to give it some thought. While you're reading those sexy books."

Give it some thought? Now that the idea was in her mind, Austin feared she wouldn't be able to think of anything else.

4

THREE DAYS AFTER his deal with the Merrills to rent the pastureland, Sawyer and his brothers had driven forty-five cows and their calves through the temporary gate they'd made in the fence between ranches. His herd wasn't anything near the size of the Bar M's, but it was a start, and looking at the black cows settling right into grazing in their new homes was more satisfying than expected. For the second time in a week, he'd felt a distant stir of life.

"They're settling right in," Ryan said as the three men sat on their horses, watching the calves nurse while their mothers' heads were lowered into the grass.

"I'd hoped they would."

Sawyer's dad had figured out long ago that, since cattle were territorial and liked staying in one place, moving them a long distance back and forth between grazing grounds, as had been traditionally done in the past, stressed them enough that they lost weight, which then took weeks to put back on. Which was when the Bar M had started rotating the fields every day or so, opening temporary gates and moving the stock to new grass. It hadn't taken long for the cows, realizing that the opening of a gate meant higher, tastier grass, to begin moving of their own accord. With the two ranches being connected, and with the fields both planted in the same grass, there wasn't that much of a change for them.

"How about a beer?" he asked.

"I wouldn't turn one down," Cooper said.

They rode the short distance to the log cabin where Sawyer had spent the past two nights.

"This is where you're going to be living?" Cooper asked as he walked into the front combo kitchen/living area, which, except for a stove, a harvest-gold fridge dating back to the '70s, and two barstools at a kitchen peninsula, was as empty as it had been when Austin had shown it to Sawyer.

"That's the plan." Sawyer went over to the fridge and pulled out three beers.

Ryan unscrewed the lid on the brown bottle. "Have you happened to notice that it doesn't have any furniture?"

Sawyer shrugged. "It's all I need."

Cooper glanced toward the hallway leading to three bedrooms and a bath. "What are you doing for a bed?"

"I have my bedroll."

"So," Ryan said, "you're camping out."

"It's not like I plan to spend a lot of time here," Sawyer said. And yes, that was defensiveness he heard in his voice. Sometimes it sucked being the youngest brother, always feeling that you had to measure up.

"If you're not going to accept Dad's offer to take some of the extra furniture from the ranch, you could at least nab some stuff on craigslist. Like maybe a table, a couch, and hey, go a little wild and get a bed."

"I don't plan to be doing a lot of entertaining."

"What about Austin?" Ryan asked.

"What about her?"

"Ry's being subtle," Cooper said. "Which is how doctors tend to talk. Being a cop myself, I'll cut to the chase. What do you intend to do about her?"

"I intend to pay her rent for the use of her land and hopefully, if she'll let me, do some of the work that's been dumped on her since Buck's polio came back."

"Yeah, that polio thing sucks," Cooper said. "Dad wanted to send over some of the men from the Bar M, but Buck's damn pride got in the way and he turned him down."

"Which only dumped more on Austin." It also explained the shadows of fatigue beneath her eyes. "How is he?" Sawyer asked Ryan. "Really?"

"It varies day to day. Although we're still learning about post-polio syndrome, evidence is pointing toward the cause being degenerating nerve cells. When poliovirus infects your body, it damages or destroys motor neurons carrying electrical impulses between your brain and muscles.

"To compensate, the remaining neurons sprout new fibers, which promotes the use of your muscles again but also puts added stress on the nerve cell to nourish more fibers. Over the years, the stress can be more than the neuron can handle, leading to gradual deterioration. Also, if you regularly perform physical activity to the point of fatigue—"

"Like any rancher does every damn day," Sawyer said.

"Exactly. Overworking already stressed-out neurons can increase the risk of PPS."

"Can he build the muscles back up with exercise?" Back in high school, Sawyer had broken his lower leg being thrown off a bucking horse. After the cast had come off, he'd been forced through weeks of flexibility and strength rehabilitation therapy.

"That works in a lot of cases, but PPS patients are advised to pace their physical activity, combining it with frequent rest periods to avoid fatigue. Moderation is the key. Overdoing on a good day can lead to subsequent bad days."

"That's got to be hard on a guy who was as tough as those bulls he breeds."

"His ego took as hard a hit as his body," Ryan agreed.

"Maybe even more," Cooper said. "He used to always show up for breakfast at the New Chance. But I haven't seen him in town since Austin dragged him out for the Christmas tree lighting and caroling."

"Since he's as stubborn as those bulls he breeds and refuses to listen to me, I'm sending Layla over to have a come-to-Jesus talk with him," Ryan said. "See if she can convince him to at least get a wheelchair or one of those scooters so he can get out and about again."

"Good plan," Cooper agreed. "I don't know many folks, especially men, Layla can't wrap around her little finger." He took off his black Stetson and sent it sailing across the room at a steer horn hook rack next to the kitchen door. Conversation paused as all three brothers watched it land exactly on point.

"Show-off." Sawyer knew his brother had started practicing that back in elementary school as a way to show off for Ellen Buchanan, who'd lived on the ranch on the other side of the Bar M. The ironic thing was that, as impressive as the skill might be, everyone had known Cooper Murphy didn't need tricks to catch Ellen's eye. The two were practically joined at the hip all their lives. Until the plane she'd taken home from visiting a friend in Denver had gone off course during a blizzard and flown into Modoc Mountain.

"I can teach you how to do it," Cooper said. "In case you want to impress your woman."

"She's not my woman."

"Hell. She's been your woman since before she *became* a woman. Same as Ellen and I were."

"You're so sure of that." Okay, once again he'd come off sounding defensive, making his brother's damn point.

"Sure am. I've watched you making calf eyes at the girl since you were wearing Pampers pull-ups and riding that wooden rocking horse Gramps made you." He pointed the neck of the bottle at Sawyer. "Nothing cuter than puppy love."

Sawyer shot him a middle finger before taking a long pull on his own bottle. "It's complicated."

"Women are complicated."

"You sure as hell aren't going to get any argument there."

"You do realize Rachel's going to ask me what this place looks like when I get home," Cooper said. Then held up a hand as Sawyer opened his mouth to answer. "And I'm not going to lie for you, little bro. This isn't like when you filched that Copenhagen from the mercantile when you were eight, swallowed too much like a damn fool, and when you spent the night barfing your guts out, I lied and told Mom you'd gotten a bad hot dog at the fair."

"Just tell Rachel it looks fine." Looking around with a more judicial eye, there might be a layer of dust on the windowsills and plank wood floor, but after two tours in Afghanistan and another in Iraq, if there was one thing he'd grown used to, it was dust.

"She'll know. Among their many superpowers, women have this eerie radar that failed to evolve in us mere mortal males. Back when I was working the rough streets, putting bad guys away in Portland, I really could have used Rachel's powers during interrogations."

"The women are going to show up here," Ryan warned. "Layla was talking about your moving in yesterday. It's not going to take long for her to drop in and check up on you."

"Check up on me? Why? I'm a grown man." He'd been to war. And, unlike too many others, had managed to make it home.

"It's what women do," Cooper explained patiently, as if he were talking to a five-year-old and not a battle-toughened Marine. "You may see this as just some place to crash for a few hours before getting back to work. I get that. But they make nests. It's in their DNA. Between Mitzi and now Rachel, our place is starting to put Scott and me at risk for estrogen poisoning."

While he was no fan of the sofa pillows strewn over Cooper's leather couch and chairs, Sawyer knew that to be an exaggeration. What the women had done was turn his brother's log bachelor's house back into a home. That certain feeling that had been missing since Ellen's passing.

"You might want to at least get a bed," Ryan suggested. "For when you get laid."

"I don't want to get laid."

"Said no guy ever," Cooper returned.

"I don't want to screw things up."

"Seems you already did that," Ryan said. "Back when you wrote her that numb-nuts email telling her that you weren't interested in tumbling her in the hayloft."

"I didn't say that," Sawyer mumbled as a vision of Austin lying in a bed of hay—her pink lips curved in a come-and-ride-me-cowboy smile—rolled across the flat-screen in his mind.

"It's obviously the message she got. Why else would she marry that loser so soon after tangling tonsils at the hospital with you?"

Sawyer shot him a searing look. "How the hell do you know about that kiss?"

"Next time, if you're inclined to indulge in some PDA, you might want to make sure you're not doing it right outside the bistro where Rachel was picking up some boxed sandwiches for the family back in the heart center waiting room."

"Shit." Sawyer scrubbed his hands down his face. "Who else knows?"

"Rachel told me because couples share stuff," Cooper said. "Heather probably knows, because they've been BFFs forever and women tell their girlfriends everything. But since neither woman would do anything to hurt Austin, I'd say that's probably it. Oh, and Ry, since I told him about it so we could double-team you and set you straight. But then Austin up and eloped before we came up with a plan we figured you might listen to."

"I didn't tell a soul," Ryan assured him. "Not even Layla, who was as surprised as the rest of us at the effed-up way things played out between the two of you."

"Well, that's something. Austin's got enough on her plate without having to worry about being embarrassed every time she goes into town."

"You know," Ryan said, "getting back to the topic of

your love life—"

"Or lack of it," Cooper interjected.

"You could always cook her dinner," Ryan continued his thought. "Women like that."

"Says the man who, from what I can tell, hasn't managed to lasso a female of his own."

"I've been a little busy going to medical school and, like you, serving in the military to pay off my ROTC debt," his brother, the most easygoing of the three of them, said mildly. "Plus, I'm particular."

"So, Mr. Particular, even if I were interested in making a move, which I'm not saying I am, what the hell would you suggest? Should I nuke her a Hungry Man frozen dinner or pop open an MRE? Because, along with calling out for pizza delivery, which I can't do because River's Bend doesn't even have a pizza joint, those are the levels of my kitchen skills."

"It's a damn pitiful thing when a man can't feed himself," Cooper said.

"Not that you have to worry about where your next meal is coming from because you just happen to be living with a New York Culinary Institute trained chef."

Cooper shot out his jaw. "I wasn't exactly starving before Rachel came to town. I can make stuff."

"How about taking her out?" Ryan tried again, obviously wanting to soothe the waters before fists started flying. As the middle Murphy, Ryan had always been a bridge between the occasionally troubled waters of Cooper's oldest-brother bossiness and Sawyer's youngest rebellion.

"Great idea. To the New Chance? Which, in case you've forgotten and unless you're talking peanuts and wings at the Shady Lady, is the only place to eat in town."

"Excuse me?" Cooper folded arms that were all muscle and sinew and could undoubtedly still wrestle a steer to the ground without him so much as breaking a sweat. His dark brows dove down toward his nose. "Are you suggesting that you have a problem with my woman's cooking?"

"Hell, no." Cooper didn't rile easily, but on the rare occasion he did, the wisest tactic to take was to back away. "From what she dished up for the party, it's a freaking miracle that she decided to settle down in a cow town like this instead of making a name for herself in New York or Vegas or L.A. Or maybe even being one of those TV chefs. She's sure pretty enough."

"And yet she chose me over the big city, flashy lights, and television fame."

"Yet another miracle."

Sawyer was happy for his brother, who seemed to have hit the woman jackpot not just once but twice. But that didn't mean *he* was in the market for a wife.

All he wanted was to be left alone.

5

AUSTIN WAS OUT in the corral, working on getting a yearling to come to her, rather than her chasing him. Last year, when he'd been a colt, she'd put in the groundwork getting him used to humans by touching him, lifting his feet, having people move in and out of the pen with him. Now she needed to build his trust and make him want her attention rather than just hanging out with his herd.

She'd bred him as a future cattle horse for the Flying Goose, who'd be putting him to work next year. Meanwhile, she was teaching him how to be a working horse and, as a prey animal with a strong flight response, how to deal with stressors. Which would be vital in keeping not just him safe and happy but the herd he'd be joining happy, as well. A disruptive horse was an unhappy horse, which no one, especially Austin, wanted.

Building up to saddle training next year would take time and patience. But when things were going well, as they were this morning, allowing her to get in a zone, it was almost as good as the meditation Rachel had taught her to do during the stressful ending days of her marriage.

As she let the horse trot awhile around the corral, Austin's gaze drifted to the far pasture, where cattle grazed. As she watched, two SUVs drove down the dusty road from what was now Sawyer's cabin. She recognized them as belonging to his brothers, who'd obviously shown up to help him move the stock from the Bar M.

Although the Merrills had built their reputation as stock breeders and she had no plans to enter the increasingly competitive beef business, the sight of the cows and calves proved surprisingly pleasing. Perhaps, Austin admitted, because they were Sawyer's cows. Just seeing them was an indication that possibly she'd been wrong about having destroyed their relationship when she'd married Jace. Maybe Heather was right. Perhaps there was some way forward for them. But first they'd have to talk about the past.

Going back to the future.

She was pondering yet again how to best attempt that when the colt stopped in front of her, nudging her, trying to regain her attention.

"Good boy," she said absently, running her palm down the front of his blaze face. "You're such a baby."

He'd always been needy for human attention, which put him ahead of others she'd worked with over the years. And while he was easy to spoil, the trick would be teaching him responsibility. Fortunately, he came from a long line of cattle horses, so herding—which was what he was doing right now, pushing against her, trying to move her where he wanted her to be—was in his blood. Even if he didn't know it yet.

"You may not realize it, but you're going to do Green Springs proud when you go off to your new home," she told him. The ranch's reputation was only as good as its next horse, and so far, over several generations, it had risen, thanks to diligent breeding and records that went back to her great-great-grandfather.

After returning the yearling to the herd, she'd just gone over to a small paddock next to the corral when a sunny yellow minivan drove up the gravel road, kicking up dust behind it. It pulled up in front of the barn, the doors opened, and two children jumped out, racing toward her, their mother following behind.

"Buttermilk had her baby!" Seven-year-old Jack Campbell scrambled up on the paddock fence, leaning so far over Austin had a momentary fear he'd go flying right over it.

"She's pretty." Sophie Campbell grabbed her younger brother by the back of his jeans. Being five years older, Sophie had always acted as a junior mother to her active brother.

"He is, isn't he?" Austin ran her hand down the foal's mane.

"What's his name?" Jack asked.

"He doesn't have one yet," Austin said.

"I know!" Jack wiggled free of his sister's hold and began jumping up and down. "You should name him Zombie Butt!"

"And we should rename you Idiot Child," Sophie shot back.

"Though Zombie Butt would definitely be an original name," Austin said, fighting back the smile that was trying to get free.

"That B-word has become the word of the day. And yesterday. And for the past month before that," Heather said. "I totally blame Santa for bringing him that copy of *The Day My Butt Went Psycho*." She ruffled her son's red head. "That was followed by *Zombie Butts from Uranus.*"

"Which he's not allowed to say out loud." Sophie scowled a warning at her brother, who'd just opened his mouth to blurt it out.

Austin ran the forbidden word through her head, separating the first two letters of the planet's name from the last four—Ur-Anus—as a young boy might relish saying. Laughing when she figured it out, she glanced over at Heather, who merely rolled her eyes with maternal patience.

"I'll bet, when we were talking about you wanting a large family while growing up, you never factored in butt books."

"No," Heather said emphatically. "I was thinking more along the lines of Dr. Seuss, *Where the Wild Things Are*, and fairy tales."

"Yuck." Jack's freckled face wrinkled up as he stuck his finger in his mouth and made gagging sounds. "Fairy tales are for girls. I like the wild things book," he allowed. "But I'm too old for it now." He started to climb on the fence again. "Can I ride him?"

"He's still too young for riders," Austin said. "He's not even a week old. But if you're very gentle and quiet, you can pat him." Austin turned toward Sophie. "You, too, if you'd like."

"Be careful," Heather warned. "He's just a baby and you don't want to upset his mother."

"I'll be super careful!" Jack promised.

"And quiet," Austin repeated.

The seven-year-old made a zipping motion against his lips, then threw away an imaginary key before scrambling over the rails to the other side. Sophie followed with much more decorum.

"He's so soft." The girl ran a hand down the side of the foal's face.

The foal's mother's ears pricked up, and she moved a little closer, but having had both children on her back before, she didn't appear to take them as an immediate threat. "I like his star."

Sophie traced the white marking between the eyes on the horse's forehead. "Maybe you could call him Stardust," she suggested.

"That's a stupid girl's name," Jack hissed in a loud whisper.

"Why don't we take some time to get to know him a little better before we decide," Austin suggested diplomatically. "Meanwhile, you both can make up lists of possible names."

"Okay." Jack's attempt at whispering appeared as unnatural as it would have been for Desperado to do jetés across the pasture. "I wanna touch his star like Sophie did."

"Sure. Just remember to be gentle."

His sister hefted him up so he could run his fingers, one of which was sporting a Darth Vader Band-Aid, over the star. The mother horse sidestepped slightly, as if realizing the perils presented by an energetic boy.

"Why don't you two go into the house," Austin suggested when the heels of his cowboy boots reached the ground again. "Winema's back and I baked some chocolate chip cookies with your name on them."

"Yay!" Jack shouted, then immediately put his hands over his mouth. "Sorry," he mumbled through his fingers.

"That's okay." Austin smiled. "His mother knows you'd never hurt him."

She watched him race toward the kitchen door, with his sister following behind.

"You're a lucky woman," she murmured.

"You always see them on their best behavior," Heather countered. "You've never had to deal with a Lego Transformer clogging up your toilet at midnight on Christmas Eve, or the mood swings of a twelve-year-old girl going on thirty-five."

"I remember that age," Austin said. "Every single thing seemed life-and-death."

"And just think, we were ideal adolescents." Heather's dry tone made Austin laugh. "Do you remember my mad, crazy crush on Maddox Mann?"

"Only too well." The skateboard-riding, leather-jacket-wearing, garage-band-guitar-playing eighth grader had been the bad boy of Mountain View Middle School. "I was amazed when he grew up to become a bazillionaire tech mogul."

"He was named the most likely to either become a rock star or end up in prison."

"He sort of did both," Austin pointed out. "Vicariously, anyway."

His first game had had players gaining levels from garage band to international rock stardom. His second, and the far more popular with players, if not their parents, had involved planning a prison break with rewards for number of days spent before capture. These days, according to the article the *River's Bend Record* had reprinted from the *Wall Street Journal*, he'd gotten into venture capitalism, of all things.

"He was so hot," Heather said with a sigh.

"Still is, from what I saw on the cover of *People* in the

mercantile." Unlike most nerd tycoons, he was still wearing the studded black leather, but she guessed the diamond flashing on his earlobe was real these days. "He also just went through a mega *War of the Roses* divorce with his supermodel wife."

"Which makes me glad that he never even knew I was alive," Heather said.

"Fortunately, Tom did."

"Yes." Another sigh. This one followed by the slow, satisfied smile of a woman who knew she was well loved. "Sometimes it's hard to believe that we've been together all these years." High school sweethearts, they'd married their freshman year of college, when Heather had gotten pregnant with Sophie.

"It isn't hard for anyone who knows you guys. You're pretty much the perfect couple. If you weren't both so nice, the rest of us would have to hate you."

Heather laughed. "Maybe I should tell you about the towels Tom leaves on the floor, his inability to return home with everything on the grocery list, and waking up to middle-of-the-night emergency calls because he decided he wanted to be a big-animal vet instead of taking care of dogs and cats. Which don't require house calls."

"If those are your only marital problems, I'm looking forward to dancing at your golden anniversary party."

"I'm fully expecting you and Sophie to plan it. And, giving advance warning, I expect it to be a blowout. I also wouldn't be averse to a destination celebration. Say, on Maui."

Which had, Austin knew, been Heather's dream wedding destination after Marcy Mann, Maddox's sister, had returned with photos from a family Christmas vacation there when they'd all been in the fourth grade. "You've got it."

"On another topic, I figured out what to do about you and Sawyer."

"Other than me showing up at his door naked and carrying a plate of double fudge sea salt brownies?"

"While they may admittedly be nearly as good as sex, I seriously doubt you'd need the brownies. But maybe there's a step in between where you guys are now and that down-the-road scenario. How about the four of us have dinner together Friday night?"

"That's your anniversary."

"I know. Which is exactly the point. We can reminisce about the wedding and how you were my bridesmaid and Sawyer was Tom's best man. And then, how, when Sophie was born, you both stood up in church as godparents, and all the other wonderful times we had together over the years. Before Sawyer screwed up by getting scared by that kiss."

"You don't know he was scared."

"As a matter of fact, I do." Heather shook her head. "He emailed Tom that he'd had second thoughts about backing away from the situation."

Running away had been more like it. "Seriously?"

"Would I lie to my best friend? He told Tom that the day after he got back to Afghanistan, but then there was a terrorist attack at his base, and unsurprisingly, he kind of freaked out and wrote you that *never mind* email right after attending a memorial for the fallen. You know, one of those where the rifle, boots, and helmet make a cross with the dog tags hanging on it."

"I know them." Austin didn't share that she'd had too

many nightmares about Sawyer's name being the one engraved on a set of metal dog tags.

"I suspect it was the first time the idea of mortality really sunk in. He didn't want to ask you to wait for him to return, then have him get killed on you."

It made sense. Not for every guy. But it perfectly fit the man who, so many years ago, had passed her that note in class, telling her how sorry he was about her mother leaving and he promised to always be her friend. And had gone on to watch out for her.

"Why did you wait until now to tell me?" Austin wasn't going to dwell on might-have-beens. But if only she'd known the reasoning behind his backing away from the door they'd opened that day at the hospital, things would have been so different.

"Because you and your dad were in Vegas. I decided to wait until you got back home so we could talk about it in person. Make plans on how you could nudge things back on track and move forward. Unfortunately, my crystal ball failed to tell me that you were going to get shitfaced and marry some cowboy you'd known all of one night."

"Waking up with the only hangover of my life. And a husband whose name I could barely remember." Austin had never been much of a drinker. An occasional beer or glass of wine, but that night, after reading Sawyer's email, she'd gone downstairs to the hotel bar and discovered cosmos. Which had been pretty, sweet tasting, and, she'd discovered the hard way, lethal.

"But that's in the past." She shook off regrets she couldn't do anything about. "My point was that you guys have a romantic weekend planned. You're going to Ashland to stay in that romantic B&B and see a play—"

"And don't forget have lots of hot, swing-from-the-chandelier sex that doesn't involve worrying a kid's going to walk in or knock on the bedroom door."

"That too. Although now that you've put that chandelier sex in my head, I really do have to hate you."

"You can have that," Heather said, turning serious after a rippling laugh. "You and Sawyer. You're both way overdue."

Austin couldn't deny that. When they'd been checking out the inside of the cabin together, she'd felt as if she'd stumbled into a pinball machine and was being bombarded with pheromones.

"Why am I feeling like high school?" she asked. "This reminds me uncomfortably of when Tom had Sawyer ask me if I thought you'd be willing to go steady with him."

"Right after I asked you to ask Sawyer to ask Tom if he was going to ask me to the Moonlight and Mistletoe Dance," Heather agreed. "And yes, it does seem freakily familiar, though may I point out that if you two had figured out your feelings back then, we wouldn't be having to go through this Kabuki theater routine now . . .

"As for our anniversary, we can leave after dinner. It's only an hour, maybe an hour and a half out of our weekend, and if it gets you two past this stupid emotional roadblock, it'll be the best present yet. Of course, I expect to be in the wedding."

"Of course." Austin waved away the idea of Heather not being her attendant. "If we do end up at the altar."

"You will."

"I can't imagine Tom would be very happy with this idea."

"He's all in. Rachel has already agreed to create a fancy

dinner at the café for the four of us, after which Tom and I will drive to Ashland and be tangling the sheets by nine. Ten, at the latest. We'll still have our fantasy anniversary, and then Monday, when we drive up to Portland with Mitzi to get our dresses for Rachel and Cooper's upcoming wedding, you can tell us all about *your* hot weekend."

The thought was too, too tempting. But Austin still wasn't sure. Although her marriage had never been a true one, at least as far as her lying, cheating, stealing ex had been concerned, once she'd awakened that morning and found the cheap gold ring on her left hand, she'd decided that she'd try her best to live up to her vows. Even as she'd had increasing indications that Jace wasn't living up to that "forsaking all others" clause, she'd wanted to make things work.

At least that's what she'd tried telling herself.

As it turned out, he hadn't been the only liar in her marriage. Because from the flood of relief she'd experienced when she received that text saying her husband had found someone else, she realized that she'd been lying to herself.

The national finals were the last rodeo she and her dad had worked before she'd finally gotten him to go to Ryan about his symptoms. While Ryan had suspected PPS, he'd sent them to Portland for extensive tests. From the moment of the diagnosis, everyone and everything else had fallen off her priority list. Which had been easy enough to do with Jace out of the country in Australia.

While her marriage might have been a farce from the beginning, Austin's divorce was still fresh. She'd already learned what could happen when you impulsively leaped into a relationship.

As happy as she was about Sawyer's return home, the timing was all wrong. It was too soon. She could be jumping from the proverbial frying pan straight into the fire.

Yet, thinking of fires, her mind reeled backwards to that flaming kiss. Of her arms wrapped around Sawyer's neck while she strained against him, wanting, *needing* more as their bodies melded hotly. Sawyer's mouth had claimed hers while his strong hands had streaked down her back, pulling her tight against his aroused body.

"Well?" Heather asked, breaking into the fevered memory.

"Okay," she said on a rush of breath before she could change her mind. "Let's go for it."

6

"I'M GOING INTO town to do some shopping," Winema Clinton said. "Want to come along?"

Buck Merrill dragged his gaze from a rerun of the 2011 NFR bull riding championships. "Why in the blue blazes would I want to go shopping for female doodads?"

"I'm getting groceries. In case you haven't noticed, we're getting low."

Buck made a sound somewhere between a curse and a grunt. Call him sexist, but unless you were talking a chuck wagon out working a roundup, as far as he was concerned, cooking was woman's work. A thought he'd started keeping to himself after Austin had surprised him by letting him know, in no uncertain terms, that for his information, most of the great chefs of the world were men.

She'd stood there, her hands fisted on her hips, practically throwing the words at him like stones. She'd been mad a lot lately. Which wasn't anything like her, but Buck had decided that it beat the way she'd been last year. When her mood had dived lower than a diamondback in a rut.

At least mad showed a spark.

"I wasn't going to drag you through the mercantile."

Being that River's Bend was a small town, he'd known

Winema all of his life. They'd gone to school together. After her husband's lumber mill had burned down, Warren had to switch gears and take up teaching machine shop at the high school. Needing the extra income, Winema had started coming in once a week to clean for Buck's wife.

It was a few months later when Britta had taken off to Sweden, leaving him with a seven-year-old daughter to tend to. Since what Buck knew about little girls could fit on the head of a pin and still have room for a thousand dancing angels, he'd been grateful when Winema had suggested that so long as her kids could stay with her when they weren't in school, she'd be willing to come help out with Austin for a spell.

More than two decades later, she was still here. Though Warren, unfortunately, was not, having keeled over from a heart attack in Young's Hardware while picking up a gallon of apple-green paint for their kitchen six years ago.

"I thought you might want to stop by Harry's, get your hair trimmed and a shave, and maybe play a game or two of checkers while you're there," she said.

"No point in spending good money when you can cut my hair." Buck rubbed his chin, feeling the scruff of bristles he'd ignored for the past week. "And there's nothing wrong with my hands. I can damn well still shave myself."

"Then why don't you?" she challenged.

Bossy woman. He was about to ask her if she'd hen-pecked Warren to death, but was able to stop the words, which had shot from his brain to the tip of his tongue, just in time.

"No reason to shave to watch TV," he mumbled.

"My point exactly. You spend too much time in front

of that boob tube," she countered. "When was the last time you got out and mixed with folks?"

They both knew that had been six weeks ago, when he'd stumbled over the curb outside Ryan Murphy's office. He'd gone sprawling, ending up on the ground, splay-legged like a helpless newborn foal.

"Going to the doctor doesn't count," she said when, instead of answering, he turned his attention to the TV, watching as Desperado sent Joaquin Sanchez—who'd been ranked second rider in the world on that day—flying off his back into the dirt.

"And another one bites the dust," he said with a spark of pride.

The animal athlete he'd bred and raised from a calf was in the pantheon of rodeo bulls, right up there alongside Bushwacker, Asteroid, and Little Yellow Jacket. Go into any cowboy bar in the country, and before caps were popped off bottles of Bud Light, you could get an argument going about which of the four deserved the pinnacle. Not that Buck had any doubt. The others were good and had their special moves, but to his mind, Desperado was the best-all-around bull ever.

Winema blew out a long, frustrated breath. "Speaking of bovine, you did know that Sawyer Murphy brought his stock over today?"

"Yeah." Buck still wasn't sure how he felt about that development. Sure, they could use the money. If he'd been willing to sell Desperado back when offers rose as high as a cool million, they wouldn't be in the straits they were. But though he didn't want anyone to think him soft or sentimental, the bull was family. And you don't sell off family.

"Maybe you might want to go look at them."

"I can see the pasture from the window." He couldn't fault the Murphys for their stock. They'd always bred for ease of birthing and quality of beef, rather than falling prey to any popular beauty contest standards many other ranchers had gone for.

"You could go welcome him home," she pressed on. Stubborn. She just never let up once something got buzzing in her bonnet. "Given that the boy's been fighting for his county and even the president called him a hero. You missed his party," she reminded him.

Since he and Dan Murphy had been best friends all their lives, Buck felt a bit guilty about that. "Couldn't help it. In case you forgot, I tripped over that damn rug."

"I've watched you take a lot harder falls. Like back in high school when you were riding that bronc at the Basin Junior Rodeo and got throwed."

"You remember that?" It had been the summer after their junior year of high school.

"Sure do. I was in the grandstands with my girlfriends. I remember thinkin' that you might need some cheering up, and Anna, who'd been there to cheer on Dan in the bull riding, dared me to go talk to you. Of course the others took up the idea."

Her dark eyes took on a momentary mist of memory. "I'd just gotten up the nerve when you up and hightailed it out of there without looking back." As that confession hit like a bullet to the brain, she shrugged. "Just as well. If you'd had an opportunity to fall for my considerable female charms, we might have ended up being the ones going steady, and Warren wouldn't have asked me to the Fall Fantasy."

Buck remembered that day all too clearly. He'd landed on his back and had lain there, helpless as a pup, unable to move with the air knocked out of him. The rodeo clowns—bull fighters, they called them these days—had gotten the bucking horse out of the arena while he'd struggled to catch enough breath to stagger to his feet.

Which was exactly how he felt right now. That revelation that might have changed both their lives had knocked the air right out of him.

He was about to spiral into regrets when he looked out the window and saw Austin working with a yearling in the corral. He might not say it enough, but from the moment the girl had drawn breath, she'd been the sunshine of his life. And the one good thing to come out of a marriage to a woman who'd never fit into his life.

When Britta had taken him to Sweden to meet her wealthy, high-society family, who was actually related to royalty, she'd enjoyed showing off her American cowboy to all her European friends. Though he'd felt a lot like a stud bull in a show ring, Buck couldn't deny that having so many females, all as flashy as exotic tropical butterflies, fluttering around him had sent his ego into the stratosphere.

For a very short time. Until they'd returned to River's Bend and settled into the routine of ranching life, which didn't involve shopping for designer clothes with her girlfriends, Saturday night clubbing and Sunday jazz brunches, or formal teas at the palace.

They'd both been miserable, and he couldn't blame his wife. There was a reason people tended to marry within their circles to people they knew well. Because that way you'd know what you were signing up for. Once the novelty had worn off, the difference between his remote western ranching life and his wife's jet-setting, free-spending lifestyle had caused the marriage to crash and burn.

Still, as rough as life had been back then, Buck couldn't regret how things had turned out, because if he hadn't married Britta, he wouldn't have Austin. Who may have thought she was hitching herself to a cowboy who'd fit into River's Bend, but had managed to screw up just as bad as he had.

Sometimes, Buck considered, life could be damn complicated. Which was why he'd never spent that much time contemplating it. Things happened, good and bad. You savored the good, got past the bad, and moved on. Just as Austin had done with whatever the hell had happened between her and the youngest Murphy boy. And like she'd shed that no-account rodeo cowboy she'd gone and married. At least that guy was half a world away and wouldn't be setting a boot back on Green Springs. And now, maybe if the Murphy kid played his cards right, he could end up Buck's son-in-law, like he and everyone else in town had always expected.

7

SAWYER WAS AT Fred Wiley's Feed and Seed when his phone buzzed with a text from Tom Campbell.

Saw your truck, it read. *How about a beer at the Shady Lady?*

Since the crowd had kept him and his old friend from having any time to talk during the party, Sawyer texted him back. *Be there in 10?*

Works for me.

The Shady Lady was one of two bars in River's Bend. Previously known as the No Name, after the sign had blown away during a winter storm, one of the many movie companies had hung up a weathered wooden sign declaring it the Shady Lady Saloon.

Tom had already taken a table in the far corner of the room when Sawyer walked in.

"Gotta love small towns." After sliding into a wooden chair, putting his hat on the spare one next to him, he looked around at the velvet couches, bordello-red walls hung with framed paintings of dance hall girls and faded sepia photographs of more girls along with cowboys, outlaws, and miners dating back to the days of the town's gold rush founding. "They just don't change."

"That's why some of us, those who either stay here or

return, like them. It's also the reason others can't wait to get away."

"Can't argue that." Sawyer plucked a peanut from the bowl in the center of the wooden table and cracked it open. "Okay," he said as a waitress dressed in jeans, a ruffled-front rodeo queen blouse, and tasseled red boots headed toward them. "That's changed."

"Not everyone would agree for the better," Tom said with a sigh and a slow, regretful shake of his head. "Maggie Washburn used this place as one of the platforms in her campaign for mayor."

Mrs. Washburn had been Sawyer's high school civics teacher. He wasn't surprised to learn when she'd come up to welcome him home that she'd gone into local politics. But she hadn't mentioned anything about the Shady Lady. "How?"

"She decided that having the waitresses dress like saloon girls didn't present a family atmosphere. And demeaned women."

"Seriously?" One of the appeals of the Lady had always been those sassy red satin dresses and black petticoats.

"I bullshit you not. She even compared it to Hooters."

"No way."

"Way," the waitress, who'd apparently overheard the latter part of the conversation, said as she plunked two bar menus down onto the table. "And it's easy for you to complain, Tom Campbell, but none of you guys had to wear fishnet stockings that dig into your skin for hours at a time. Not to mention the fact that those damn dresses needed corsets." She efficiently swept away the nearly empty bowl and slammed a freshly filled one down next to the menus. "You try doing your job without breathing and see how you like it."

"Hey, I get it." Tom held up both hands in a gesture of surrender when she looked inclined to throw the peanuts at his head. "I really do. And I admit that men are pigs. My wife has reminded me of that on more than one occasion. And, if it gets me off the hook, I voted for Maggie."

"That, along with the fact that you still treat Heather like she's the queen of the world after all these years, is a point in your favor," she allowed. Then shot Sawyer a look. "How about you, cowboy?"

"I was out of town," he said. When her eyes narrowed dangerously, although he wasn't willing to go as far as to use his hero status, he did decide it was time to play another card. "Serving my country."

"Oh. Well." This time the look she swept over him wasn't so much challenging but speculative. "Welcome home, soldier." Her smile was as smooth and inviting as her voice. "And the first drink's on the house."

"I'm a Marine. And thanks, but it's not necessary."

"Oh, I insist." The exaggerated batting of her lashes, after that sharp, feminist lecture, had Sawyer thinking yet again that he'd never understand the complexities of the female mind. "It's the very least I can do to thank you for keeping our homeland safe."

After taking their order for two bottles of Bud Light and some wings, she left with a seductive sway of those jean-clad hips. "You do realize," Tom drawled, "that you could get so lucky."

"I'm not looking to get lucky."

"She's definitely hot."

"And you're married."

"I love Heather and would never, ever even contemplate cheating on her," Tom said easily. "But just because a guy puts a ring on it doesn't mean he locks his balls away in cold storage. There's nothing wrong with looking. It's not that different than when Heather and I went to Eugene for a Tim McGraw concert a couple years ago. It didn't bother me at all that she was practically drooling over him in those tight black leather pants. Because I knew that she'd be going home with me."

"You're the lucky one." Sawyer meant it.

"And don't I know it." Tom looked up and offered another conciliatory smile to the waitress, who'd already arrived with their order. "Thanks, Harley."

"No problem," she said without sparing him a glance as she zeroed in on Sawyer. "You all enjoy now." The hint of Texas twang in that sugared tone explained why he hadn't recognized her.

"Funny." Tom held his hand up in front of him and studied it thoughtfully after she'd sashayed over to another table with two bottles of beer and a mountain of fried onion rings. Then he waved it in front of his face. "I don't feel invisible, but you seem to have become the only guy in the place."

"Not interested," Sawyer repeated.

"It's just as well," Tom decided. "Her ex, who, word has it, hasn't exactly gotten over the breakup, is a long-haul truck driver the size of the Merrills' Desperado, but with a lot meaner personality."

He tilted the wooden chair on its back legs and ran a finger down the condensation on the outside of the brown bottle. "So," he said finally, "Heather sent me here on a mission."

"Heather did?"

"Yeah." He cracked another peanut. Chewed. "She wants me to invite you to dinner Friday at the New Chance."

"I thought Heather said you guys were going to Ashland for the weekend."

"We are. This would be earlier in the evening."

"Why?"

He shrugged. "Who knows a woman's mind? I'm guessing the anniversary has her feeling sentimental about our wedding. God knows she's been talking about it enough. She took a selfie last night wearing her old wedding dress."

"She still has it after all these years?"

"It's obvious you've never been married. We guys don't make a big deal about what to wear to a wedding. Most of us just do what our women tell us. We rent a tux and take it back after the ceremony is over.

"But to the female of the species, a wedding dress falls into a strange category of sentimental keepsakes. Like I told you the night of the party, we're living in a frigging construction zone while Brody Ames remodels our house, and every day some new 'must-have' pops up.

"Last week Heather decided that we needed two walk-in closets in the master bedroom. So, I took my life into my hands and dared to ask her why, if we weren't going to have enough closet space with the one ginormous walk-in already on the plan, she was keeping a dress she'd never wear again. One that just happens to take up the entire back of the closet we're currently using."

Sawyer took a bite of the hot wings and felt his tongue burst into flames. "What did she say?" he asked after cooling it off with a long drink of beer.

"She told me it was still sentimental and important to her. Especially since she made it herself."

"That makes sense. Remember that ground dummy practice calf I made in shop class back in high school?"

"Sure. It was as good as the store-bought ones Fred sells at the Feed and Seed."

"Well, Dad kept it all the time I've been gone, and I'm bringing it over to Green Springs with me."

"Okay." Tom blew out a breath. "If you ever tell Heather I said this, I'll call you a damn liar, but that calf's a helluva lot more functional than a dress. But that's okay, because I figured that she'd eventually decide it can go to the thrift store. Like maybe sooner rather than later and save us some remodel costs. But she says she expects her feelings to grow even stronger as the years pass."

"Huh."

"Well said. And now maybe you can see why I didn't interrogate She-Who-Must-Be-Obeyed on why we're inviting you to dinner."

Sawyer thought of the frozen Hungry Man meatloaf in that old gold fridge's freezer and decided there was something to be said for a dinner with friends. "Sounds like a plan."

"Great." Tom nodded. "She'll call you to give you a heads-up on the time and stuff." He paused for a moment, looked inclined to say something else, but grabbed a wing instead.

There'd been more times than Sawyer could count that his life had depended on reading people. He might not possess superpowers like his brothers claimed women did, but he could tell when something was off. He lifted a brow. "What else?"

Tom held up a hand as he finished off the wing. Then he swallowed, took another long pull on the bottle, and looked as if he wished he were anywhere else.

"Nothing. Now there's another thing that hasn't changed," Tom said, glancing over at the mechanical bull that had sent a lot of drunken cowboys and tourists flying onto the sawdust-covered floor. "Maggie wanted to get rid of it because she said it didn't fit the decorating time period and could be a liability problem. Everyone revolted. When was the last time you rode a bull?"

"Probably not since the summer after my junior year of college. And as a diversionary tactic, that one's pretty lame. What aren't you saying?"

"Hell." Tom rolled his eyes toward the ceiling, as if seeking divine inspiration. Which didn't seem to come. "Okay. Here's the deal. I'm stuck between pissing off my wife and staying true to the bro code. So, I really need your word that you won't tell Heather I told you this part."

"We made a blood oath," Sawyer reminded him of that time in the fourth grade when they'd taken his Buck pocket knife, made cuts in the tips of their index fingers, and mingled their blood, swearing to always be brothers. "That trumps even the bro code."

"Austin's going to be there." The words came rushing out as if he wanted to put them behind him.

"At the New Chance. On Friday night." As that idea hit home, Sawyer realized this dinner could be *his* new chance. He also knew that, once again, the timing sucked.

"Yeah. Heather already asked her and she's okay with it."

"Then the real reason we're here having wings and brew is because your wife wants to play matchmaker."

"No. The real reason is what I said. That we didn't get time to catch up at the party. And yeah, there's a secondary agenda."

"Okay."

"But here's the deal . . . What? Did you just say okay?"

"Yeah. As long as neither of you try to marry us off between the appetizers and desserts."

"I'll try to rein my wife in," Tom promised.

Sawyer laughed. Then realized he'd forgotten how something as simple as a laugh could loosen knots that had been tying up his guts for so long. "Good luck with that."

8

NERVES TANGLING, HER mouth as dry as sawdust, Austin knocked on the door of the cabin. Sawyer's truck was parked outside, and she'd seen him working in Duke's stall earlier, but when he didn't immediately answer, she wondered if he might have gone off with one of his brothers. She was just about to leave when he opened the door, wearing only a pair of Wranglers and a towel looped around his neck.

He looked surprised to see her. But not all that disappointed, which Austin took as encouragement.

"Sorry. I was in the shower." He ran a hand down his chest. Above the unfastened button, it was hard and dark and wet. The thought of him in the shower, one hand braced against the tile she'd helped her dad install, while hot water streamed over his naked, ripped body, had her swallowing hard.

"I can come back. After you get dressed." *Or, hey, maybe, since you're already nearly naked, maybe you'd like to drag me into the bedroom and have your wicked way with me.*

"Why would you want to do that?" He moved aside. "Come on in. It is, after all, your place."

She looked up at him, searching for an edge of resentment that she'd ended up his landlady. But his eyes gave nothing away.

"I thought I'd bring you a moving-in gift." She held out the wildflowers she'd stuck in a mason jar.

"Thanks." He took them from her and crossed into the kitchen area. Some things never changed. Sawyer Murphy still had the best Wrangler butt of any cowboy she'd ever known.

"You're welcome." She was feeling a little foolish about having brought them over. More so when she noticed the cabin was as empty as Jim and Janet had left it. A man who didn't care about furniture probably didn't have any need for posies. "Though it would be helpful if you had a table to put them on," she said pointedly.

He shrugged, calling her attention to the raised silver scar from a past surgery for a broken clavicle running across his bare shoulder. The sight brought back the memory of him crashing into the gate as the bull exploded from the chute. It wasn't long after that the rogue animal had been taken off the circuit. Challenging bulls were what made the sport what it was. But there was no place for ones who'd try to kill the riders.

Austin didn't want to think about how he'd acquired those new scars marring that beautiful chest.

"Not much need for a table when I've got this counter," he said. Another shrug sent a bead of water off that curve between his neck and shoulder. When it disappeared into the happy trail of dusky hair that disappeared under that unfastened waistband, sorely tempted to follow it with her fingers, she slipped her hands into the pockets of her jeans to keep them out of trouble.

"And this stool beats sitting on a rock or my helmet to

LONG ROAD HOME   71

eat."

"You're not in Afghanistan anymore," she reminded him. Without waiting for permission, she went down the short hall to the larger of the three bedrooms. "You don't even have a bed."

"Again, not needed."

Which told Austin all she needed to know. If he'd intended to make a move on her, wouldn't he at least want a mattress to tumble her on?

A silence as wide as Black Bear River during a high spring runoff stretched between them. Although it might have been a trick of the sun streaming into the window, she thought she saw his eyes darken.

Was he thinking the same thing she was? Was he remembering that impulsive kiss they'd shared? Could he, like she'd done countless times, be imagining taking it deeper, hotter, to its natural conclusion?

Which, she admitted, as heat from Sawyer's eyes warmed her skin, wouldn't need a proper bed.

"I was just thinking about you," he said, scrubbing a hand over his military-short-cropped hair.

"Were you?" *When you were in the shower?*

"Yeah. I got a call from Heather earlier."

"Oh?" Pretending that she had no idea what it might be about, Austin took her hands from her pockets and ran her thumb back and forth over a nail she'd chipped earlier on a fence gate.

"Did she call you?"

"Not today," she hedged. Damn if this wasn't getting more and more like high school. "But she dropped by yesterday with the kids."

"Did she mention going to dinner with her and Tom at

the New Chance?"

"It came up in passing." It was Austin's turn to shrug. "We pretty much left the idea up in the air."

"Well, she said she'd like us both to come. On Friday."

Her heart hitched. For a moment, Austin forgot how to breathe. "What did you say?"

"At first I said I didn't think it was a good idea."

Which, from the fact that he hadn't come over and said as much as hello since leasing the pasture, wasn't that much of a surprise. If he'd wanted to spend time with her, it wasn't exactly as if they were still living on different continents.

"I suppose you have a lot to do," she said helpfully. "Getting back into the swing of civilian life."

"I'm adjusting okay." The firm set of his chin suggested that the statement through tight teeth wasn't the whole truth, but Austin wasn't going to challenge him on it. "But it was the idea of crashing their anniversary that seemed weird."

"That's what I thought," Austin admitted.

"Then she said how she'd been wanting time to talk to me at the party, but she'd been too busy helping dish up the food, then cleaning up, for us to have any time alone."

"You said it was quite a crowd."

"Yeah." He rubbed his jaw. He hadn't had that light beard when he'd kissed her, and now, watching the absent gesture had her wondering what it would feel like. Against her face. Her breasts. And, dear heaven, lower still. "Hanging out with the two of them again could seem like old times, I guess."

"I always have fun with them. And, of course, their kids." Although she was still nervous, worried that he might sense that he'd been set up, Austin felt her lips smiling. As they always did when she thought of Jack and Sophie.

"They've grown up a lot," Sawyer said. "And changed. Sophie's nearly a young lady, and Jack, well, he's a firecracker."

Austin laughed at the spot-on description. "He is. He reminds me of you at that age."

He lifted a brow. "I may have presented a challenge to my folks, but I never had to be rescued from a tree."

"A tree?"

"Yeah. He climbed a big old apple tree in the orchard at the party while no one was looking and got himself so far out on a limb he couldn't figure out how to turn around and get back down again."

"Oh, dear." And so Jack. "Did someone go up and get him?"

"We debated that and worried that too much could go wrong. So Coop drove over to the county maintenance lot and brought back the cherry picker the linemen use."

"I'll bet he was in seventh heaven getting to ride in that."

Sawyer's answering laugh sounded rough and rusty. As if he hadn't used it a lot lately. "The trick will be to keep him from climbing up more high places just to get rescued again. Both Tom and Cooper gave him a stern lecture once his feet were back on the ground."

"Maybe it'll actually take." Austin wasn't holding out a lot of hope.

"So, you want to go?"

"To dinner?"

"Yeah. Friday night. At the New Chance."

Yes! "It sounds nice," she said mildly. "You haven't eaten there since Rachel took it over, have you?"

"No. But I had some of her food at the party. It was really good and Cooper tells me she's turned the place around."

"She's beyond fabulous. I could see her as one of those TV Iron Chefs. People were afraid she was going to serve fancy New York City food. Not that they don't have steak in New York, but you know."

"Yeah. Which would've gone over about as well as a vegan sprouts place," he said.

"True. But she somehow manages to take the western food people around here expect and are used to and elevate it. She even got Jake Buchanan to eat juniper-berry-encrusted venison with a red wine and crimini mushroom sauce."

"That sounds pretty damn good."

"It's amazing. But you're talking about a guy who's always eaten his steak charred to the texture of a burnt boot."

"A cowboy mortal sin."

"Isn't it? I've always found that strange since he's a lifelong cattleman. Anyway, Rachel actually has him up to ordering medium well."

"By the time he's a centenarian, he might have worked his way up to eating beef like it's supposed to be eaten."

Austin laughed, feeling the knot in her stomach begin to loosen. This was more like old times, just two friends having an easy conversation. "I said she's amazing. Not a miracle worker."

Sawyer seemed to be relaxing, as well. Those wide shoulders weren't squared away as if he were standing at attention, and his smile appeared more genuine. More the way she remembered it. It was a half-smile that had always seemed to say, "You know that I know you want me."

Austin had seen it work its charm on baby girls in strollers to teenage girls to elderly ladies, like Edna Graham, who'd retired from her job as River's Bend's librarian back when they'd been in high school but still showed up a few hours a week to ensure that things continued to run properly.

"So," he said, breaking into a memory of Edna getting into tussles with a few of the less open-minded locals over her prominent display of banned books every year, "since we wouldn't want to cause them to head out of town on their way to Ashland too late, I figured I could pick you up around five."

"You're going to pick me up?"

"Sure. We're both going to the same place."

This time when he shrugged that tanned, scarred shoulder, Austin had a sudden urge to lick it. Then take a nip. Not a hard one. Just enough to leave her brand. "Doesn't make sense to take two rigs," he pointed out.

Could it really be this easy? Deciding that when Heather got back from her anniversary trip, she was going to treat them both to a spa day over in K. Falls, Austin smiled. "Five sounds great." Deciding to leave now, before he changed his mind or she caved in to the impulse to just jump him, she said, "I've got to go feed the horses."

"Thanks again for the flowers," he said as he walked her the few feet to the door.

"No problem. They were just growing there, after all." She was on the porch when she turned and looked back at him. He was standing in the doorway, the lowering sun gilding his naked flesh a gleaming copper. Once again her fingers tingled with the urge to touch his chest and see if it was as warm as it looked. "Oh, and Sawyer?"

"Yeah?"

"Buy yourself some furniture. You're not in Afghanistan anymore. Or roughing it on a roundup."

Her business done, she headed toward the barn. And although she didn't look back, Austin could feel Sawyer watching her walk away.

9

BY FRIDAY MORNING, Austin was a nervous wreck. She was trying to stay low-key. After all, it was just a dinner with friends. No big deal. Right?

Wrong.

Not helping was Heather dropping by and vetoing the jeans and blouse she'd planned to wear.

"I don't want him to think I'm trying to lasso him," Austin protested.

"That's exactly what you're doing," Heather said. "Guys aren't that adept at nuance. You have to hit him between the eyes." She was deep in the closet, shoving hangers aside. "This skirt." She pulled out a short washed-denim skirt with a swirly line of rhinestones edging the hip pocket.

"That was an impulse buy from our day at the outlet mall last summer." One that still had the tags.

"I remember. Layla and I had to spend all lunch talking you into going back to the store to buy it."

"I knew I shouldn't have had that margarita with my taco salad."

"If that's what it takes to loosen you up, I'm ordering a pitcher for the table tonight." Heather continued searching.

"What happened to the blouse you bought to go with it?"

"I don't know."

"Good try." She unearthed it from beneath a thick cardigan rag sweater. "Here it is."

The cream-hued crocheted top was just barely lined for modesty. But its neckline dove low to showcase cleavage that Austin didn't have. "It's tacky."

"A bit," Heather agreed. "But guys respond really, really well to tacky." She tossed it on the bed beside the skirt. "Especially ones who've spent the past year being around women wearing camo or burkas. Wear your rodeo queen boots."

"I'll look like I belong in a country music video," Austin complained.

"All the better. Desperate times call for desperate measures."

"I'm not desperate."

"Aren't you? Look." Heather crossed her arms. "You and Sawyer have screwed this up too many times. So now you're back to square one, and if you don't do something to get the man off the dime, you may end up losing him to someone else."

Okay. Austin hadn't considered that possibility.

Which was why, seven hours later, she was still second-guessing the entire idea.

"Pacing a path in the floor isn't going to speed the clock up any," Buck pointed out.

"I just don't want to be late. This is a big weekend for Heather and Tom." She really needed to change back into jeans.

"The boy isn't late yet." He tapped a hand on the face of his wide, leather-banded watch. "He's still got time."

"I realize that." She'd only checked the clock about ten times in the past ten minutes.

Her father's eyes swept over her. "You're pretty spiffed up for the New Chance." Austin held her breath, waiting for the inevitable criticism. "Murphy's toast."

"It's just a dinner with friends," Austin insisted. The outfit was definitely overkill. It'd be like walking into the New Chance with a neon Do Me! sign over her head.

"Which explains why you and Heather spent all that time in your room this morning." He lifted a brow. "Reminded me a lot of when you two were back in high school."

Which was just what Austin didn't need to hear since she couldn't deny how close to those days this situation was. The only difference was back then she was the one helping Heather choose outfits to wow Tom Campbell.

"You and Sawyer Murphy have been waltzing around each other most of your lives," he said, surprising Austin, who hadn't even realized he'd been paying attention. Perhaps there was that rare dad a girl could talk with about boys, but Buck Merrill had never been him. " 'Bout time one of you made a move."

She was about to insist that she had no intention of making a move, when Sawyer's truck—which she knew he'd bought used from Radley Biehn, who'd moved up to an SUV because his wife was pregnant with a surprise fourth baby—pulled up in front of the house.

"I've got to go." She grabbed her jacket from the hook by the front door.

"Not till he comes in and gets you proper-like," Buck said.

"Dad." Austin rolled her eyes. "I'm not sixteen."

"And neither is he. Which is why he should know that a gentleman doesn't expect a lady to come running out to his truck like some girl in a country song."

"Interesting analogy." Who'd have thought her dad and Heather would be on the same page about anything? Even as she watched Sawyer climb out of the cab of the red truck and come around the hood, headed toward the door, Austin laughed. "My life seems to have turned into a country song the past couple years." Including marrying a man whose last name she could barely remember the next morning.

Her father's rugged features softened in a way that she hadn't seen since she was ten and Matilda, the loyal Australian shepherd he'd allowed to sleep on her bed after her mother had left them, had died of old age.

"You've been through a rough patch," he said, not even trying to deny what everyone in River's Bend already knew too well. "But country music is about a helluva lot more than crying in your beer. Some of those tunes have happy endings." He nodded decisively. "Which, if you ask me, you and that boy are overdue for."

Love flooded through her like a river. Buck Merrill might not be one to toss compliments around like confetti, he might be gruff and stubborn as one of the mules he used to use for packing supplies up to high pastures, but Austin had never, for one minute, doubted that she was well and truly loved.

She bent down and hugged him. "You're the best dad ever."

She knew she'd disappointed him by up and marrying Jace, but he'd never, not once, said anything negative about her impulsive behavior. Even when she'd filed for divorce, all he'd had to say about the situation was, "Good riddance to bad rubbish."

She was about to ask him not to share their conversation with Sawyer, when there was a knock on the door. Smoothing down the front of the skirt—wishing her fairy godmother would suddenly show up and add three, make that six inches to it—Austin went to let him in.

"Hey." His gaze, as it moved from head to toe, lingered for a heartbeat on her cleavage. Or lack of it, not that he appeared to care. "You look great."

"Which is another way of saying I clean up well?" Realizing that she may have sounded defensive, she tried to move on by skimming a look over him. "You look pretty good, too, cowboy."

This time she'd managed a teasing tone, like one old friend ragging on another. "I like that shirt." Instead of the expected snap-front western shirt, he was wearing a black Sleater-Kinney band T-shirt topped with an open green-and-black watch plaid shirt with his Wranglers and Tony Lama boots.

"The girls have made a comeback," he said, flashing that quick grin that had started making her toes curl back in middle school. "And high time."

Although he listened to country like everyone else Austin knew, Sawyer had stood out in high school with his band shirts, some of which had gotten him sent home to change. Which was yet another trip down memory lane.

Which, in turn, had Austin wondering if, just maybe, he'd worn the shirt to send a message. Maybe that while a lot had changed, he wasn't all that different? And even, perhaps, that she wasn't the only one wishing they could go back in time and take a do-over?

Glancing past her to Buck, who was still seated in the La-Z-Boy, Sawyer took off his straw Stetson as he entered the house. "It's good to see you again, sir."

"Same here." Putting both hands on the wide arms, although it took an obvious effort, her father managed to push himself upright out of the chair and held out a rough and work-gnarled hand. "Glad you made it back home in one piece."

"That makes two of us," Sawyer said. Although his smile stayed in place, Austin, who was watching him carefully, noticed the shadow drift across his whiskey-brown eyes. "Thanks for the lease of your pastureland."

"Makes no damn sense having it sit idle," Buck said gruffly. "Good to see cattle on it again." He glanced over at Austin, then back to Sawyer as he gingerly lowered himself to his seat. "Heard you're a hero."

"You won't be hearing that from me," Sawyer said mildly.

"Modest, too." He shot Austin a pointed look that had her holding her breath that he wouldn't get into their relationship. Whatever it might be. Then, to her relief, he turned his attention back to Sawyer. "War's never easy."

"And yet governments keep having them."

While his legs might not be as strong and steady as they once were, her father's intimidating stare could still blister paint off the barn from a hundred yards. "I was in Lebanon for the barracks bombing. Came home with what these days they're calling *issues*. You got any PTSD problems?"

"That must have been tough." Sawyer didn't flinch beneath her father's probing gaze. "But I've no issues that I can't deal with, sir." He paused a beat, as if choosing his words carefully. "As I expect you did with yours."

"Yeah. I did. But it took time."

"Something I've got plenty of," Sawyer pointed out.

Her dad blew out a breath, apparently signaling the end of the third-degree parental interrogation.

"Well, you'd best get going," he said. "You two have a good time. And"—he jabbed a finger at Sawyer—"you're going to have my little girl in that rig, so don't go driving the way you used to. Like you were trying out for pole position at Talladega."

"Dad," Austin murmured.

"Yessir," Sawyer responded politely while Austin's cheeks burned with embarrassment. "And I promise to have her home by midnight."

"Didn't necessarily say that," Buck qualified, making the blush flame even hotter in her face before moving down her chest, which she feared Sawyer could see due to that damn low-necked blouse Heather had pushed on her. "My daughter's a grown woman. How she spends her nights would be her own business."

After blowing her father a kiss goodbye, Austin made her escape.

"I'm sorry about that," she said as they walked out to the pickup.

"Can't say I'd blame him." Sawyer shrugged as he opened the passenger door. "I'd probably feel the same way if I had a daughter I was sending out on a date."

"Not that this is a date," she felt obliged to say as she climbed up into the seat.

"It's been a long time since I've been on a date," he said. "But I do know when a woman dresses up in rhinestones and lace and brings out the pots of girly stuff for her face, she's not thinking of burgers and beer with her buddies."

He'd closed the door and gone around the front of the truck before that comment sunk in.

Even as she was grateful he'd noticed the effort she'd gone to, Austin wasn't certain either of them were ready for this. "Heather talked me into the outfit," she said when he'd joined her in the cab.

He gave her a sideways glance. "Remind me to thank her."

"This is complicated," she said as they turned onto the paved road leading into town.

"It shouldn't be. But, yeah, it is," he agreed. "Especially since, like I told your dad, I came home with some stuff I'm dealing with."

"I'm sorry. If you need someone to talk with—"

"Thanks, but it's not anything I can't handle." His curt tone had her envisioning a forest of oversized No Trespassing signs springing up across the landscape.

"At least you have your brothers, who undoubtedly understand, having both served." When he didn't respond, Austin feared this dinner idea could end up a drastic mistake. "Meanwhile, I'm just glad that you're back."

"You're sure as hell not alone there," he said.

As they drove down Front Street, Austin thought, again, how much she couldn't imagine living anywhere else. While with a population a bit under four thousand, River's Bend might not have all the amenities of a city like Portland or even Eugene, she loved its quaint western charm.

Seeking tourism dollars, an earlier town council, long before she'd been born, had come up with the idea of billing itself as "Oregon's Most Western Town—where spurs have a job to do and cowboy hats aren't a fashion accessory." The ploy had worked. While ranching remained the top industry, tourism was coming close, thanks to the outdoor lifestyle, growing proliferation of dude ranches, and the number of western movies that had been filmed there.

Gene Autry, John Wayne, and Clint Eastwood had all ridden horseback down Front Street. So had Doc Holliday, Wyatt Earp, along with both Butch Cassidy and the Sundance Kid. But other than Butch and Sundance, the make-believe cowboys had bigger displays in the local historical museum.

One of the pluses of being a go-to location for western films was that typically crews would return the storefronts to an even better condition than they'd found them, which had proven a good deal for local merchants over the years. An admitted downside was the fact that more and more movie people were offering top dollar for a piece of paradise to escape to.

The trees along Front Street had greened up, and perky-faced purple-and-yellow pansies tumbled over the flower boxes below the store windows.

"Harry and Hank are still playing checkers," he murmured as they passed Harry's Barber Shop, where the barber and hardware owner were seated outside on a wooden bench with the board between them.

"Some things never change. They've been doing that nearly every day for as long as I can remember."

In the winters, when she'd go to town with her dad, she'd see them through the window, playing next to the woodstove that Harry had once used for heat. After an errant spark had nearly burned down the shop—and risked setting the entire block of wooden buildings on fire, he'd given in to the county fire marshal and switched to electric.

While many things stayed the same, the New Chance, which had been gutted by a fire last fall, was nothing like the tumbling-down restaurant Rachel Hathaway had bought, sight unseen, while living back east with her young son.

"The steer's gone," Sawyer said as he pulled into the parking lot. The fiberglass steer on the roof of the New Chance Café had, for many years, been a River's Bend landmark.

"It was one of the first things to go. But Rachel saved it and put it in the backyard of their rental house. Then they took it to your brother's when they moved in with him. Cooper's been using it to teach Scott to rope."

"Never too young to learn."

Which was true enough. But the missing steer was just yet more proof that the planet hadn't stopped spinning during all those years he'd been away.

10

"IT DOESN'T LOOK like the same place," he said as they walked in the door. The entry had been widened, and although Sawyer wasn't a gardener, he figured the skylight must provide sun for whatever kind of potted pine tree sat next to the hostess stand.

"In a way, the fire proved a blessing in disguise. Since the place was left a gut job, Rachel was able to design her dream restaurant."

"She definitely pulled it off." Cooper had shared the story of how the entire town had pitched in, not only to ensure residents would continue to have a restaurant but to help a young widow and her son settle into the community.

"Hey, Austin." Janine Walker, who was behind the hostess stand, greeted them with the megawatt smile she used to flash to folks in the bleachers during her cheerleader days. "It's good to have you back home, Sawyer."

"It's good to be back," he said for the ten-gazillionth time over the past week.

"Heather and Tom are already here. They reserved a booth so you guys can have some privacy."

The smile turned a bit sly, Sawyer thought. As if she knew about Heather's matchmaking scheme. Then again, maybe she was just remembering that July summer night they'd shared a kiss atop the Ferris wheel at the county fair when they were both trying to make someone else jealous.

Which had worked for her when Dave Ellingson had come crawling back to her after a fling with a fellow counselor while at the Presbyterian church camp at Crescent Lake. Meanwhile, if Austin had even noticed him dating Janine for that two-week period, apparently it hadn't bothered her, because she'd never said a word.

For as long as he could remember, the New Chance had been a westernized version of any small town's greasy spoon. It had been dark and dingy, and the menu, while not actually offering up a side of ptomaine as locals had long joked, had done nothing to stimulate any appetites.

Rachel had opened up what he remembered to be a smoke-stained popcorn ceiling to the high rafters, which highlighted antique embossed copper tiles. The old log walls, which had undoubtedly been embedded with decades of nicotine going back to when smoking was allowed, had been covered with sheetrock and painted a warm gold that enhanced framed paintings celebrating the town's western heritage.

Heads swiveled toward them as they wound their way past the hand-carved bar from an 1800s Gold Rush brothel Sawyer knew Mitzi had unearthed in a Jacksonville antique shop.

"I think we're now number one on the gossip hit parade," Austin murmured as they passed the open kitchen, where meats grilled on open flames and stews bubbled away on the stove.

"They're looking at you." Who wouldn't? The pertinent question was what the hell was wrong with the men of

River's Bend that they'd let Austin Merrill get away all these years?

She shook her head. "You'd think I'd never worn a skirt before."

"I like it." He refrained from saying that he'd never seen her wear a skirt like that before. The clunk of his heels against the original tongue-and-groove wood floor Rachel had uncovered beneath the peeling old avocado-green linoleum was a familiar, distinctive sound that combat boots had never replaced. Like the rushing Black Bear River and the soft lowing of cattle at sundown, that clunk was another welcome sound of home.

"You're here!" Heather jumped up from a back booth snuggled next to a beehive fireplace. She tackle-hugged Austin, then Sawyer. "What fun to have the gang back together again!"

After hugging her back, Sawyer shared a half guy hug with Tom. "Good luck," his friend murmured as the women leaned back, checked one another out, and complimented each other on their outfits.

Which, in Austin's case, had been a major surprise. Sawyer had known she was leggy from the way she'd started to spout like a weed back in fourth grade. And later, all those years swimming in the natural hole at the river's bend that had given the town its name had caused his adolescent hormone-driven body all kinds of misery. But he'd forgotten that those strong, slender legs went all the way up to her neck. And he'd never, that he could remember, seen them in a skirt that short.

When his pheromone-hammered brain had imagined unbuttoning those flat metal jean buttons down the front of the skirt, he'd slammed the vision shut, afraid Buck, still being a guy himself despite his health problems, might be able to read his mind.

From the way her father's wiry gray brows had dived toward a nose that had been broken on more than one occasion during his rodeoing days, Sawyer knew he'd been busted.

"I hope you haven't been waiting long," Austin said as she slid into the booth. The skirt scooted up a bit, causing a lightning bolt of heat to shoot below Sawyer's belt.

"We just got here," Heather assured her.

"What'll you have?" Tom asked as a waitress in black jeans and a starched white shirt arrived with her pencil and pad ready.

Sawyer glanced over at Austin, realizing that he had no idea what she liked. It was odd how, in some ways, being with her felt like just yesterday, while a Grand Canyon-size chasm had opened between those days and now.

"I'll have a margarita, please," she said, smiling up at the waitress, whom he belatedly recognized as having gone steady with Ryan during most of his brother's sophomore year of high school. "Frozen. With salt."

"A Bud Light for me." Despite what he'd been told about Rachel's home-style cooking, given her background catering to the East Coast's one percent, Sawyer wondered if she carried anything but pricey artisan craft brew.

The waitress didn't bat an eye. "A frozen margarita with salt and every cowboy's label of choice," she said, sounding resigned as she wrote the order down. The beer, like the boot clunk, was a basic part of life. Just like you wouldn't catch a cowboy wearing designer jeans or pimping up a pickup.

"Thanks, Laci," he said, after they'd all agreed to order

what Heather assured him was the café's signature spinach and artichoke dip with grilled flatbread and tri-color tortilla chip appetizer.

She'd just slipped the pad into the pocket of her short black apron and looked up, seeming surprised. "You remembered me."

"Sure. I always thought you were too good for Ry," he said as more memories had filtered through the fog of years. There'd been a time when the two teenage lovebirds had looked as if they might actually be getting serious. Which might have been too young, but not unusual in small towns, where everyone knew everyone and people tended to pair up early.

Then their mother had died of ovarian cancer, and Ryan, who'd always planned to be the first astronaut from Oregon, had changed direction, instead focusing every atom of his attention toward becoming a doctor.

"I'm not sure about that. I always knew that I wanted to get married and have kids, while Ryan had other, bigger plans. Especially after . . ."

Her voice drifted off, as she realized that the topic of their mother dying wasn't a topic conducive for a fun evening.

"He's always been single focused," Sawyer agreed, wanting to help her out.

"Which worked out well. For both of us. He became a doctor like he was determined to do, and I settled down and had three kids with Garrett Henley. Who, by the way, brews that cold-filtered, no preservatives or additives, made with four different kinds of malt Rogue Rodeo Red Ale you didn't order."

"Well, hell," Sawyer said, flashing her a grin that pulled

at the muscles in his face and felt decidedly rusty. "Why don't you change my order and I'll give it a shot."

She tossed a grin right back at him. "You won't be sorry."

Although the café was nearly filled, she was back in a couple minutes with a margarita the size of a swimming pool and a stubby brown bottle with a bucking bronc on the label. Because he knew Ryan's old flame was waiting, Sawyer tipped the bottle back and swallowed.

"This is good stuff." It was. Robust, complex, but satisfying.

"Of course it is. That's why Rachel stocks it. She also likes that it's natural, which makes it good for you. In moderation."

He took another taste. "You and Garrett had better get ready for your simple life to amp up," he said. "Because this brew could take off."

"From your lips. We've got kids to send to college down the road." She laid down four tan menus with dark brown script, which were a long way from the yellowed, laminated, food-stained plastic Johnny Mott had used forever. "Take your time. The booth's booked for you guys as long as you want it tonight."

"Small towns," Tom said as they watched her walk over to a table across the room.

"My favorite kind," Heather said. "I enjoyed living in Corvallis when we were in school, but although it's a nice college town, and Portland was fun to visit, it never felt like home.

"So." She blew out a breath. "Because this is a special occasion and it's been so long since we've all been together, I brought a memory book to share."

She pulled out a small blue photo album embellished with the family name and dates on the front in a calligraphy Austin remembered her teaching herself back in middle school. She'd always been the creative one of the two of them. Give Heather Campbell a glue gun, tape, and some cardboard and the woman could probably build a house. "Of course you both remember this day."

"Best day of my life," Tom said.

She dimpled prettily. "And isn't that exactly what you're supposed to say?"

"We look so young," Austin murmured, looking down at the wedding photo. So filled with hopes and dreams of happily-ever-afters. Which Heather and Tom had managed to achieve, despite marrying right after their freshman year of college.

She was standing next to Heather, holding a smaller version of the bride's pastel bouquet created from hydrangeas, roses, and peonies. Although the flowers had come from Tom's mother's garden, they'd managed to talk Heather into allowing Lily Sullivan, who owned Blossoms, the local florist shop, to arrange the bouquets. As Mrs. Campbell had wisely pointed out, even Wonder Woman had her limits.

Lexi O'Halloran, the other bridesmaid, who'd arrived for the wedding from Nevada with blue hair and a pink toolbox filled with mysterious pots, tubes, and brushes, had pulled Austin's hair into a tidy figure-eight knot at the back of her neck. She'd also insisted on painting all their faces, which had made Austin nervous, given that Lexi had spent the past two years glamorizing showgirls in Vegas. Yet, somehow, although the hair stylist/makeup artist had put enough gunk on to spackle a barn, she'd magically made

Austin look just like a better, sexier, almost hot version of herself.

Sawyer, wearing a white rosebud in the lapel of the dark suit he'd bought for high school graduation, was standing in the best man spot beside a beaming Tom, who looked like a kid who'd just had Christmas arrive six months early. Standing next to Sawyer was Brody Ames, another lifelong friend.

"We were mere babies," Heather agreed. "I was a baby having a baby." She reached over and laced her fingers with her husband's. "But I wouldn't change a thing."

"Me, neither."

Tom lifted their joined hands to his lips in a moment so intimate Austin looked away, only to have her gaze clash with Sawyer's. His eyes were shuttered, revealing nothing, while she feared that everything she'd ever felt for him, was *still* feeling, was flashing for everyone in the New Chance to see.

"And, not that I'm tooting my own horn or anything," Heather said with a laugh, breaking the suspended moment, "but after two kids and a dozen years, I can still fit in the dress."

"You were, and still are, gorgeous," Austin said. "And I'll be eternally grateful that you didn't make me dress like Annie Oakley."

Instead of going for western wedding attire, which tended to be popular in ranching country, Heather had worn a floaty, snowy cloud of tulle over an eight-month baby bump. She had, unsurprisingly, made the dress herself, and somehow, despite a rapidly approaching due date, she'd even managed to bead the bodice during finals week. She was wearing the simple pearl necklace and earrings that her mother had worn at *her* wedding.

The blue bridesmaids' sleeveless sheaths they'd found on a day trip across the mountains to Shirley's Bridal was simple and classic and, atypical for many bride's attendant dresses Austin had since worn, suitable for wearing after the wedding.

"Since I only expect to get married once, I decided I deserved something princessy," Heather said. "Like you and I always dreamed of wearing when we'd play wedding." Belatedly realizing how that lighthearted comment might sound, given Austin's quickie marriage and divorce, she winced. "I'm sorry."

"Don't worry about it," Austin assured her. "I was thrilled you wore your princess dress. Especially since you guys definitely set the standard for fairy-tale happily-ever-afters."

"It hasn't exactly been all a bed of roses." As if wanting to get beyond the delicate subject of weddings, Heather literally turned the page to another day three months later, in front of the altar at Our Lady of the River. "And here you both are again. At Sophie's baptism."

Austin was back in the blue dress, Sawyer in his suit. Sophie was wearing a long white baptismal gown that had been passed down through Heather's family from her great-grandmother. Austin remembered the lace being so frail they were afraid if the baby had decided to start kicking too hard, the dress would shred.

"That little girl had a set of lungs on her, that's for sure," Sawyer said, reminding them of the baby girl's ear-splitting objection to having water poured over her head.

"It's ironic," Tom mused. "Sophie screeched like a banshee when she was born. But Jack was as peaceful as a baby lamb."

"And look how that's turned around," Heather said. "Sophie is my little helper, and her brother's a perpetual motion dynamo from the moment his feet hit the floor in the morning until he crashes into bed at night." She grinned over at her husband. "Your mom always says Sophie was a screamer because she could sense our fear."

"There was sure enough to sense back then," Tom agreed. "From the moment we put her in the car outside the hospital, I was scared spitless."

"You stayed that way almost until her first birthday," Heather recalled. "It took a week before he didn't go pale as paper just holding her," she told the others.

Austin laughed, even as she vaguely recalled those first days when Heather had always been the one to hold their daughter. "That's hard to imagine." This was, after all, a man accustomed to treating animals that could roll over and crush him while he knelt on a bed of straw turning a breech calf around.

"It's true," he said. "I finally got comfortable. But now that she's turning into a young woman way too fast, I'm starting to worry all over again."

"Because, having been a teenage boy yourself, you know exactly what to worry about," Heather said.

They all shared a laugh as a dark flush rose on the back of Tom's neck, confirming the comment.

"And here's when your dad stood proxy for you for Jack's baptism," Heather said to Sawyer as she turned another page.

Since it had been winter, Austin was in a heather-hued sweater dress Heather had woven, while Dan Murphy, wearing a western-cut brown suit, had looked like the hot, older Mark Harmon. He still did, giving Austin an idea of what Sawyer might look like when he was his father's age.

"I was sorry to miss it," Sawyer said. Which was definitely true since he'd been on a covert mission to Somalia at the time. A place that had seemed about as far away from River's Bend as a guy could get.

"We totally understood," Heather assured him. "You were fighting to keep our children safe." The smile she bestowed on him was as warm as August sunshine, making Sawyer think, yet again, what a lucky son of a bitch his best friend was.

You could've had that, a too familiar mocking voice reminded him. *If you hadn't blown it. Big-time.*

Sensing that Austin was as studiously avoiding his gaze as he was hers, Sawyer was relieved when his brother's fiancée delivered their appetizers herself.

"Here you go," Rachel said cheerfully, putting the platter in the center of the table. "Enjoy and feel free to spend as much time as you'd like. And, by the way, don't hold back ordering. The meals are on the house."

"You don't have to do that," Tom and Sawyer said together.

"It's my pleasure. The entire staff is so pleased to be able to share, in some small way, in such a special night for you all. You and Tom celebrating your anniversary," she said to Heather.

Then her eyes zeroed in like a laser on Sawyer. "And you finally being back home where you belong. With your family." She glanced briefly but so pointedly at Austin, Sawyer could practically see the flashing red arrow. "And friends."

Both dip and message delivered, she smiled. "Again,

take your time. And although it's not on the menu, we have rainbow trout so fresh it's practically jumping out of the pan. It's pan roasted with brown sage butter and Meyer lemons."

"That sounds great," Heather said. "And again, thanks so much for keeping the kids for us."

"It's my pleasure. When I left the house, Jack and Scott were beating the socks off Cooper at Mario Cart, and Sophie was mixing up some oatmeal cookies. She's becoming quite a baker."

"Thanks to Austin," Heather said. "I like to think I have many talents. But get me near a kitchen, and I'm downright dangerous."

"Anyone can burn fried chicken," Tom said loyally.

"True. But how many nearly burn the house down?"

"It was only a couple cabinets."

As she rolled her eyes and they all shared a laugh over what sounded as if it could have been far more serious, Sawyer felt a tug of envy.

How was it, he wondered, that some people could get it right? Tom and Heather, Coop and Rachel, and hell, even his dad had fallen into love with a woman who adored him right back not just once but twice. Most of the guys he'd gone to high school with were already settled down, seeming happy enough, from those who'd shown up at the party. Some, their wives and a couple of rug rats in tow, had been downright smug.

So, why couldn't he seem to get things right? He'd known Austin Merrill all of his life. Surrendered his heart to her a very long time ago. And yet, as they'd spent all those years dancing around each other, they always seemed just a beat out of step.

Maybe, Sawyer considered, remembering back to stumbling over his feet while his dad had tried to teach him the box step when his eighth-grade class was required to attend a school dance, he'd been doing it all wrong.

Maybe, this time around, instead of worrying about fancy steps and smooth moves, he should do like he'd been taught.

Lead.

He was pondering that idea when the sudden backfire of a truck driving by caused him to nearly dive beneath the table.

Or maybe not, he decided as, heart hammering, he ignored the concerned gaze he felt Austin directing his way.

11

AUSTIN'S LIFE HAD revolved around worry for so long—worry about her dad, her marriage, followed by a divorce that was sadly far less painful than it probably should have been, bills, and the ranch—except for those monthly escapes to the book club, she'd forgotten what it felt like to relax and have fun.

The food—the trout for Heather and her, racks of dry-rubbed ribs for the guys—was, as always when Rachel was cooking, delicious. The company was easily familiar and as comfortable as sliding into a warm Jacuzzi at the end of a long day's trail ride. They shared stories and laughter and were making plans to get together again as soon as Tom and Heather got back from Ashland when Tom's cell chimed.

"Oh, no," Heather said. She shook her head. "Not tonight."

Tom's expression echoed the chagrin in her tone. "I need to check it."

"I know. The fact that you can't ignore a work call is only one of the reasons I love you," she said on a long, deep sigh. "But there are times, and this is one of them, that I almost wish I'd married an accountant."

"Then you'd have a husband you never saw during tax time," he reminded her as he pulled the phone from the pocket of his jeans. "This is Tom Campbell." He listened a bit, then, frowning, covered the phone. "Sorry. I have to take this outside."

"Who's the patron saint of veterinarians?" Heather asked rhetorically as he made his way through the tables to the door. "Because if there was ever a time for an intercession, this would be it."

"Hopefully it's not too serious," Austin said. But watching Tom out the new big windows, pacing the parking lot, wasn't encouraging.

"So," Sawyer said, in an obvious attempt to distract Heather's attention from thoughts of plans for a romantic weekend possibly being blasted to bits, "are either of the kids into sports?"

"Sophie plays soccer," she said, dragging her gaze from the parking lot. "Jack's in T-ball. He's technically age-eligible to play in Little League minors, but since he's still a bit of a wild card, Tom and I decided to put that off until next year."

"Sounds like a good idea." He was talking to the side of her head as her attention swiveled back out to the lot. "If it's any consolation, I wasn't exactly the easiest kid, either. But I turned out okay."

"That's encouraging." She straightened and Austin watched her breath hitch as Tom shoved the phone into his jeans pocket and came back into the café.

"It's okay," he said as he returned to the table.

"Really?" Hope was written in bold script across her face. Unlike Austin, who'd learned early on, when she'd been trying not to make her mother unhappy, Heather had never been one to hide her feelings.

"Well, mostly." He scooted back in beside his wife and put his arm around her shoulder. "Barry Carpenter's mare is having a difficult delivery. He tried to turn the foal, but it's not budging. I told him we'd stop by."

"I knew it." She shook her head.

"It didn't sound as if it'll take all that long," he assured her. "Barry's wife says the spring rains have his arthritis flaring up, so he's not as dexterous as he could be. Bottom line, I'll flip the foal and we'll be on our way."

Austin could see the pique of annoyance slide away as Heather put her hand on her husband's cheek and briefly touched her lips to his. "My hero," she said.

Rachel returned to the table as they stood up to leave. "I boxed up some cake," she said, revealing that she'd been watching events unfold. "I hope you'll enjoy it."

"I know we will," Heather said. "Thank you. For the amazing meal and deciding to move here to River's Bend. We never realized what we were missing until you bought this place."

Rachel laughed. "*I* never realized what I was missing until I bought it. Although I'll admit that the first sight of that cow on the roof gave me a moment's doubt."

After more promises to get together next weekend with the kids for a cookout at Green Springs, Heather gave Austin another hug.

"Text me," she said, as Tom and Sawyer made plans for some spring fishing on the river.

And then, taking their anniversary cake with them, they walked away, leaving Austin and Sawyer alone.

A little silence stretched out. Apparently, she considered, they still needed a buffer of other people. Things had been flowing so easily, but now that they were on their own, that gap, or wall, or whatever it was, had sprung up between them again.

"Feel like dessert?" he asked.

"I couldn't eat another thing," she said. "Plus, it's funny, but I spend so much time taste-testing all the baked goods I make for here and the bookstore, dessert has lost a lot of appeal. But don't let me stop you," she said.

"I'm fine."

"Good."

"Well, then." He took some bills from his wallet and slipped them under his plate for the waitress. "I guess we should be going."

"I guess so," she agreed. If for no other reason than to escape this inane conversation.

As they walked out of the restaurant, they passed the hostess stand, reminding Austin of that summer she'd seen Sawyer kissing Janine Walker atop the Ferris wheel.

It was funny, her date for the fair had been so unimportant she couldn't even remember who it had been. The only reason Austin had agreed to go with him was because Heather had, once again, set her up so she wouldn't feel like a third wheel going with the two lovebirds.

Now, watching the cheer-queen smile Janine flashed Sawyer's way, Heather's warning that if she didn't snatch him up, someone else would beat her to it, struck home.

If she wanted Sawyer Murphy, and she did, she'd be wise to cowgirl up and make her move. Before she ended up having to buy a set of monogramed towels for his wedding.

12

IT BEGAN TO drizzle as Sawyer drove out of town, headed back on the empty road to the ranch with Alan Jackson's "Remember When" drifting out from the radio.

Under different circumstances, Austin would have found the lyrics, advising them to cherish all memories, the good, the bad, and the romantic.

"Well," he said. "Except for the abrupt ending, that turned out well." And that flashback that he'd hoped to hell she wouldn't bring up.

"It did, didn't it? It was nice to all be back together again. And Rachel was sweet to gift the dinner."

"I always knew it would take a special woman to fill Ellen's place," Sawyer said. "Coop's a lucky man."

"From what I've seen, they're both lucky." Austin wondered if Cooper had shared his and Rachel's desire for another child, and decided it wasn't her business to mention it.

As if by unspoken agreement, the conversation shifted to safer topics: Cooper and Rachel's upcoming wedding, the Run the Rapids race on the river, the Readathon fundraiser for the library, and the annual Modoc County Fourth of July rodeo—with Green Springs providing the horse stock—and fireworks at the fairgrounds. Unfortunately, except for his brother's wedding, all those other occasions brought back memories of summers past. Summers Austin had watched Sawyer going out with seemingly every girl in the county and wondered if he'd ever open his eyes and notice her as more than just a friend.

Now, after all these years, weren't they right back in that same place?

As they reached the ranch house, as if tonight were country music theme night, Jason Michael Carroll began crooning "We Threw It All Away," a reunion song about former high school sweethearts. Not that she and Sawyer had been boyfriend and girlfriend back then. But still.

Austin was about to get out of the truck, when he caught her arm. "I'd catch hell from your dad if I didn't walk you to the door."

"I'm not sixteen, Sawyer," she repeated what she'd told her father earlier.

He gave her a slow, hot sweep of a look, the kind she'd gotten from him once before. Right before he'd pushed her up against the brick hospital wall and kissed her. "Believe me, I'm well aware of that."

So she waited for him to open her door, then walk her to the front porch. Just like, she thought again, this was a real a date.

"I had a good time," he said.

"Me, too."

There was a long pause, sometime during which Austin entirely forgot to breathe.

The drizzle, which had softened to a mist, added moisture to the evening air, which caused little ghosts of fog to drift in from the river. The mountain air was rapidly cooling, which didn't explain the crackling, like heat lightning, sparking between them.

He wanted her. Oh, he might not be willing to admit it, but Austin could read it in his eyes. He really had wonderful eyes. Like a yummy blend of warmed brandy and gold flecks.

She wanted him. He wanted her. They were both adults, so why didn't she just put a stop to all this dancing around and make her move? The idea was so, so tempting. But just then, the wooden porch began to sway.

Before her brain could sort out what was happening, Sawyer had pulled her off the porch into the driveway, safely away from the house. Then they stood there in the open, his legs braced and his arms tight around her as the rolling earth settled.

The slight tremor, which was not unusual for this part of the country (she'd learned in school that micro ones happened all the time without anyone feeling them), only lasted seconds. But while it had driven her into his arms, it had definitely shattered the mood.

"We haven't had one of those for a long time," she said as she took a single step back. A step that caused those shields, which had lifted during dinner, to lower over his eyes again. Not wanting the evening to end this way, she decided to try again. "For a second I thought it might be us."

"I suspect we could do a lot better than that." He might have shuttered his gaze, but that low, raspy, *hungry* voice caused her nipples to perk up.

"Would you like to come in for a beer?" she asked. "Or maybe coffee?" Although she hadn't seen any indication during dinner that Sawyer's "issues" included alcohol, Trace Eastwood, a former president of 4-H who'd earned a trip to Washington to meet the president back in high school, had returned from Iraq with a drinking problem.

"I'd better not. I've got a lot of work to do tomorrow, and you probably do, too."

It was barely past six thirty, and while ranchers got up earlier than most of the world, even her father stayed up until almost nine. So much for making her move. Even having Mother Nature throwing her into his arms hadn't had any effect. So, that was that.

"Well. Thanks for the ride to the café." Her cheeks ached from the pain of the forced smile. "Have a good evening."

She was climbing the three steps back onto the porch when Sawyer said, "I'm thinking of going furniture shopping tomorrow."

She looked back over her shoulder. "Good idea."

"So everyone keeps telling me." He jammed his hands into his back pockets and gave her a hot, direct look that she was surprised didn't set off at least a 5.3 quake. "I thought I'd begin with a bed."

Leaving her with that enticing idea, he straightened his hat and strolled back to his truck. Damn, he did have the best. Cowboy. Butt. Ever.

Austin stood in the doorway, hand to her hopeful heart, watching until his taillights disappeared past the house.

Fortunately, her father must be watching TV in his bedroom, leaving her to practically waltz down the long hall to her room, where she texted Heather, as she'd promised.

He's buying a bed.

And that, she thought, said it all.

When an answering text still hadn't come in by the time she went to bed, Austin decided that Tom must've solved the problem with the foal and the anniversary couple had already begun their celebratory weekend.

Smiling at that romantic idea, Austin decided that Sawyer wouldn't be the only one shopping tomorrow. She needed to score some lacy underwear, just in case she'd have an opportunity to show off her girls anytime soon.

13

I T FELT LIKE *one of those old movies his dad liked to watch on*
the Western Channel. He and his team were walking through a
box canyon with almost vertical walls. Looking up at the top of the
cliffs, Sawyer wouldn't have been surprised to see a tribe of Apaches
illuminated by the faint predawn light. With high vertical cliff faces to
the east and west and the end of the box at the north, the situation
was tailor-made for an ambush.

This was definitely serious bad guy territory. They'd already
passed signs of what, from all the spent shell casings on the ground,
appeared to be a terrorist practice range.

This wasn't good. When Sawyer saw the imprint of a sniper on
the ground—body, elbows, toes—as the insurgent had been shooting
his rifle, he called in a report to HQ. This wasn't his first rodeo.
He'd been through enough battles that he knew what were normal
adrenaline-spiked nerves and what were instincts developed in training
and battle.

Instructed to stay with the mission to locate the insurgents' camp,
then call in the drones, he told his men, none of whom looked any
more optimistic about their situation than he was, to keep on
humping.

As they pushed on, he kept checking out the tops of those cliffs.

"Damn." Internal alarm sirens started blaring when they found

the goat trail they were using as a roadway blocked by a disabled Humvee. Before he could get on the radio, they were hit by a tsunami of gunfire from machine guns, rifles, and—oh, shit!—rocket-propelled grenades.

It was bedlam, which quickly descended into hell.

The able-bodied team members dragged the wounded behind the Hummer as the corpsman, who'd been hit in the shoulder in the first barrage, struggled to treat the injured while the others provided cover and threw up smoke grenades. Meanwhile, the aircraft that had been called in struggled to hit constantly moving targets in the difficult terrain. The voices echoing in the canyon made communication near impossible.

Of the two dozen members of the combined team of U.S. and Afghan National Army troops, eight were wounded. Their only hope was the medevac helicopters that couldn't land while the kill zone was being bombarded with fire.

"Fuck this." Fed up, Sawyer ran, zigzagging between rocks and stunted trees, whatever bit of cover he could find, while the remaining members of the team provided cover from behind the vehicle.

As a bullet pinged off a rock just next to his head, he decided this dodging attack method looked a helluva lot easier when John Wayne or Clint Eastwood did it.

Those miserable days of Special Forces training under actual fire, along with years spent scaling sheer rock faces in the mountains back home, paid off as he finally managed to climb the cliffs to an outcropping that allowed him to blast away with his machine gun.

Which provided enough distraction that the wounded could be carried to the copters and airlifted out.

Meanwhile, he'd taken a lot of fire that had peppered his arms and legs with rock fragments. A direct hit through his pant leg above his knee burned like a son of a bitch. Other shots had been stopped by his armor, which had left his ribs feeling as if he'd been gored by a bull.

But as Sawyer made his way back down the cliff, he was congratulating himself on still being alive when—shit—a bullet slammed into his shoulder, causing him to lose his death grip on the rocks.

Jerked out of the all-too-familiar falling nightmare, Sawyer realized that the hammering pounding in his head wasn't gunfire but someone knocking.

While he wouldn't object if Austin had shown up for a bootie call, he doubted that was the case.

Not taking time to pull on his boxers, he yanked the sheet off the bed, wrapped it around his waist, and stumbled into the other room to open the door. Cooper was standing there, illuminated by the spreading yellow glow of the porch light.

The time of night, along with his brother's uncharacteristically grim expression, told Sawyer that the news was bad. "Is it Dad?"

"No."

"Not Rachel or Scott?" Coop had already lost one woman to tragedy. Sawyer couldn't imagine him losing another.

"It's the Campbells."

Sawyer raked a hand over his hair. "Heather and Tom? What about them? We just had dinner with them. They had to leave before we finished because Tom got a call about a breech foal he had to turn before they left for Ashland."

"That explains what they were doing out on Duck Pond Road."

Sawyer's blood, which was already cold from lingering shadows of that night in the Afghan mountains, turned to ice. "They couldn't tell you why they were there?" Even as he asked the question, he knew the answer. The unthinkable, impossible, very bad truth was written all over his brother's face.

"They couldn't because a boulder fell from the cliff onto the top of their car. A witness who'd been driving a lumber truck a ways behind them saw it happen and said that it was when that tremor hit. Which was probably what shook it loose."

"Jesus." Sawyer had managed to convince himself that once he got home to River's Bend, he wouldn't have to ever hear news like this again. Coming on the heels of the nightmare, it slammed straight to the gut like an iron fist, nearly doubling him over.

Then, another thought hit. "You haven't told Austin yet."

"No. I figured it would probably be better if you were there when I did."

"Jesus," Sawyer repeated. "Yeah . . . Right. Just let me put on some clothes."

Cooper followed him into the bedroom as he pulled a pair of knit boxer briefs from the duffle bag he was still using for a bureau and scooped the jeans he'd worn to dinner off the floor.

"We just had dinner with them," he repeated, knowing how inane that sounded. But was there anything more effing inane than two best friends being killed on their way to an anniversary celebration? Two parents leaving their children . . .

"Aw, shit. The kids."

"I stopped by the house on the way over here, and Rachel's going to keep them away from the TV in the morning and not answer the phone unless it's one of us. I figured you, Austin, Rachel, and I would tell them together."

"Good idea." Sawyer pulled a T-shirt, which was lying on the floor next to his jeans, over his head. It was the one he'd worn yesterday to clean out a stall and smelled like horse and sweat, but he figured that was the least of his problems. "Good," he repeated numbly.

Thoughts were bombarding his brain like incoming shrapnel. "We were looking at photos," he said as he sat down on the sleeping bag and pulled on a pair of socks that didn't smell too much like a wrestling locker room before reaching for his boots. "The wedding, the kids' baptisms."

As Cooper's news sunk in even more, memories of standing in front of helmets, inverted rifles, boots, and dog tags of the fallen flashed before his eyes. "Hell. Now we're going to be going to their damn funerals."

"It sucks," Cooper agreed. "You okay?"

"Yeah." As much as Sawyer felt like hurling up his guts, he had to stay strong for Austin. He stood up, put his hands on his thighs, and drew in a deep breath. Sent it exploding out.

His head cleared, his vision focused, he grabbed his jacket, which he'd tossed over the doorknob when he'd come home. "Let's go get this over with."

❧

A MOMENT AFTER Cooper's knock, the porch light came on. There was another pause, then Austin opened the door.

"Sawyer? Cooper?" Dressed in a pair of pale blue pajama pants with clouds printed on them and a knit camisole, she looked sleepy, tousled, and delicious. On any other night, Sawyer would be tempted to take her back to bed and make up for lost time. But this was not any other night. "What's wrong?"

"I'm sorry to disturb you, Austin," Coop said. "Could we come in?"

"Oh." She backed up and opened the door wider. "Of course." Sawyer watched as comprehension on why they'd be showing up at her door at this hour of the night clicked in. "What's wrong?"

"Maybe you'd like to sit down." Cooper's tone was kind but, Sawyer noticed, had shifted into cop mode. Which had him wondering how many times in his life, first as a military cop, then working for the Portland Police Bureau, then here, his brother had been required to make a visit like this. As hard as the visits Sawyer had made to the families of his fallen teammates had been, this had to be far worse.

"Do I need to?"

When Coop appeared prepared to give some oblique cop answer, Sawyer decided this was one of those bandage cases. Ease it off, taking more time and dragging out the pain, or just rip and get it over with. He decided Austin would rather just have it rip.

"Heather and Tom were in an accident after leaving the Carpenters' place," he said, earning a sharp look from Cooper for having interfered in his official police business. "A boulder fell onto their car out on Duck Pond Road. Coop says they died instantly."

"Died?" Even as Austin's heart denied it, her head knew that Sawyer had no reason to lie. "No." Feeling as if she were about to shatter, she folded her arms across the front of her tank top, trying to hold herself together.

When she'd been a little girl, younger even than Jack, all the yellow diamond *Watch for Falling Rocks* signs along the upper river road had made her nervous because she'd never known what she'd do if she actually saw one crashing down the side of the cliff. Austin had never shared her fears with her father because she didn't want to sound like a scaredy-cat. Over the years, after having never heard of anyone being killed there, she'd put her concerns aside and had gotten so she didn't even notice those signs anymore.

"I'm sorry." Sawyer drew her into his arms. "So damn sorry."

Austin was cold. So very cold. The last time she remembered feeling like this, chilled to the very marrow of her bones, had been eight years ago, when a devastating blizzard had blasted down from Canada and Washington.

Barreling through the mountains like a freight train, it had brought snow, ice, and sixty- to ninety-mile-an-hour winds that buried cattle in snowdrifts, some measuring eighteen feet high, leaving a trail of destruction and dead animals in its wake as it headed eastward into Idaho. Her teeth had chattered near to breaking as she'd joined her neighbors for days out looking for thousands of missing animals.

Unlike back then, tonight she was inside her warm and cozy home, safe in Sawyer's arms. But she still couldn't stop her teeth from chattering.

"I'm sorry," he murmured, over and over. She could feel his lips on her hair. Hear the steady, solid beat of his heart beneath her cheek while her own heart was wildly kicking against her ribs like a bucking horse.

"Oh, God, poor Heather. And Tom." Trying to block out the vision of the sunny yellow minivan Tom had agreed to drive to Ashland instead of his old veterinarian pickup, Austin pressed her fingers against her eyes, so hard that all she could see were crazily floating spots.

"We just had dinner with them," she said, as if stating that truth could reverse time back to when they'd been laughing together at the New Chance.

"I know." His hand was soothing her back. "I said the same thing when Coop told me."

She lifted her head and saw the truth in his somber gaze. Once again, like old times, they were on the same wavelength. And how terrible was it that this was the thought they'd have to be sharing?

She looked over at Cooper, who was still standing there, hat in hand, looking as if he'd rather be anywhere else. Or, more likely, she thought, back in time, before he'd gotten that call. "You told Rachel first." It was not a question.

"Yeah. We figured you, Sawyer, she, and I would tell the kids in the morning. But she's going to tell Scott first."

Although her heart had slowed down to a more normal rhythm, her chest felt so painfully tight. Austin rubbed the heel of her hand against it as her cottony brain tried to sort that out.

"Because he lost his father." Despite having only been together since early last fall, Rachel, Cooper, and Scott had bonded so well it was as if they'd always been a family.

"Yeah." She knew he was uncomfortable when he dragged his hand through his hair. "She thought Scott would be able to share empathy. And let them know it gets better."

"That's fortunate they'll have someone there who'll truly understand." Her mother abandoning her family had felt like a death at the time. But Sawyer had always been there, like a rock for her. And from then on, Austin had always been able to rely on him. Except for after she'd cut him out of her life by marrying Jace. "But reliving that time is bound to be terribly hard on him."

"Yeah," Cooper repeated on an exhaled breath that had her realizing that what she'd first thought to be discomfort was deep concern for the boy he loved like his own flesh-and-blood son. "Rachel's an amazing mom. We're going to do our best to ease any hurt, but we're notifying the school so they can watch for any problems. We're also setting up appointments with a therapist I've used for kids in bad situations before. One just for him alone, so he can share whatever he's feeling without having to worry about us judging him. And another with him, Rachel, and me together as a family."

"You're a good dad, Cooper Murphy."

Austin felt the moisture burning her eyes and blinked it away. Although she wanted to just go back to bed, hide under the covers, and sob until she was all cried out, between Sawyer's strong arms and Cooper's steady, reassuring attitude, she was able to clear her head enough to concentrate on what all needed to be done.

"Where will the kids stay? With you and Rachel?"

"For now. I called a woman I've worked with before at Child Protective Services on the way over here. We've been cleared as emergency temporary custodians until a permanent home can be found."

"Tom's parents are in Hawaii and not well enough to travel."

Tom had been adopted at birth by older parents, who were now both in their eighties. His father was suffering from Alzheimer's, and Heather had worried about his mother wearing herself out taking care of him twenty-four seven. When the elderly woman had broken a hip last winter, she'd had no choice but to place her husband in a long-term care home. The same one she'd ended up in.

"And, of course, Heather's parents died when she was pregnant with Jack." Another painful thought struck like a lightning bolt. "Heather hated driving on Duck Pond Road because that's where they swerved to miss an elk and hit a tree."

She closed her eyes again when she realized she'd just spoken of her best friend in past tense. How could that be? It wasn't fair. Even as she wanted to scream, to sob, Austin struggled for calm because the children—her godchildren—were going to need her. And Sawyer.

"The location makes it even worse," Sawyer said.

"It does. It's so, so tragic."

Austin drew in a breath.

Shook off the pain.

Okay. There was planning to be done, and one thing she'd always been very good at, even more so since having to scrape up income for the ranch, was to figure out ways to handle all this.

Then only once Heather and Tom were—how could this be happening?—buried and the children settled in with a new family, most likely with Rachel and Cooper, especially since Rachel had mentioned wanting another child, would Austin allow herself to weep.

14

AUSTIN DRESSED HURRIEDLY in jeans, a shirt, and boots. After pulling her hair into a tail, she wrote a note to her dad, telling him what had happened, left it next to the coffeepot, then rejoined Sawyer and Cooper.

As she and Sawyer followed Cooper's SUV, the butterflies she'd felt fluttering in her stomach when they'd headed off to the dinner that may or may not have been a date had returned. But this time they were giant condors, flapping oversized wings that had her feeling on the verge of throwing up.

"Are you okay?" Sawyer asked, slanting her a look as they turned onto the two-lane road. It had begun to rain again, which Austin found appropriate. It also started a "Tears in Heaven" earworm she feared she'd be hearing a lot over the next days.

She started to assure him that she was fine. Then decided there was going to be enough pretense for the kids' sake. If she didn't have someone she could be honest with, vent to, she'd never make it through this.

"No. I'm not. This is wrong in so many ways and on so many levels I can't even wrap my head around it yet. I'm crushed, angry—no, make that pissed off—heartbroken, and scared to death because I'm afraid I'm going to screw this up and make things even worse for Jack and Sophie."

"You won't screw it up."

"And you know that how?"

"Because you love those kids. And they love you. Heather told me at the party how wonderful you are with them. How you're like a favorite aunt."

"They don't have any aunts. Or uncles." The children were more alone than she'd been when her parents divorced. At least she'd had her father. And Sawyer.

"Family doesn't necessarily come from blood. We make it. The way you were family with Tom, Heather, and the kids."

She turned from looking through the rain-streaked window toward him. "If I'm like their aunt, you'd be a surrogate uncle."

He shrugged. "It's not the same. They haven't seen me for over a year. A lot changes in a kid's life in that length of time."

"Like you said the other day, life happens," she said. "They may have grown up some, but they're still children. Who are going to need you."

"I'm not going to bail on them."

"I wasn't suggesting that." Sawyer, like his brothers and father, had always been faithful to the bone. "And I wasn't lecturing you." Though it admittedly could have sounded that way.

"They'll be living with Coop and Rachel," he said as he turned off the road onto the long driveway to the ranch house. "My brother's good with kids."

Austin felt a niggling of nerves at the back of her neck. "But he's older," she said carefully. "He didn't know Tom as well as you do. Did." Damn, there it was again. How could she possibly think about the couple as only existing in the past?

They had plans. She had them all written into the planner on her desk and, as backup, on her phone's iCal. There was bridesmaids dress shopping with Heather for Rachel's upcoming wedding. After that was Sophie's thirteenth birthday party, which was taking place in a new tea shop that had recently opened on Front Street. Heather, naturally, had already gotten the pattern for her daughter's dress and had shown Austin sketches of the hats she was making for each of the girls invited to the party. Although there would be the usual tea sandwiches and sweets, Austin was making the birthday cake.

Then came the Fourth of July rodeo, with Tom not only providing veterinarian services but taking part in the calf roping, the same way he had with Sawyer back in high school. Though Sawyer, being the more reckless of the two back then, had also done bronc and bull riding.

And that didn't even cover typical Sunday picnics at the river, trail rides, barbecues. The patterns of Austin's life had become so interwoven with the Campbell family she couldn't have separated the threads if she'd wanted to. Which she hadn't.

But that wicked bitch fate had stepped in and ripped her life to shreds, just when she was starting to get it together again.

And how could she be pitying herself while two children lay sleeping in the log house Sawyer was pulling up in front of, unaware that, come morning, their own young lives, and their hearts, would be shattered?

She was, Austin decided as she jumped out of the cab, not waiting for Sawyer to go around to open her door, a very bad person.

15

COOPER'S HOUSE WAS made from logs milled on the ranch property, the same as the one Sawyer had grown up in with his brothers at the Bar M. Since the night had grown seasonally chilly, Rachel had started a fire going in the river-rock fireplace.

She greeted Austin with sad, red-rimmed eyes and a hug. "I'm so sorry."

"I keep swinging back and forth between feeling as if I've broken into a million pieces and a cold numbness," Austin admitted.

"That's the way I was when I lost David," Rachel said. "Later, I learned that it's a defense our minds take on to protect us from more pain than we can deal with. The numbness gives us a chance to reboot."

Sawyer had never heard the numbness that had settled over him like a cold blanket of snow after that last battle described that way. But it fit. Rachel's words also reminded him that he wasn't the first person to experience these feelings. He also hoped to hell that his future sister-in-law had escaped the grinding, soul-sucking survivor guilt he'd been slammed with.

Which brought his mind to his brother, who, as sheriff,

had headed up the search party that had located the plane that had crashed into Modoc Mountain. The one carrying Coop's high school girlfriend and first wife.

Maybe, he considered, he should talk with him. The Marine shrink had warned him that guys who tried to handle things on their own were the most likely to contribute to the rising military suicide statistics. At the time, Sawyer had said whatever he'd needed to get through his separation testing without having to spill his guts to anyone.

But Cooper wasn't just anyone. He was someone who'd seen a lot of horrible shit and seemed to be handling life just fine. And Ryan had been a surgeon in a field hospital. If he'd been deployed when the Ranger team got ambushed, all those wounded would have first been brought to him.

Hell, Ry had probably dealt with more death than he and Cooper together. And he was doing great. So what was wrong with him? How about the fact that he was wallowing in self-pity when his best friends' kids were going to be hit with a tsunami of pain in a couple hours?

"I've been thinking," Rachel was saying to Austin, when he dragged his mind back to what was really important, "that you should be the one to tell them."

"Me?" Austin paled.

"I can do it," Cooper said. "It's my job and I've had experience."

"No." Sawyer watched her stiffen her spine. The same way she had, he remembered, when Kendall Cunningham had come up to her on the playground at recess and teased her about her mother having run off. "I appreciate the offer, especially since they know and like both you and

Rachel. But their mother is—was—my best friend. They've practically grown up on the ranch. I'd appreciate any advice you have on how best to break the news, but Rachel's right. It should be me."

A flash of memory came back. Winema Clinton had been the one to break the news to Austin. In the beginning, Buck had told her that her mother had taken a trip back to Sweden, as she had several times before. Finally, as the days spun into weeks, then a month, Winema had sat her down and told her the truth.

Later she'd asked her father why he hadn't been honest in the first place, and from what she'd told Sawyer, he hadn't known the words to say that wouldn't hurt her. If Austin had ever considered that perhaps Buck Merrill had been protecting himself from having to deal with a heartbroken little girl, she hadn't shared that with Sawyer.

"I just remembered something," she said now. She rubbed her forehead with her fingertips. "I'm listed as a potential guardian in her will."

"You are?" Sawyer wondered why he'd never heard about that.

"I am," she confirmed. "It was years ago, right after Jack was born and they were, as Heather put it, suddenly feeling like grown-ups. They bought life insurance and had wills drawn up. She asked if I'd be willing to take the kids if something ever happened to them."

"Of course you said yes," Sawyer said.

"Of course. But it didn't seem at all likely at the time. No one really ever believes they're going to die when they write up wills, do they?"

"I didn't even when the Marines made me list my primary next of kin before deployment." Since his brother had always been a take-charge type of person, and it wasn't as if Sawyer had a wife or kids, he'd named Cooper as his PNOK.

"Although Tom's parents were older than most of our parents, they were still in good health, so, again, I never thought this"—Austin choked up, struggling to say the words—"this would ever actually happen."

"So your guardianship is written into the wills?" Cooper asked.

"I suppose."

"We need to make plans," Rachel said. "Let's continue this in the kitchen while I make us all breakfast."

They gathered together around the old farm table that had seen many family discussions over two generations. Rachel had already brewed coffee and gotten out a box of tea bags and, apparently subscribing to the idea that there wasn't anything a good meal couldn't make better, began scrambling eggs and frying bacon. She'd delegated Cooper to making the toast, and watching his brother getting out the butter and marionberry jam, Sawyer realized that the two of them had developed a comfortable routine. Glancing over, he saw Austin watching them and wondered if she was comparing their relationship with her own failed marriage.

"You need to be straight with them," Rachel advised Austin as she dished up the plates and set them on the table. "When David died, one of our friends told Scott that God loved his daddy so much that he wanted him to be in heaven with Him. Which was well meaning, but that got Scott thinking that God must not love him enough to let his father stay here with him. I was lucky that he brought it up with me, rather than worrying that he hadn't been good enough to keep his father from dying."

"That must have been a terrible time," Austin said.

"It wasn't easy," Rachel admitted. "One of his friends at school, whose mother was more New Agey than most, told him to watch out for David coming back as a ghost. Having not grown up with séances in our house, he started sleeping with his bedroom light on. He told me it was so he wouldn't miss seeing his father.

"Which was just one more thing to deal with during a time when his life was in upheaval. Not only had he lost his father, I had to take him out of private school, which cost him some friends, and since we were left with a lot of debt, I had to return to catering full time. And then, after paying off our creditors, I uprooted him and dragged him across the country from Connecticut to here."

"For which, despite the circumstances, I'll be eternally grateful," Cooper said. He bit into a piece of crispy bacon.

Rachel's smile warmed the chill the tragedy had brought into the house. "Don't feel like the Lone Ranger, Sheriff."

Austin cradled her mug of tea in her hands, and although she listened intently to Cooper and Rachel's advice, when they heard the children stirring upstairs, Sawyer could see the concern edging toward fear in her eyes.

"You'll handle this," he assured her after Rachel and Coop had gone upstairs. Rachel to break the news first to Scott, and Cooper to supervise the morning teeth brushing.

"So you say. Just between us, I'd rather be dragged by a horse over a rocky road."

"I know." He took her ice-cold hand between both of his, rubbing the blood back into it as he'd used to do when they'd stay out too long ice skating on Glass Lake.

She sighed. Closed her eyes and let out a long breath. "I'm glad you're here," she said as they heard the footfalls coming down the stairs.

Although once again the timing was off, Sawyer lifted her hand and pressed the back of it against his lips. Not to seduce but to comfort.

"Me, too," he said. And meant it.

16

JACK, DRESSED IN *Jungle Book* pajamas, came racing into the room so fast Austin was amazed he hadn't taken a header down the stairs. As usual, Sophie, in hot pink polka dot cropped pajama pants and a pink tank with *Be Your Selfie* written in purple glittery script, followed him at a more reasonable pace. Bringing up the rear, Scott was holding Cooper's hand. Rachel had told Austin how, when her husband had first died, he'd insisted that he was now the "man of the family."

Although the nine-year-old's eyes were more serious than she'd ever seen them, more than any young boy's should be, it was readily apparent that he'd willingly surrendered that role to his new dad. Which gave Austin hope that Jack and Sophie would be able to get past this terrible time without too many emotional scars.

"Austin!" Jack hurled himself into her arms. "Are you here for breakfast? Rachel's going to make blueberry pancakes!"

"That sounds wonderful." She touched her lips to the top of his head, breathing in the bracing scent of spearmint. She looked up at Sophie. "Good morning, Sophie."

"Morning." Sophie tilted her head, studied the group

around the table. Clouds of suspicion, like smoke from a wild fire, rose in her hazel eyes. "What's wrong?"

Hoping that it would be the hardest thing she'd ever have to do, Austin met her gaze. *Please help me, Heather.* "There was an accident," she said with far more calm than she was feeling. "I'm so horribly sorry, honey. And you, Jack. But I'm afraid your mom and dad are dead."

Silence descended like a steel curtain. Heather's daughter's head jerked back, as if she'd been struck in the face. Sawyer was there in a flash, his arm around her in case she passed out.

"Dead?" Jack scratched his head, ruffling his bedhead red hair. "Like Riley?"

Riley had been their old beagle, who'd finally crossed that rainbow bridge last summer when he was eighteen. He'd been into middle age when Tom and Heather had adopted him from a beagle rescue group when she'd been pregnant with Jack. They'd already had Daisy, an orange marmalade cat who'd, unfortunately, since died of cancer, but Tom had insisted that all boys needed a dog.

Austin decided not to quibble the difference. "Like Riley."

"What happened?" Sophie asked as she allowed Sawyer to lower her into the chair Cooper had pulled out.

"They were driving to Ashland when they had a car accident."

"Like Grandma and Grandpa." Since Sophie had been five at the time, Austin wasn't sure how much she remembered about Heather's parents. Unlike Heather and Tom, it had taken time for each of them to succumb to injuries. During those difficult days when Heather practically lived at the hospital, only going home when the nurses and doctors insisted, Sophie had stayed at Green Springs.

"Yes. A bit like that. But Cooper assured me that it was very quick and they didn't suffer."

"Where were they?"

"Along the upper lake." Concerned that Sophie might know about the Duck Pond Road connection, Austin decided not to share that detail. "Your father had just helped birth a foal."

"That's what Daddy does," Jack said. "He delivers baby horses when their owners get in trouble."

"Yes," Austin said. "He was special that way."

Watching the sheen gloss Sophie's eyes at her deliberate use of past tense, Austin wished there was something, anything, she could do to turn back time to earlier yesterday. Before Tom had received that call.

Which had her thinking that if she and Sawyer hadn't had dinner with them, they would have been on the road earlier and not been on Duck Pond Road when the tremor hit.

"Are they going to be buried?" Jack wanted to know. "Like Riley?"

Austin exchanged a quick, questioning glance with Rachel, whose answering nod advised being straight from the beginning. "Yes. That's what your parents wanted."

"How do you know what they wanted?" Sophie was rallying, her pain giving way to anger. Austin couldn't blame her. Not one bit. "Did they talk about dying? Did they tell you?"

"Actually, your mother did," Austin said gently. "When I agreed that if anything happened to them, you'd come live with me."

"On the ranch?" Jack asked.

"Yes."

Sophie folded her arms. "Why can't we stay in our own house?"

"Because," Sawyer suggested, "it's kind of torn up from remodeling right now."

"It's an effing wreck," Jack said. Then, when his sister shot him a killer look, he said in defense, "That's what Dad said."

"It's not that bad," Sophie said. Not if you considered no kitchen, the parents sleeping on a couch in the living room, one functional bath, and both kids sharing a bedroom with excess furniture moved from other rooms. "We were doing fine, and when the remodeling is done, the house is going to be perfect." Which was exactly what Heather had kept saying during the past three months of what, to Austin, had looked like chaos. "If Mom and Dad were alive, we'd be there."

Austin was so over her head here.

"I had to move when my dad died," Scott broke in to try to help out. "We moved all the way out here, and I had to leave my friends back in Connecticut. But it turned out okay."

"But you still had your mom," Sophie said.

"Yeah. I did." Scott's apologetic look told Austin that he'd tried, but the ball was now back in her court.

"Why don't we talk about this later?" Rachel suggested. "After you've had breakfast."

"Like I'm supposed to be hungry?"

"We're still having pancakes, right?" Jack asked.

"You can have anything you want," Rachel agreed.

"Right. Let's everyone be nice to the poor orphans,"

Sophie muttered.

Knowing the tween was using anger as a defense didn't make Austin feel as if she was making any headway. "This sucks," she said, opting for total honesty.

"Mom says you're not supposed to say *suck*," Jack said.

"I think she'd allow it this one time," Austin responded. Then turned back to Sophie. "I lost my mother when I was Jack's age, but she didn't die. She went away."

"So she could have come back," Sophie countered.

"She could have, yes. Though she didn't." And hadn't Austin spent years wishing and waiting?

"At least she wasn't in the ground." The girl swallowed as she blinked away tears. "Like Mom and Dad will be."

"Are we going to bury them at the ranch? With Riley?" Jack asked. Since the couple's small yard hadn't allowed room for animal burial, Riley's final resting place had been in a pasture where generations of cattle dogs, barn cats, and even ranch horses had been buried. Although she'd refused to call it a pet cemetery, Austin had always found visiting the pasture comforting.

"Don't be a moron," Sophie, who'd always shown remarkable patience with her younger brother, snapped. "You don't put people in the same ground as you do dogs."

"Why not?"

"Because River's Bend has a special place for people," Sawyer took that question. "My mom's there."

"She is?" Sophie appeared to soften a bit at that. "How old were you when she died?"

"Thirteen."

"I'll be thirteen next month."

"I know. It's a big milestone."

Her hazel eyes welled up. "And my parents won't be there."

"I know." He crouched down beside the chair and took both the tween's hands in his, just as he'd done with Austin earlier. "But Austin and I will be. And Rachel, and Cooper—"

"And me," Scott said. "Austin's right. It does suck, but you've got lots of friends so you won't be all alone. And," he added, "I didn't believe it would ever be okay when my dad died. But it doesn't keep hurting like it does now."

When Rachel's eyes misted, Austin knew that the tears she was holding back were due as much to pride in her son as sadness.

"Are we going to have a funeral?" Jack asked. He'd begun kicking his legs back and forth, hitting the chair leg. "Like we did for Riley? We kids got to plan it and it was really cool. Mom and Dad said Riley would've really 'preciated it."

"He was a stupid dog," Sophie snapped, the understandable anger making a comeback. "Adults plan people's funerals. Kids just show up and try to sit still for more than two minutes. Which, like anyone would expect you to be able to do."

"You don't have to yell at me!" Great. Now the waterworks began to flow.

"Mom and Dad are dead," Sophie shouted back. "And you just don't get it!"

He jumped to his feet, small hands fisted on the hips of his pajamas. "I do, too! I just want to know what's going to happen!"

And couldn't Austin identify with that?

She bent and hugged the little boy whose world had

been so tragically turned upside down. "I know you do. And to be perfectly honest, I'm not sure, either. But I promise you, we'll figure it out the best we can and let you know everything that's going to happen."

"But we're having a funeral?" he asked in an uncharacteristically subdued voice.

"Yes, because funerals are a way to celebrate people's lives."

"Like my parents dying is something to celebrate," Sophie muttered.

"No," Austin said, struggling for patience. "It's not. But your mom and dad can't be defined by that single terrible moment. They have so many friends whose lives they touched who'll want to be there with you."

"What if I don't want to be there with them?" Sophie countered.

Rachel had told them, over the eggs and bacon, that this would be a possibility. She'd also suggested that they try, without pushing, to encourage the children to attend the funeral. Because someday they might look back and regret, or worse, feel guilty for not having been there to say goodbye to their parents.

"That's your choice," Austin said mildly. "But there's still time to make a decision. Meanwhile, we'd appreciate your help with the planning."

"As if."

"I'll help!" Jack waved his hand as if he were trying to get called on in class.

"Thank you." A wild, possibly crazy thought occurred to Austin. "Perhaps we could have a special service just for you and your friends before the grown-up one."

"I've never heard of that," Sophie said. But Austin

could tell that she'd caught the girl's interest.

"I haven't, either," she admitted. "But I could ask Father Cassidy. And if we can't do it at the church, we could hold it at the ranch."

"We made a great funeral for Riley," Jack told Sawyer, swiping away at his wet cheeks with the backs of his hands as the idea began to take hold. "We all said nice stuff about him and put his favorite toys with him in the box Dad made. Then we played 'I Feel Love,' from the *Benji* movie. Mom really liked that, didn't she, Austin?"

"We all did," Austin agreed. "It was a very special day." The bittersweet funeral had made a sad occasion memorable. "I'll definitely see what we can work out."

"I want to see them," Sophie said.

That sudden request, which Austin realized they should have seen coming, blindsided her and caused a sudden silence to hit the room.

"I understand, but I don't think you really want to do that," Cooper suggested.

Heather's daughter tossed up her chin. "I do, too. I *need* to see them."

From what she knew about the accident, Austin didn't think this would be a good idea. Especially since Cooper was so obviously against it.

"Is it because you need to make sure they're really gone?" Sawyer asked.

She could only nod as the tears welled up again. Understandable anger aside, Austin was reminded that Sophie was still a child. A child who'd undergone a horrible, life-altering loss.

"How about this," Sawyer suggested. "You trust Cooper, right?"

She looked up at Cooper. "I guess. Because he's the sheriff."

"Right. And taking care of things is his job. So, what about if he goes to the funeral home, in his official capacity, and makes sure that the paramedics got it right? That it was your parents in the car."

"Minivan," she corrected. "A yellow one."

"That's what I saw," Cooper said in a quiet but assuring tone. "But I'll definitely go and double-check to make sure."

"And I'll go with him," Sawyer said.

They all held a collective breath as she considered that offer.

"O-k-k-kay," she decided.

"You've got it," Cooper said. "Unfortunately, I've had to do this before. I know what I'm doing."

"I know you do." She ran her hand beneath her nose, causing Rachel to hand her a tissue from the box she'd put on the counter earlier. "It's just that I've *never* done this. So *I* don't know what to do."

"You're not alone, honey." Austin knelt down beside the chair next to her. "We'll all miss your mom and dad terribly. But I promise that we'll get through this sad time together."

Austin could only hope.

17

THEY AGREED THAT the kids would stay with Rachel and Cooper while Austin and Sawyer returned to Tom and Heather's to pick up some personal items. Then, although she'd already called Buck, they'd go back to the ranch to fill her father and Winema in on the details.

The Campbells' house was a Craftsman bungalow on Mountain View Drive, just a block away from where Rachel and Scott had first moved to when they'd arrived in River's Bend. With its blue siding, red front door, and white pillars and porch, it always reminded Austin of the Fourth of July. The lawn had greened up, red-and-white petunias brightened the front garden bed, and a huge dumpster for construction debris took up most of the driveway. Next to the dumpster was a white Ford pickup with *Ames Construction* written on the side beneath a silhouette of Modoc Mountain.

The remodeling had been going on for three months. It had become such a part of the couple's life, Austin wasn't surprised to enter the house and see Brody up on a ladder installing crown molding.

"Hey, guys," he greeted her with a quick smile as he slipped the hammer into the loop on the tool belt he wore low on his hips. "What's up?" His expression sobered as he took a longer look at their faces. "You're not here to make sure I paint this room the buttercream yellow Heather picked out," he guessed.

"I wish." As Austin tried to tell the story as succinctly as Sawyer had told her, she wondered how many times she'd have to repeat it over the next days. Like all small towns, River's Bend wasn't immune to a swift and far-reaching gossip line, but like that old game of telephone, it wasn't always accurate.

"Damn." He backed down the ladder. Then looked around, not with the eye of a contractor but a man who'd just lost two close friends. "The kids can't really stay in this place," he said. "Not without Tom and Heather."

"No," she agreed. "Not that I'm criticizing your work—"

"Don't worry. I get it. Living in a construction zone is never easy. Doing it when you're a kid who's lost his parents would be untenable."

"That's what we decided, although Sophie wanted to come back at first."

"That makes sense. Especially since hers is the only room that's not a wreck. Although Jack's been sleeping in there for the past two weeks because we blew out his wall to add a bath so he and his sister won't have to share anymore."

"Heather told me that Sophie's getting to that age where sharing a bath with a younger brother is becoming more and more of a problem," Austin said. "They're moving to the ranch and can have their own rooms there."

"They probably won't want to be separated," Sawyer said.

"Probably not," Austin agreed. "Their rooms have a Jack-and-Jill bath in between, so they can work out the sleeping arrangements as the days progress."

"Good idea." Brody took off the Hank's Hardware cap he'd been wearing backwards and ran his fingers through his hair. "What's going to happen to the house?"

"If you're worried about getting paid—"

"Hell, no. I was just thinking of how many hours I spent with Heather on details. It's rough that she's never going to see it completed."

"There's a lot she's going to miss."

Like Sophie's and Jack's graduations from middle school, high school, college. Their weddings, holding her first grandchild. Christmases with her children's growing families filling this house that she'd planned to stay in forever. All the holidays that no one celebrated quite as wonderfully or fully as Heather Campbell. The list of losses seemed to stretch past forever.

"You might want to hold off doing any more work until the ownership situation with the house is settled," Sawyer said, looking around at the half-painted room. A room interrupted. Just like its owners' lives.

"I'm going to call Colton Kane right after we leave here," Austin said. "He's handled all their business legal stuff and wrote their wills, so he'll undoubtedly have more facts."

It had never dawned on her until now exactly how many details were going to have to be dealt with. She also belatedly wondered if the property guardianship was separate from guardianship of Jack and Sophie. And if so, who'd be taking care of that. Especially since Tom's family being able to handle anything was out of the question.

"If you want to help keep Jack occupied," Brody said, "I bought him a small hammer a few weeks ago. It's probably up in his room or maybe Tom put it in the garage. I'll look out there while you're collecting other things, and if you'd like, I can give you some short nails to take back to the ranch. He really enjoys pounding them into boards."

"If it makes noise, Jack's all over it," Austin agreed.

"Buck and I can come up with some fake chores that'll help him transition to living on the ranch," Sawyer said.

"That would be great." Jack was still young enough that Austin wasn't certain the finality of his situation had hit home. Sophie's adjustment, she suspected, would prove more problematic.

She'd had the kids make a list of their must-have items. Not only had it given them something else other than their parents' deaths to think about, as well as she knew them, she wouldn't have wanted to make that important a selection on her own.

Together it took them twenty minutes to locate everything. Although Sophie hadn't put her diary on the list, when Austin saw it on the bedside stand, she added it to the things in the oversized suitcase she'd brought along with her.

Leaving Brody to clean up the house, they dropped off the suitcase with Rachel, then returned to the ranch.

"OH, THOSE POOR babies." Winema wiped her damp eyes with her apron as Austin filled her and her dad in on what had happened. "You just handle whatever needs to be done, and I'll get things ready for them and take care of them when they arrive."

As she'd taken care of Austin. Some women, like Winema, Rachel, and Heather, seemed to be natural-born mothers. Austin decided she must've been hanging out with horses the day that gift had been handed out, but surely it was something that could be learned. And it wasn't as if she would be doing it alone. Along with a strong group of friends, there was also Sawyer.

Who, although he'd assured her that he'd be there for the children, also had his own problems he was obviously struggling with. He'd always been the most outgoing of the Murphy brothers, the one who lived life as fully as he rode his bulls and broncs. But the man who'd returned from war was quieter. More distant. And, from the way his entire body had stiffened at that backfire outside the New Chance, like preparing for a body blow, she wasn't certain how serious those "issues" might be.

Maybe she could talk to Rachel and ask her to have Cooper talk with him. She didn't want to be overly dramatic. But neither did she want to put the children at risk. Not that she believed Sawyer would ever hurt anyone. But Jack and Sophie were emotionally fragile right now. They didn't need any other problems to deal with.

And didn't just considering that possibility cause a twinge of guilt?

This was Sawyer. A man she'd known all her life. Yet now he'd become a man seemingly incapable of talking to her without the buffer of friends. Friends they'd lost. Which brought her mind full circle back to the children. Who had to remain the most important aspect of this problem.

"I'm not sure how long Jack and Sophie will be staying

with Cooper and Rachel. Sawyer and I are going to the funeral home and the church to make arrangements, then to Colton Kane to learn the logistics of petitioning for custody and hopefully to find out what Tom and Heather wanted done with the house."

"What about the cemetery?" Buck asked. "Do you know if they pre-bought plots?"

Damn. All that earlier talk about burying and it hadn't even occurred to her. "I doubt it." Heather and Tom may have been feeling like grown-ups when they'd asked to include her in their wills as a secondary guardian, but who in their twenties spends hard-earned money on a cemetery plot? Taking out her phone, she added that to her list of things to ask Colton. "But I'll check."

"Why don't you bring the kids over here?" Buck suggested. "They like the horses."

"They do," Austin agreed. "But—"

"Dad would be happy to help out by sending one of the hands over," Sawyer broke in before she could share her concern about her father being able to handle an energetic Jack on horseback. "Colt Bartlett and his wife had five sons before Marybeth finally gave up trying for a daughter. He's great with boys."

Having known the Bar M foreman for years, Austin found that a perfect solution.

"Sophie can help me plant the annuals I picked up yesterday at The Plant Place," Winema said. "Gardening is such a positive activity, because you take a little bitty plant, stick it in the ground, treat it nice, and before you know it, you'll end up with something good to eat or some pretty flowers you can enjoy in the garden and bring into the house. That way, when the girl sees a garden ablaze with flowers this summer, she won't look back on this time as all bad."

"That's a wonderful idea."

Austin wasn't surprised that Winema had come up with a perfect plan. She was, after all, a natural at this mothering stuff. Tom and Heather might have laughed at how he'd been so afraid of even holding their infant daughter, but she was finding the idea of living up to Heather daunting. And why, oh, why, didn't kids come with a manual?

18

THE EARLE FUNERAL Home was located on Foothills Drive, which, as the name suggested, was one of the higher streets in town, offering a view of the valley. When it had first been established in the early 1900s, Jacob Earle had moved the business to higher ground after a spring runoff had the river flooding his initial establishment. Fifty years later, one of his descendants had created a park-like garden space, complete with a circulating waterfall tumbling down a back wall and seating for those who'd enjoy outdoor memorial services. It had proven so popular there were even couples who'd chosen to get married there.

Earl Earle IV, who had been two years ahead of Tom and Heather at Eaglecrest, had collected their bodies from the hospital morgue. He'd assured her that his team could make any body, no matter the condition, available for viewing, but Austin suspected that, since she, personally, wouldn't want people looking at her after she was dead, her best friend would feel the same way. So, they'd opted for closed caskets.

Choosing that casket was yet another thing she'd never expected to be doing. There were so many of them, in all price ranges. Many were so fancy she was tempted to ask which one King Tut had chosen, but since Earl was being so genuinely kind, she kept her thoughts to herself.

"This is nice," Sawyer said, standing next to one of the simplest caskets in the showroom. While Earl had been showing off a hunter-green twenty-gauge steel model with a choice of ivory velvet or cream crepe, Sawyer had wandered away to browse on his own.

"It matches the new cabinets," Austin said. While pine might not be trendy, Heather had believed that the kitchen was the heart of the home, and nothing said heart to her more than country.

"That's definitely not your old-time pine box." Earl, who was probably not thrilled with the less expensive choice, deftly switched gears. "It's our American Heritage green model. The manufacturer uses local lumber from a Clackamas County timber company that follows sustainable forestry practices and air-dries its own lumber. The water-based paints, stains, and finishes are VOC-free. Which makes them safe for the environment."

"Heather and Tom were part of this year's Earth Day planning." Another point in this choice's favor.

"I know. And you probably didn't spend that much time at our booth, but this model was the one we featured. Heather mentioned that it reminded her of the cabinets she'd chosen for Brody to install."

Austin exchanged a look with Sawyer and knew he was thinking the same thing. That, ironically, Heather had ended up choosing her own casket.

Earl ran a palm over the top. "As you can feel, it's smooth as glass."

When he paused and looked at them, Austin realized he was waiting for them to feel the glassy surface. So, they obliged.

"Nice," Sawyer said.

"If you want to stay green—"

"We do," Austin said.

"Then you have a choice of organic cotton, linen, hemp, or Lyocell, which is a soft wood pulp-based fabric."

Heather was the seamstress and weaver. She would know which to choose. Feeling in over her head yet again, Austin went with the organic cotton.

"Good choice," Earl said. "Though not as upscale as the velvet or crepe most people end up choosing."

"Heather and Tom weren't most people," Austin and Sawyer said together.

The price was higher than Austin would have expected. Death, she was discovering, was not inexpensive.

"Did I mention the company also plants one hundred trees for every one of these caskets they sell?" Earl asked as he wrote up the sale.

"That's a lovely gesture."

"It's also wise business practice since they're ensuring themselves material long into the future. This is their third decade in business, so they're no fly-by-night like some others out there."

"That's good to know." Sawyer's flat tone suggested that he was about casketed out and had no plans to be shopping for body boxes again anytime soon.

After the selection, they went into Earl's office (which also had a smaller version of the outdoor fountain, which Austin guessed was intended to soothe ragged nerves) to go over what turned out to be mountains of paperwork. Not only was death not cheap, it came with myriad complicated hoops to jump through. Fortunately, despite their not having chosen the Cadillac of caskets, Earl took his time, walking them through the guidebook the funeral home had put together.

Two exhausting hours later, after he'd helped them prepare the forms necessary for Sophie's and Jack's Social Security survivor benefits, arranged to get the necessary copies of the death certificates they'd need, and assured them he'd write the obituary for the *River's Bend Register* from the facts she gave him, she and Sawyer were on their way with a to-do list stretching into the next county.

"Damn. I could use a beer after that," Sawyer said as he drove back down the hill toward Eureka Way.

"I could use a dirty martini."

He shot her a look, reminded yet again that, while they'd known each other forever, there was a lot about her he didn't know. "I didn't know you drank martinis."

"I don't." She rubbed her temples where he suspected a headache mirroring his own had begun to throb midway through the funeral meeting. "I'm not even sure what, exactly, a dirty martini is. I just saw Daniel Craig drink one in *Spectre*, and it looked very good."

"By good, you mean sexy."

"He's James Bond," she pointed out. "The man can't be anything but sexy. But it seems the olives would add a salty tang."

"They do."

"So you've had one?" She sounded surprised, which made sense because, while alcohol was readily available at those Saturday night parties on the river, he'd always stuck to beer. While Austin, who was much more of a straight arrow and had probably never been drunk in her life, had stayed with Coke.

"Yeah. On my last deployment. But the vodka tasted like kerosene, so I'm not sure that counts." One of the U.N. soldiers he'd served with had managed to smuggle the rot gut in from Turkey that had him puking up his guts the next morning.

"I'm not much of a drinker," she said. "But I'm beginning to see the appeal." She reached out and touched his leg, the way she had the first day when they'd ridden out to see the foreman's cabin. "Thank you for helping me with all this."

Sawyer shrugged. "No problem. It's a lot for one person to do." Although he'd rather be dodging bullets in Afghanistan than making funeral arrangements for two more dead friends, at least he was feeling somewhat useful for the first time in a very long while.

❧

COLTON KANE WAS Ryan Murphy's age, and after graduating Willamette Law, he'd landed a prestigious job at a top Portland firm where, after an initial year clerking, he'd begun to gain a reputation for being a rainmaker, which had him fast-tracking up the ladder to an eventual partnership.

But to hear him tell the story, the constant need to acquire more business, along with eighteen to twenty billable-hour days had cost him any semblance of a life outside work and caused him to begin to lose sight of what had made him go into law in the first place. Which had been to help the law work for ordinary people who found themselves understandably perplexed by the often byzantine legal system. And who never could have afforded his Portland fees.

So, he'd sold his condo with its doorman, concierge, two pools, saunas, gym, twenty-four-hour security, and incredible views of the city, Mt. Hood, and Willamette River, and returned home to River's Bend, where his family had been running Hereford cross cattle since shortly after World War I near lower Glass Lake.

While he lived in a house he'd had built on the lake, which allowed him to spend Sundays fishing from his front porch, he'd set up his office in a 1907 Craftsman with two round white pillars flanking a wide front porch.

All the beautiful original wood detail was intact, including the pocket doors closing off what would have been a formal front parlor from a dining room. Colton was using the parlor as a reception area, and Brody had combined the dining room and a second family parlor to create a spacious office.

After offering them something to drink, which they turned down, rather than sit behind the desk, he chose one of the armchairs that was diagonal to the sofa they'd taken.

"First, as I told you on the phone," he told Austin, "Heather and Tom were more than clients. They were friends and I'm devastated I'm having to do this. Writing wills is a steady source of business, but I always hope the people are pushing a hundred before I have to have this sit-down meeting with the heirs." He ran a hand through his hair. "This is just wrong."

"You'll get no argument from me about that," Austin said. "So, the first question on the table is obviously guardianship of Jack and Sophie. Heather asked me if I'd be secondary guardian, after his parents, back when Jack was born. Of course I said yes, but I don't know if she ever did anything official about it."

"She and Tom both named you in their wills," he confirmed. "As you said, behind his parents, who aren't up to taking on the care of two young children."

"Have they been told?"

"I'm planning to call them later today. There's a three-hour time difference between here and Hawaii, and I have a contact name for Tom's mother's niece. I worked with her when Mary needed to be moved into a care center, so it would probably be better if she told them. Though I'm not sure his father will understand."

"That's so sad," Austin said.

Sawyer, she noted, didn't say anything. As soon as they'd entered, she'd felt him retreating back into whatever place he'd been going to since returning home. Which wasn't encouraging and made this very bad, horrible situation even worse. Having him provide emotional support and serve as a surrogate father would be an enormous help during this difficult transition time. But if he did take a role in the children's lives, he'd have to stick with them. Abandoning them, the way he'd abruptly cut himself off from her after that kiss, would only make things worse. They'd already lost their parents. Once again she wondered if she could risk them getting attached to a man who might not always be there for them.

On the other hand, she also had to think of Sawyer's well-being. How badly had the war damaged him? Not just his physical wounds but any emotional ones. Would putting the pressure of helping to care for two minor children only make those issues he'd admitted to worse? Which wouldn't be fair to him.

"I'm sorry," she said, shaking her head when she realized she'd missed what Colton had been saying. "Could you please repeat that?"

"Sure." Colton's easy attitude suggested that he was accustomed to clients' minds wandering. After all, people didn't tend to need lawyers when their lives were going smoothly. "Generally, what happens after parents of a minor child die is that anyone wishing to claim guardianship, who, in this case, would be you, must petition the court to be appointed guardian. Since you're named in the will, that's evidence that the children's parents wanted Sophie and Jack to be with you, so the judge will grant this pretty easily."

"How do we petition?"

"It's similar to a divorce or adoption and takes place in family court. First you need to hire a lawyer."

"Who would be you."

"Okay. Great. I'd be glad to take it on. Pro bono, because, quite honestly, it's not a lot of work, and I figure I already made my fee when I wrote their wills. Not that you'll run into any problems, but I can also attest to their sound state of mind when they made the wills.

"I'll have the niece email me Tom's parents' medical records, and will have a local attorney get his mother to sign off on any claim. Since the judge will rule in the 'best interest of the children,' you shouldn't expect any problems. You're a lifelong resident of the community, you've got a stellar reputation, you were close friends with the parents, and the kids love you."

"I'm also their godmother."

"Even better."

"And Sawyer is their godfather."

"Interesting." Colton put his elbows on the chair arms and steepled his hands as he turned his attention toward

Sawyer. "Are you planning to petition, as well?"

"No." The quick, one-word response spoke volumes, and Austin saw something that looked like panic momentarily flash in his whiskey eyes. He rubbed his hands on his thighs. "But I'm living at Green Springs, so I'll be there to offer any support I can."

"Good, good," Colton said. "So, you're staying in the house with Buck, Austin, and the kids? For now?"

"No. I'm living in the foreman's place."

"I'm not saying it will definitely happen," he warned. "But you might want to be ready for a visit from the DHS caseworker."

"To me? Why?"

"Because you're their godfather and you're living on the property with them."

"Not *with* them," Sawyer argued. "They're going to be in the ranch house. With Austin and her dad."

"I understand. But the fact that you're here right now and went to the funeral home demonstrates that you're going to take an active part in their lives. Which is a good thing. But, since the court has to dot all the i's and cross the t's, you may have to be checked out. Not that there'll be any problem."

He paused a moment and gave Sawyer a long look. Realizing that Colton had probably been at the party, Austin wondered if he might have witnessed something that could prove a cause for concern.

Sawyer lifted his chin. Squared his shoulders as if standing at attention. Any fear or panic was gone, and in their place was steely Marine fortitude. "No problems at all."

"Great." The lawyer blew out a quick breath. "Okay, moving on, Tom and Heather left a few smaller bequests to people, which we'll get to at the official reading of the will after the funeral. Which will be when?"

"We're going to the church to figure that part out next," Sawyer said.

"Probably Monday," Austin said. "I don't suppose, when they wrote their wills, they mentioned anything about buying cemetery plots."

"No. And just in case, I called John Breebart at Evergreen Memorial Cemetery. He assures me that he's got a double space not far from Heather's parents with a nice view of the lake that he'll save for you to come by and see.

"Meanwhile, I'll pencil Monday in and just let me know if it changes. If for no other reason than I want to be there as a friend."

After agreeing there was no point in having the children attend the official reading of the will, Colton turned back to legal details.

"Except for those bequests I mentioned, Tom and Heather left everything of value to the kids in trust until they're eighteen. If you choose, you can also assume fiduciary guardianship of the estate. Which means dealing with the house, other personal property, paying bills, whatever else comes up. And, of course, reimbursement for the support of the children."

"I'm not taking money for that," Austin said.

"It's an option."

"No." About this she was very firm. "Whatever money comes in, from Social Security or the estate, it's going to be put away for them. This isn't like a foster parent deal, Colton. I agreed to try, the best I can, to be Jack and Sophie's mother. Last time I looked, that's not a paying job. Nor would I want it to be."

"Children aren't cheap."

"Nor is friendship. Heather was the closest thing I'll ever have to a sister." Emotions clogged her throat as she folded her arms. "The children are family and that's that."

"Fine. We'll deal with the details another day. In the meantime, as soon as the court approves your petition, I'd advise you to at least use the money in the checking account to pay current bills. Which," he pointed out, "you know Heather would want. She wouldn't want to stick you with her bills any more than you'd want to leave her with yours."

"Point taken," Austin said reluctantly. There was also the fact that both hers and the ranch's checking accounts were getting down to the bottom as they neared the end of the month.

"Sometimes creditors will void the accounts in case of a death, but not always. And you'll probably want to have Brody finish the remodel so you can sell the house. And bank the profit from that for their future," he said before she could state that she wasn't going to take any of the house money. "I can also arrange for a fund to handle construction draws."

"Brody and I already talked about him finishing," she said. "I think the idea makes sense. When can we petition the court?"

"If the funeral's Monday, except for thirty minutes or so to wrap up the will reading with everyone, you'll probably want to be with the kids that day. I should be able to get a court slot for Tuesday morning to start the proceedings."

"Thank you." Austin managed a weak smile. "You've no idea how glad I am that you moved back home." She glanced down at her watch. "We'd better get going. If that's all for now."

"That'll do it. If I run into anything we haven't covered, I'll call. Also, if you have any questions, you can call any time, day or night." He handed her a card with his office, cell, and home phone numbers on it.

After thanking him again, she and Sawyer were off on their last mission of the day.

"I guess we'll have to go to the cemetery first thing tomorrow morning," she decided. "And why do they need a view lot?"

"Beats me. Maybe so people will have something nice to look at when they visit the graves? Mom's is under a tree. Dad had a bench put in and used to go sit there a lot in the early years after we lost her."

"That's nice. Well, not nice, but, you know."

"Yeah. I do."

"How long has this day been?" Austin asked as they headed toward the church and their meeting with Father Cassidy. "It's got to be five o'clock somewhere."

"You're not going to get an argument from me," he said, thinking he'd kill for a beer—or six—right now.

19

OUR LADY OF the River Church was situated on a bluff above Black Bear River. After the original church had burned down due to an unfortunate candle accident in 1910, it had been rebuilt of brick with gray stone accents hauled in by mule. Five years later, a room had been added for the resident priest, along with a barn, no longer standing, for his horse.

Later additions included classrooms for catechism instruction and a meeting hall that served as a wedding reception and funeral luncheon room, along with being a venue for seasonal plays put on by the youth groups. From its position above the river, the steeple bell tower could be seen from nearly everywhere in town.

It didn't seem right, Austin thought as she and Sawyer walked up the stone steps to the tall double front doors. Father Cassidy had suggested meeting at first in the church itself, so they could talk about casket and flower placement. Which had her thinking back to when she and Heather had come here to discuss the altar wedding flowers and the bouquets on the main aisle ends of all the pews. That had been such a fun and happy day that rather than risk anything Johnny Mott might be serving at the New

Chance, she and Heather had driven to Klamath Falls for a celebratory lunch at the Blackbird Bistro.

"I feel just like one of those citified ladies who lunch," Heather giggled as she unfolded the white damask napkin and put it on her lap, which, as her pregnancy progressed, seemed to be disappearing more and more by the day.

"You deserve it. This may be the last time you get to go out without baby spit-up on your clothes."

Heather wrinkled her nose in a way that had earned her the nickname of Bunny until she'd decided it was too childish for high school and had returned to her given name. "Thanks for the positive affirmation."

Austin grinned. "What are best friends for?"

"Are you okay?" Sawyer leaned down to ask.

"I'm fine." Austin furiously blinked her swimming eyes. "No. I'm not. But at least this is the last stop for today."

"Until we go back to the ranch and face the kids."

"And aren't you just a beacon of positivity?" she asked, once again thinking back on that day.

She'd been so happy for her friend. But she couldn't deny that a part of her had been envious. Not jealous, she'd assured herself then and did again now. That would suggest that she didn't want Heather to have a happily-ever-after marriage with the man she loved. What she'd wished then, and yes, dammit, now, was that she could have that same type of relationship. Not with Jace. That had always been a reckless, impossible hookup that she'd allowed to drag on way too long.

But with Sawyer. At the time, she'd wildly hoped that both of them being attendants at the wedding of their close friends might give him some ideas. Like proposing. But after they'd danced their last reception dance, she'd returned home to the ranch. Alone.

The side door that led to the suite of church offices opened, and Father Donovan Cassidy entered the nave. Like most of the residents of River's Bend—even Cooper, who seldom wore his official sheriff's uniform—the thirtysomething priest could often be found in jeans, a starched cotton shirt, and boots. That he was wearing black slacks, a black shirt with his white clerical collar, and dress shoes showed how serious he took this meeting.

"I'm so sorry I'm late," he said. "Phyllis Gardener is coordinating next month's parish picnic, and there seems to be a problem with the variety of side dishes."

"We just got here," Austin said. The priest, usually punctual to a fault, was only three minutes past their meeting time.

"Still, your time is valuable." He blew out a breath and seemed to be gathering his thoughts as he switched from the mundane of picnic potato salad to the sacramental. "I'm well aware of how many things you have to deal with right now." He held out his hand to Sawyer. "And as unhappy as this situation is, it's good to see you back home again safe and sound, Sawyer."

"It's good to be back home."

When the shadow crossed his eyes again, Austin, who was starting to get a handle on the baggage Sawyer had brought home with him, suspected he was thinking of those he'd been in battles with who hadn't made it home. She still couldn't quite get past the idea that if only she hadn't gone along with Heather's plan for dinner, perhaps none of the sequence of events that had brought them here to Our Lady today would have happened.

"I hear you're staying at Green Springs," the priest said.

"In the foreman's cabin," Sawyer pointed out for the second time today.

"Good, good. Jack will be needing a man he's comfortable talking with during this sad time. Earl called from the funeral home after you both left. He said you were thinking of a Monday mass."

"Is that a problem?" Sawyer asked with an edge to his tone Austin wasn't accustomed to hearing from him.

"No, of course not." The priest slipped his hands into the pockets of his black trousers. "Today's Saturday. You could have the visitation Sunday night. The only problem with a Monday funeral is that you won't be able to have the obituary posted in the *Register* before the mass. Which may not be important to you, but—"

"I hadn't thought of that," Austin said. Nor could she remember Earl mentioning it in his list of things she and Sawyer would have to take care of. But, then again, her mind hadn't been as sharp during that meeting as it might have been.

"Yes, I'd like the obituary printed before the funeral." That way she wouldn't have to spend hours this evening and tomorrow calling everyone who might want to attend. Which would also involve repeating the horrible details of the accident over and over again.

She did, she realized suddenly, have to call Lexi. As soon as she got back to the ranch. Just as there was no way she would have missed taking part in Heather's wedding, she'd want to be here, as well.

"If you move it to Tuesday or even Wednesday, Earl can send the obit to Dan Brewer at the *Register*. The church's newsletter editor will also put a notice in the Sunday bulletin and post it to our Facebook page."

"The church has a Facebook page?" Sawyer asked.

"Of course. It's pretty much a requirement these days," Donovan Cassidy, who'd married the couple on that lovely June day, said. "I always post my homily there on Sundays for those who, for various reasons, such as the opening day of fishing season, can't make it to mass."

After a short discussion of where the caskets would be placed and how many flower arrangements might be expected, which reminded Austin that she needed to ask Earl to mention that, in lieu of flowers, people donate to the local food pantry, where Heather had volunteered two mornings a week, he led them into his office. Once again they refused the offer of coffee or tea, and after going through the basic procedure of the funeral mass, the priest asked if they had any special requests.

"Although eulogies aren't part of Catholic tradition," he said, "more parishes and bishops are bending the rules if it helps a family through this difficult time."

"I'm fine with not having to speak," Austin said. "Even if I could think of what to say, I'm not sure I could get through it without crying, which wouldn't be any help to Jack and Sophie."

"I'm fine with that, too," Sawyer agreed.

"There is one thing that occurred to me this morning," Austin said. Had that only been this morning? It seemed like a lifetime ago. Worried that the priest would think she was totally going outside the centuries-old traditional funeral box, she nevertheless shared a brief idea of a children's funeral for Jack's and Sophie's friends before the actual service.

"That's a wonderful idea," he surprised her by saying without a moment's hesitation. "In fact, my sister Anne had a similar one for our grandmother, who passed last year. My nieces and nephews had been very close to her, and unlike Jack and Sophie, they'd taken part in the dying process by visiting her in the hospital and then the hospice.

"Anne, her husband, Dave, and I could tell that the children received a lot of comfort from being able to have their friends with them in the same way the adults had their friends. And children love rituals. Both the planning and taking part in them help as a distraction from the sadness."

He turned in his swivel chair and reached to a bookcase behind his desk. "Here are a couple books on the topic to help you get ideas. One that was especially popular with my family was blowing bubbles into the air instead of the more harmful balloons. Also, the deep breathing and exhaling required of blowing bubbles serves as a stress reliever."

"That sounds wonderful," Austin said.

"I'm sure you'll find many helpful ideas, but if you'd like, we've been planting trees in the garden park area behind the church in a living memory of those we've lost."

Austin exchanged a look with Sawyer and knew they were once again thinking the same thing. Of Jack climbing the tree at the barbecue welcome home party.

"That'd be cool," Sawyer said.

"You could take them to The Plant Place to pick out the tree on Sunday or Monday. This being spring, the nursery will have a good selection."

Austin had been feeling horribly depressed and more than a little overwhelmed after the funeral home and legal meeting. While both Earl and Colton had been patient and helpful, they'd had her feeling a lot like Sisyphus faced with pushing that eternal rock up the mountain.

For the first time, she was feeling optimistic. She

couldn't bring Jack and Sophie's parents back. But together, she and Sawyer, Winema and her father, and the Murphys could all help make the funeral a more positive experience for the children to look back on.

"I'm feeling better," she said as they left the church after pausing on the way out to light a candle.

"Yeah, me, too. This, I think we can do."

"You said 'we.'"

"I said I'd be here for you."

"I know. But you're also dealing with your own situation, and—"

"Which isn't anywhere near as important as this," he cut her off. "And I was talking about twenty years ago."

When he'd passed her that note written in his big, second-grade scrawling print. *Dear Austin, I'm sorry your mom went away. But I'll always be your friend.*

Whatever happened between them, Austin knew that Sawyer Murphy was a man of his word. He'd meant those words then. And he meant them now.

"What would you say, while we're on a roll, of taking care of the cemetery?"

"We might as well," Austin agreed, thinking that, despite what he'd said about the tree and the bench, it didn't seem as if the location really mattered all that much. "That way we'll be able to concentrate more attention on the kids."

"Great." He turned a corner, taking them back to Front Street, where he stopped in front of Blossoms.

"You're getting your mom flowers," she guessed.

"Yeah. I haven't been there since I got back. So, this seems sort of appropriate. Want to come in and help me choose?"

"I'd love to." Austin realized that, like the candle she'd lit for Tom and Heather, the flowers for his mother were an act of faith that somehow, somewhere, death was not the end but yet another stop on life's eternal journey.

20

WHEN THEY GOT back to the ranch, they discovered that, rather than send over his foreman, Dan Murphy had come himself. He was in the corral with Jack as they drove up. Buck, leaning heavily on two hand-carved wooden canes, was standing by the fence. Seeing a man who'd once been as strong as one of his bulls being so weakened ripped a big piece off Sawyer's heart.

"Guess what I can do," Jack said as he ran over to the fence.

"What?" Sawyer asked.

"I can rope a steer."

"Really?"

"Yeah! Mr. Murphy said you made this dummy steer to practice when you were in high school."

"I did. It was my year-end project."

"I wish my school had cool stuff like that." Jack's mouth turned down and he scuffed a booted foot in the dirt. "We have to study boring stuff like spelling and arithmetic."

"Those are important," Austin felt the need to point out.

"I'm going to be a cowboy and rope and ride in the

rodeo," the seven-year-old argued. "I don't need to know all that."

"Sure you do." Sawyer climbed over the fence, took the branding rope from Jack's hand, tossed it out, and progressively coiled it with the same muscle memory he'd learned to shoot a rifle with. "If you don't know how to spell, you're going to look like a blame fool when you're filling out your entry forms. And if you think it's humiliating to land on your butt two seconds into a ride, just think how you'd feel to have the announcer sharing some of your spelling screw-ups over the loudspeaker for everyone in the grandstands to laugh at."

Jack's eyes widened. "They'd do that?"

"You bet." As he refined his loop, Sawyer remembered the pleasure he'd once received from roping. Maybe, he thought, he'd sign up for some July Fourth rodeo events. "Rodeos are partly for practicing necessary cowboying skills, but they're entertainment, too. And people like to laugh. So it's best that you don't give them any more reason than necessary to laugh at you."

It had been years since he'd had any reason to rope a steer, but some things you never forgot. "And you're going to really need arithmetic."

"Why? That's the worst."

"In the first place, you've got to keep a running track of yours and your competition's scores. Sure, you're going out every time to win, but so does every other cowboy. So, you need to know what times and scores you're shooting for."

"Don't forget how entry fees cost money," Buck—who as a stock contractor, had always preferred taking other cowboys' money to paying it out—said.

"There is that." Sawyer flipped the rope loop over his

body, two or three times, getting accustomed to the extra-soft beginner's rope his father had apparently brought over for Jack. "So do gas, meals, motels, vet bills, and either horse feed or horse rentals, depending on whether you're using your own horse or stock like Austin and Mr. Merrill bring to rodeos."

Swinging the rope, he walked up to the dummy, hooked it under the right horn, then brought it back up around the left. "And you can never count on payouts. Only the top finishers end up in the money, so since even the best horse and cowboy can have a bad day, a miles-long drive can result in nothing but racking up more experience and expense. If you can't do math, you can get in the hole really fast. I've seen more than one guy's career end because he's racked up a bunch of debt.

"Right, Dad?" He exchanged a look with his father, who'd given him much the same lecture when he'd been Jack's age.

"Right as rain," the older man said.

"Okay." Jack blew out a resigned breath. "I'll learn to like school, even though I'd sure rather be outside. Do you think I'll ever be as good as you?"

"Sure you can, if you put your mind to it." Sawyer coiled the rope back up and handed it to his father. "It just takes a lot of practice. After you get your homework done," he tacked on when he felt Austin's sharp look.

He remembered her not feeling a bit sorry for him when his own father had made him study when he would've preferred to be riding or out in the corral swinging rope all day. Being a superior form of being, Austin Merrill had somehow managed to get nearly straight A's in school while still making time to become good

enough at barrel racing and roping to have shelves filled
with trophies and gold buckles.

"I don't have to do homework today," Jack said. The
reason for him being here at the ranch swept back to
swamp the fun distraction Sawyer's dad had created for
him. "Because my mom and dad died." His freckled face
fell and his eyes shone.

"I know." Sawyer felt so at sea here. And damn if the
others weren't just standing there, putting it on him. "And
that's as bad as it gets. But Austin and I just came from the
church, and Father Cassidy really likes the idea of a kid's
funeral. We'll need your and your sister's help to plan it."

"We can do that." Jack ran the back of his hand below
his nose, which had begun to run.

Austin reached into her bag and pulled out a tissue.
"Blow," she said gently.

He did, with a loud honking sound. "Sophie's in with
Mitzi and Winema." He sniffed. "They planted some
flowers. Now she's making brownies for dessert tonight."

"Nothing better than brownies," Sawyer said. "But I
think they could use some ice cream. Want to help me
make some?"

"Okay." He sniffed. "Mom's favorite was vanilla bean.
Can we make that?"

"You betcha, pardner." He took off his Stetson and
plunked it down on Jack's carrot-orange head, deciding that
as soon as they got past this mess, the two of them were
dropping in to the Stockman's Shop and getting the kid a
real hat of his own. Like Cooper had done for Rachel's
son. "Now, let's put this rope back in the tack room, and
we'll go track down your sister."

SOPHIE'S LONG HAIR had been done up in some sort of fancy braid thing Austin wouldn't have been able to pull off in a million years, revealing that Mitzi Murphy was in the house. As drained as she was by the events of the day, Austin was even more grateful the citified real estate agent had fallen in love with Dan and moved to River's Bend.

She and Sawyer began by explaining about the caskets and showing them the brochures.

"They're just like the cabinets Mom picked out," Sophie said.

"That's what we were thinking," Austin said. "Sawyer was the one who spotted them."

"Thank you." Sophie looked over at him, and for a split second, Austin thought she'd seen a flash of a beginning crush in the girl's gaze.

Which wouldn't be surprising. Sawyer Murphy was a drop-dead-gorgeous man. Making him even more appealing was that either he didn't realize how good looking he was or it didn't matter to him. She'd always suspected it might be the latter.

Whichever, Austin had enough trust in the man to know that if Sophie tumbled, he'd treat her gently so someday she'd look back on her crush with fondness rather than embarrassment. She was also pragmatic enough to think that a little bit of falling in love might help dull the inescapable pain these next days and weeks would entail.

"I'm glad you approve," he said easily.

They moved on to the next item on Earl's list. The clothing.

"I think Mom should be buried in her wedding dress,"

Sophie said. "Because she tried it on again for all of us and was really proud she could still wear it."

"She loved that dress," Austin said, and although she knew the children had heard the story many times over the years, she shared the tale of the making of the dress and all that beading during finals week once again.

"She wore it every year for before their anniversary." Sophie's bottom lip began to tremble. "She always looked so pretty I wanted to wear it for my wedding. She said it would be her happiest day."

"Perhaps we should keep it," Mitzi suggested gently.

"No." Sophie swiped furiously at her glistening eyes. "I don't want to anymore. Because Mom won't be there to see me get married in it. So it wouldn't be the same."

"Whatever you want, honey," Austin said.

She wrote down the dress on the list but decided to wait until the very last minute to take it to the funeral home, just in case Sophie changed her mind. Meanwhile, she was going to make sure to take lots of pictures. That way, at the very least, a clever seamstress could make a duplicate dress if Sophie wanted to recreate it.

"And what about your dad?" she asked. There was so much to get through, she was hoping they wouldn't get bogged down on each item because no way did she want the children as emotionally drained as she felt.

"I think he should wear the zombie costume he wore last year when we went trick-or-treating downtown," Jack said.

"What?" Sophie turned on him, eyes now blazing. "Why would anyone, anywhere on this planet, want to be buried in a zombie costume?"

"Austin said it was supposed to be about happy times.

And we all laughed and laughed when he did his scary zombie walk." He stuck his thin, freckled arms out and began lurching across the kitchen floor.

"In case you've forgotten, idiot child," his sister shot back, "zombies are the undead. Dad can't be a zombie because he's dead!" She stood up so fast she tipped the chair over and ran out of the room. A moment later the sound of the front door slamming reverberated throughout the house.

"Well," Mitzi said on a long sigh. "That went well."

21

SOPHIE WAS HALFWAY down the driveway when Austin came out on the porch. The girl could definitely run. Austin thought about chasing her, then considered the truck instead. Maybe they could take a ride and talk things out. Of course if Sophie climbed the fence and cut across a pasture toward the river or mountain, she'd have to ditch the rig.

Starting to appreciate what Heather had been talking about those times she'd insisted her life wasn't as perfect as it might seem to outsiders, Austin opted for the truck.

It took less than a minute to catch up with Sophie on the road. Austin rolled down the driver's window. "Where are you going?"

"Home." Sophie didn't look her way.

"I don't think your mom would want that."

"My mom isn't around to want anything. Because she's dead. And we don't always get what we want. I didn't want her to die, either. And now that we're damn pitiful orphans, I'm stuck with being idiot Jack's mother."

Austin decided to let her calling her brother an idiot pass and focus on the more important issue. She remembered what Rachel had said about Scott believing he'd have to be the man of the family after his father's death. Sophie was going to have enough to deal with without having that burden put on such very slender shoulders.

"No, your brother isn't going to be your responsibility. At least not that way, though he will need your love and support."

"He doesn't even care."

"He does. But at his age, I'm not sure he totally understands the permanency of the situation."

Sophie stopped marching down the gravel at the side of the road and spun toward the truck. "He's having fun planning our parents' funeral!"

"Father Cassidy said young children get caught up in the detail of ritual. I suspect it's a form of coping mechanism."

"Lucky him." She kicked the ground, scattering gravel. "I hate this."

"I do, too. Your mother was my best friend for as long as I can remember. I have this big, huge, aching hole in my heart and am afraid if I let myself cry, I'll never be able to stop."

"Really?" That got the girl's attention. "I figured since you were a grown-up, you knew how to deal with stuff like this."

"I haven't a clue," Austin said. She might not have any idea how to handle this situation, but decided honesty couldn't hurt. "Neither does Sawyer."

"He's a Marine. He probably saw lots of people die in war."

"I suppose he did. But the Marines undoubtedly have a very organized and detailed system to deal with battlefield losses. In civilian life, we only have guidelines and have to learn how to get through the maze as we go along."

"Well, that's fucking encouraging."

Austin wasn't wild about the f-bomb, but she did welcome the snark. At least it was communication. "How about going for a ride?" she asked. "I always feel better down by the river."

"Do you really believe that's going to make all this go away?"

"No." A cattle truck, loaded with fifty thousand pounds of beef on the hoof, roared past between them in the other lane. "But at least we can talk in quiet."

"I don't want to talk."

"Fine." Austin pulled off the road onto the gravel shoulder. "I'll talk and you can listen."

"And if I don't want to?"

"You can always cover your ears."

Sophie tilted her head. "That reminds me of something Mom would've said."

"I know." Austin managed a smile. "She was a lot better at it than I am."

Heaving a huge sigh, Sophie trudged across the road and climbed up into the passenger's seat. When Austin gave her a pointed look, she scowled back but fastened her seat belt.

Neither spoke as they drove past the Bar M, headed toward the river. There was a small, grassy park on the bank, with picnic tables, a drinking fountain with icy water from the spring right beneath it, and horseshoe pits. She pulled into the empty parking lot and cut the engine. Then rolled down the windows and opened the moonroof, allowing the tangy scent of pine and the rushing sound of the river into the truck.

"I know no one will ever be able to replace your mom," she said carefully. The sun was lowering. One wrong word and Sophie could bolt, possibly getting lost and, even worse, be forced to spend the night out here in the woods alone.

"Duh," Sophie muttered, staring straight ahead.

"But Rachel, Mitzi, Winema, and I are going to do our best. Just like Sawyer, Cooper, Ryan, Dan, and my dad are going to try to help fill in for your dad."

"It won't be the same."

"No. It won't. Winema is wonderful and I've always loved her as much as I would a mom. But that doesn't mean that I don't still miss my mother. Less as I've gotten older, but when I was Jack's and even your age, I thought about her every day. And missed her."

Sophie turned to look at Austin. "Did you hope she'd come back?"

"Every day for years." Which was something she'd never told her dad. And had even stopped mentioning to Sawyer when she'd been Sophie's age. "Sometimes, while I'm out working with a horse in the corral, or baking for the bookstore or the New Chance, I'll wonder if maybe this will be the day she decides to check in and see how I turned out." And hadn't so much of what Austin had done all these years been about trying to prove to an absent mother than she'd grown up to be worth keeping?

"You could go see her."

Austin had often thought of that. Too many times to count. "She knows where I am," she said mildly. "If she wanted to see me, I suspect she'd have come by now."

"Maybe," Sophie allowed. "Maybe she feels guilty and doesn't know how to come back home."

"I've thought of that, too." Had Sophie always been wiser than what Austin would have expected a twelve-year-old to be? Or was she special? Of course she was. She was Heather's daughter. How could she not be exceptional?

"Why does shit happen?"

The pain in the question tore ragged strips off Austin's already broken heart. "I don't have any idea."

"Do you think it's like God's plan?"

"No." Austin had thought about that. "I think it's more random than that. I don't believe God would take your parents."

"I saw a movie where these kids' parents were killed in a plane crash on Christmas Eve, and the grandmother told them that the mom and dad died because God wanted them in heaven with him."

"No one has the answers, but that sounds pretty selfish of God to me."

"Yeah." Her shoulders slumped. "That's what I thought." She picked at a hangnail. "Then I wondered if it was my fault."

"Oh, honey." When Austin reached out to her, the girl pulled away, back against the door, away from comfort. Perhaps because she didn't think she deserved it? "Of course you're in no way responsible."

"I got mad because Mom wouldn't let me spend the weekend they were in Ashland with Madison Graham instead of at Cooper and Rachel's."

"She didn't tell me about that."

"We had a fight. The Grahams were going to be away at some sort of business conference that weekend, and Mom didn't trust me enough to let me sleep over without 'parental supervision.'" She made air quotes with her fingers.

"I doubt she was worried about *your* behavior," Austin treaded carefully, wishing she'd had advance warning of the death and could have at least gotten some advice from that therapist Cooper knew.

"But things happen. I was at a party in the eighth grade when Karyn Morse's parents were out of town. Of course, I didn't tell Winema or Dad, and neither of them thought to ask if the party would be supervised. But they found out when some high school guys showed up at the house and got wild enough the Morses' neighbors called the police. You can imagine how horrible it was to have Cooper's father, who was sheriff at the time, call my dad to pick me up at the jail."

"Wow." Finally, something she'd said that impressed the tween. But did it have to be her hour-long stint as a jailbird? A stint that could have been shorter, but Buck had decided to let her stew for a while to teach her a lesson. It had worked.

"Yeah. Wow," Austin repeated. "I was grounded for two weeks. During the summer."

"I told my mom I hated her."

"I suspect everyone tells their mom or dad that. I did." And had wondered for years if that had been the reason her mother had left. Fortunately, one autumn afternoon while baking apple pies with Sawyer's mom, she'd shared that worry. Mrs. Murphy had assured her that her mother's leaving had nothing to do with her. "Not everyone is cut out for ranch life, dear," she'd said mildly. "But that doesn't mean that she doesn't love you." She'd reached over and brushed some flour off Austin's cheek with what had felt like a mother's tender touch. "But your father,

Winema, Mr. Murphy, and I certainly do." Remembering that frozen-in-time moment had Austin hoping that she could be half the surrogate mom Sawyer's mother, whom they'd lost way too soon, had been to her.

Sophie went back to picking at the hangnail again. "And I said I wished she weren't my mom." When she lifted her face, tears began trailing down pale cheeks. "So, maybe God punished me by taking her away."

"Oh, no." This time Austin wasn't about to let her back away. She scooted over on the bench seat and took Sophie in her arms, holding her tight to try to calm the tremors. "It was an accident, darling. A horrible, terrible accident. And all any of us can do, what your mom and dad would want us to do, is to try our best to move on and find a way to be happy again. Because that's all Heather ever wanted for you. From the moment she knew she was pregnant."

"It's hard."

"Yes, it is. Horribly hard."

"Maybe Mom would want me to be happy, but I don't want to. It doesn't feel right to even think about being happy when she and Dad are dead. I want to be mad." She pulled away again and wrapped her arms around herself, as if trying to hold her tumultuous feelings in. "Because if I'm mad, then I won't be so sad I start crying and, like you said, never stop."

The tears were flowing again and her nose had started running. Unfortunately, Austin had left the house without her purse. Which also meant that she was driving without a license. Which was the least of her problems. Especially since she had an in with the sheriff.

"But I know she doesn't want me to be angry and

mean to Jack, and just in case she's watching, I don't want her to feel bad."

Austin was madly trying to think of what to say to that when Sophie said, "So, I guess maybe I could try not to be so mad. But." She lifted her chin in a determined gesture so much like her mother's Austin had to fight back water-works. "We are not going to let Jack put Dad in a zombie suit just so he has something to laugh about."

"Maybe you can play the Halloween video at the kids' funeral." Heather had dressed totally out of character as Cruella de Vil in a black-and-white wig, long red gloves, and a faux fur Dalmatian coat that she had, of course, made herself.

"That's another thing. Do I have to do that stupid kids' funeral? I'm not a kid. I'm almost thirteen."

Another important milestone Heather would miss. "No, you're not a child. But your brother is, and I'm pretty sure Jack will feel a lot better if you're there with him."

"I can sure see why you and Mom were best friends," Sophie huffed. "Because she was just as good at playing the guilt card."

Austin surprised herself by laughing at that. "We can't help it," she said. "We're Catholic. It's probably in the genes."

Although Sophie didn't laugh, her lips did move just a bit at the corners. And she'd gotten some color back. And that, Austin figured, as she started the engine and headed back to the ranch, was a start.

22

ALONG WITH COMING over to keep Jack occupied, Dan had brought along a hand who'd taken care of feeding the horses that evening. When he'd assured Austin that all the day-to-day ranch work would be taken care of by his crew until everyone's life settled down, she nearly burst into exhausted, grateful tears.

This was one very strong part of why she'd never wanted to leave River's Bend. It was a strong, interlinked community where not only did everyone know their neighbors, along with celebrating the happy events, they looked out for one another during the hard times. Which inevitably came.

After a comfort-food dinner of stewed chicken and noodles Winema had cooked, Sawyer and Austin drove the children back to Cooper and Rachel's house. The seemingly never-ending day had worn everyone out. Jack had fallen asleep the moment he'd been buckled into his car seat and didn't wake even when Sawyer carried him upstairs to Scott's bedroom, where Jack had spent last night in the bottom bunk.

How different that night had been, Austin thought sadly.

She was trying to decide whether she should go into the guest room with Sophie, when the girl solved the problem by walking into the room and shutting the door in her face.

It was dark by the time Sawyer drove them home.

Insisting she didn't need him to walk her to the door tonight, Austin jumped out of the truck and went inside. Winema had gone home, and the locomotive-loud snoring coming through her father's door told her that he'd been just as wiped out as the rest of them.

She washed her face, brushed her teeth, put on her pajamas, and climbed into bed, but made the mistake of turning on the news to see what they were reporting about Tom and Heather. When they showed the flattened minivan, Austin knew that image would stay frozen in her mind for as long as she lived.

꙳

AFTER DROPPING AUSTIN off at her house, Sawyer drove on to the foreman's cabin, where he found Ryan's forest-green Expedition, with an empty utility trailer hitched to it, parked in front.

"You come to rustle my cattle?" he called out as he opened the door. Then stopped and stared around in stunned surprise at the inside of the cabin that, except for a stove, fridge, microwave, and his bedroll, had been deserted when he'd left the house this morning.

The furniture was covered in bark-brown leather, wide cushioned, and worn enough that he wouldn't need to feel like he had to shower before sitting on it.

Austin's wildflowers claimed the center of an old pine table that he recognized from the Bar M. It'd been distressed from generations of Murphys living with it, and Sawyer knew if he looked closely at the kitchen table, he'd see his initials and USMC on the underside. He'd carved those the summer he'd turned twelve and, drawn by the posters while delivering copies of the afternoon *River's Bend Record*, had dropped into the Marine recruiting office.

Patterned rugs in earth tones were scattered over the floor.

"What the hell?"

It was like a reverse robbery. Instead of coming home to an empty house, he'd walked into one that looked as though it belonged in one of those magazines rich folk bought about how to decorate their weekend country cabins.

Brown muslin curtains framed windows that offered an expansive view of the foothills and mountain in one direction, the sprawling Merrill ranch house in the other. He glanced up at a second-story window, remembering climbing up the old oak tree to Austin's window when they'd been kids. He'd stopped those night visits during high school, when being alone with her in her bedroom tempted the bad, sex-crazed devil who'd taken up residence on his shoulder.

He checked out the bedroom, which had a black iron queen bed and the knotty pine dresser he'd grown up with. One of the other bedrooms had bunk beds and another had two twins covered with pink and purple girly-looking floral comforters. If he hadn't known better, from the bedding and furniture, he'd have sworn a real family lived here.

Ryan was sitting on the floor surrounded by hand tools, screws, and bolts putting together a white bookcase in the room with the twins. "The women put you up to this, didn't they?"

"Don't blame me." Ryan held up his hands, one of which was holding a screwdriver. "I just did what I was told. Besides, not only was I outnumbered by Layla and Jenna, who hatched up the plan with Rachel, Mitzi, and Gram, it was hard to argue when I agree with them."

"I was going to buy furniture." A bed, anyway.

"Well, now you don't have to. Look," he said, "Cooper called and told me about how the social worker's going to pay you a visit. Everyone decided that if you were going to pass muster, you had to look halfway civilized.

"So, while you and Austin were running all over town taking care of the funeral and legal stuff, Brody, Jake, and I were picking up a few things from the ranch and buying out the basin's craigslist." Jake being Cooper's father-in-law from when he'd been married to Ellen Buchanan. "They brought along their trucks to help haul it all back here. Then the women swept in like Ninjas and did their decorating thing."

Sawyer had returned to River's Bend wanting to be left alone. Sure, he'd admit having been conflicted where Austin was concerned, but he'd figured that they had plenty of time for him to get his head back on straight, banish the big black dog that had been following him around for months, and start living again.

"This wasn't what I'd planned," he said, as much to himself as to his brother.

"Hell, kid," Ryan replied, with all the superiority of their two-year age difference, "you should've figured out by now that the gods laugh when men plan."

Like their mom dying too young and too hard. Or the

fog of a war Sawyer still couldn't understand. Families shattered by the men who'd been cut down in the prime of their life during battle. Tom and Heather leaving behind two kids who needed him to step up.

Semper fidelis wasn't just some motto signifying dedication to the Marine Corps and country. It was a way of life. And as much as he'd tried to convince himself that he was just a civilian now, the fact was that Semper fi wasn't relative. It was absolute.

While he still intended to start his own spread, fate had stepped in and given him another mission. Taking care of two kids would not only be a monumental task, it was the most important he'd ever undertaken.

And failure was not an option.

Fortunately, he thought as he crouched down and started putting books onto the shelves Ryan had just finished putting together, he wouldn't be doing it alone.

∾

AUSTIN TOSSED AND turned for what seemed like hours, finding sleep an impossible target as past memories kept turning in her mind like the facets of a kaleidoscope. Finally giving up, she went downstairs to the mudroom, put a corduroy barn jacket on over her pajamas, and pulled on her boots. After grabbing a box of long matches, she went outside to the back porch and lit a candle in the iron lantern.

She was sitting on the porch swing, rocking slowly, looking up at the swirling sky of diamonds, when she heard the familiar crunch of boots walking toward her.

"I hope I'm not interrupting anything," Sawyer's voice came swirling out from the darkness. "I couldn't sleep, and when I saw the candlelight, I thought you might be up for some company."

"I am." She scooted over, making room for him. "I made the mistake of watching the news."

"Yeah. Me, too."

"The minivan was such a cheerful color. When Heather first picked it out, Tom was embarrassed to drive it. He called it the Banana Mobile."

Sawyer sat down beside her and stretched his long legs out in front of him. "A yellow minivan doesn't exactly say cowboy tough."

"No. But Heather said just looking at it made her happy. Which was all he needed to hear."

"They had a special bond."

"They did." As she and Sawyer had once. Until they hadn't.

They sat there, side by side, not saying anything as the night sounds filled in the silence. In the distance they could hear the river continuing its journey to the sea. The hoot of an owl, the lonely call of a coyote, and a whistle of the midnight southbound train.

"I was drunk," she said into the darkness. Sawyer didn't say anything, but Austin sensed him listening. "The night I married Jace."

Again, no answer, but she knew that she had his full attention.

"I thought," she continued haltingly, "after that kiss at the hospital, that maybe you finally saw me as more than just the girl next door. That you were thinking you might want me." She paused, needing a moment to get the rest out. "The way I wanted you."

"I did." His deep voice was like Irish coffee topped

with cream. Warm, smooth, and potent, awakening parts of her body that had been sleeping far too long.

"But the email—"

"Was a mistake. And a lie. I didn't mean a word of it." He dragged a hand down his face. "Well, in a way I did. Some of it was true."

And wasn't that a revelation? "What part?"

"The part about the kiss being an impulse."

"One you regretted."

"Yes. No. Damn." He stood up and walked over to the edge of the porch and put his hands on the railing. "Look, I didn't regret the kiss," he said, still not looking at her. "What I regretted was the timing."

"You were upset about your dad. It had you act out of character."

"Sure, I was worried about him. That, plus jet lag and guilt for leaving my team back in those mountains, tore down some barriers. If things had been different . . .

"I told myself that it'd be better to say that the kiss hadn't really meant anything, that it had been a mistake, that we didn't have a future, than to cause you even worse pain if we'd gotten involved and I didn't make it back."

"What?" Austin dragged her hand through her hair. "You didn't think that I'd be devastated if you died? Or were injured?" Her head spun at the idea that whether or not they were lovers would make any difference. "Just for argument sake, what if I'd been hit by a logging truck, or had a boulder drop on me while you were deployed?" And ended up dead. Like Tom and Heather. "Are you saying you'd be any less upset than you would be if we'd slept together?"

"Of course not." He turned back toward her. "The real

mistake wasn't the kiss. It was that email, which was a major fuckup, okay?"

Like many cowboys, Sawyer didn't cuss around women. It might be considered an old-fashioned attitude in this day and age, but long-held habits die hard. The fact that he'd done so now told Austin how tangled his emotions were.

"How the hell was I supposed to know that you'd elope with some guy before I could fix things? I had no idea you were even dating." He left unsaid that she sure as hell hadn't kissed him like a woman who was in a relationship.

"I wasn't dating anyone." He was right about it being effed up. On both their parts. "I met Jace the night I married him."

He'd been slick, handsome, and compliments had come trippingly off his tongue, unlike most of the men she'd grown up with. Those pretty words, along with the cosmos, had, for a few dizzying hours, put a temporary patch on her broken heart.

"Getting married was the biggest mistake of my life," she said. "But the worst part of the debacle was that I lost you."

"Hell. I'm sorry." He flung his body back down beside her and took both her hands in his. "I screwed things up. Big-time." His voice was as rough and gravelly as a rutted logging road after a harsh mountain winter.

"It wasn't just you," she said. "I was a grown woman. I should've been honest about how I felt."

"And now?"

"I want you." There, she'd said it. "I've never stopped wanting you."

"We're on the same page there. Me wanting you," he clarified.

"That's a start." Austin had been giving their situation a great deal of thought ever since that New Year's email. "And if you were anyone else, we wouldn't even be having this discussion. But we have a history, and I don't know if some quick, sweaty rounds of hot hookup sex is the answer."

"Hello. I'm a guy," he reminded her. "To us, sex isn't a bad answer whatever the question. And trust me, there'd be nothing quick about it."

She slapped his arm, even as she knew he'd said that to lighten the mood. "I'm serious."

"So am I. And thinking about those sweaty rounds of hot sex that are going to keep me up the rest of the night, now that you've put all those pictures in my mind. But I'm also serious as a heart attack about you."

"Not everyone can be like Heather and Tom."

"We're not them. They tumbled into the ever-after kind of love when they were too young to appreciate it. We may have wandered off onto separate paths these past years, but that doesn't mean that we can't meet at the crossroads."

The way they always had at the meeting place between their two ranches.

"I'm not much of a risk taker," she said.

"Says the women's breakaway roping champion. Not to mention that crazy barrel racing at thirty miles an hour."

"My top speed was thirty-four coming home," she murmured.

"See? That's flat-out crazy. And I hate to tell you this, sweetheart, but if you're looking to be risk averse, you're in the wrong business."

"You're talking about work. Not life."

"Maybe others can compartmentalize. But for you and me, ranching is life. Green Springs, your horses, even that mangy old bull—"

She tossed up her chin. "Desperado is not mangy."

"See." He reached out and ruffled her hair in an easy, familiar gesture. "Here we are, sitting in the dark, wading through a minefield of a conversation about regrets, hot sex, and God help me, the dreaded R word, and you sidetrack the conversation to defend livestock."

"While you can't even say the R word," she pointed out.

"I can, too."

She folded her arms, gave him a hard look, and waited.

"Okay." He sucked in a breath. Whipped off his hat and raked his hand over his hair. "Relationship." He nodded. Job done. "Satisfied?"

A smile was tugging at her lips, but not wanting him to think she was laughing at him, Austin merely said, "Congratulations. Another milestone achieved."

"How about one more?"

As Sawyer framed her face in his hands, she forgot to think. Forgot to breathe as he tilted his head and kissed her, slow, soft, and sweet, while the night breeze sighed in the tops of the pine trees and brilliant stars spun overhead.

She could have wept as he eased back and brushed his knuckles down her cheek. "We're dealing with a lot of stuff right now. So, although thoughts of tangling the sheets with you are going to have me taking a lot of icy showers, maybe you're right about letting things spin out. Take our time to get it right."

"It's not my first choice, either," she admitted, touching her palm to his cheek. "But with the funeral and the kids and everything . . ."

Heather and Rachel were turning out to have been right about children being the ultimate birth control.

"Yeah. They get priority." He exhaled a breath. "We've got a busy day tomorrow. I'd better let you get some sleep."

"You, too." The regret she'd heard in his rough tone was echoed in her own soft voice.

Sawyer stood up, held a hand down to her, and when she took hold of it, pulled her to her feet.

As they stood there, Austin felt as if she were standing on a rocky escarpment at the top of Modoc Mountain. One false step and she'd go tumbling over. Displaying a self-discipline that had undoubtedly made him a great Marine, Sawyer simply walked with her to the door.

"Sweet dreams."

"You, too," she said.

"Mine will be," he assured her as he ran his palm down her loosened hair. "Because I'll be dreaming of you."

Then he stepped away as Austin walked back into the house instead of flinging herself into his arms. As she'd been aching to do.

Then she stood there, her hand pressed against the glass of the French door, watching as he headed back to the foreman's house.

23

S OPHIE WAS IN bed when the ding of her phone signaled a text. She wasn't supposed to be texting or talking with friends after ten o'clock at night, but it wasn't as if her mom was here to stop her. She did pull the blanket over her head, just in case Rachel might go by the door and see the light.

The text was from Madison. *RUOK?*

My parents are dead.

I saw the news. *OMG!!! RU devastated?*

Sophie thought about that for a minute. *I was mad. Now I just feel like an invisible nothing.* Like a ghost. Maybe instead of her parents haunting her, she'd spend eternity haunting herself. Kill me now.

YUR probably in shock.

Maybe. We're having 2 funerals.

Srsly? Y???

Kid 1 & regular 1.

Yu R not a kid.

I have to go 4 Jack.

NW

Way

Sux

Wanna come?

Sophie held her breath. After what seemed like forever, she tried again. *I'll die w/out friends there.*

K What time?

Dont know yet.

Text when U do.

She blew out a relieved breath. *TY!!!*

U R BFF What RU wearing?

IDK

Hadn't she already been forced to help plan the stupid kid funeral and fight to keep Jack from dressing their dad like a fucking zombie? Now she was supposed to think about a funeral outfit? Thanks to *Seventeen*, she might know fifty-two ways to have the best first kiss ever and fifteen foolproof ways to snag her crush (number one: find out where he goes, and stalk him so he'll come up and talk to you), but she'd never read a single "What to wear to the funeral after your parental units get squashed by a giant boulder" article.

Stay + I'll CU 2moro we'll figure it out.

Sophie felt her stupid eyes stinging again. *THX*

<3<3<3

Wishing she could stay hidden beneath the blanket forever, she pushed herself out of bed and went into the guest room's adjoining bathroom, where she stared at herself in the mirror for a long time. Looking hard. Looking deep. Trying to find some sign that she'd changed, but except for her eyes being red-rimmed and puffy, she looked just the same as when she'd got up this morning. Before her entire world had crashed down around her and burst into flames. And now she was just left with the ashes.

How could she not look any different?

She went back into the bedroom and cracked open the door. And listened. When she couldn't hear anyone talking or moving, she crept down the hallway in her bare feet and went downstairs into the kitchen, where her near perfect life as she'd known it had ended.

Thanks to the moonlight streaming in from the window, she didn't have to risk turning on the light. She did stop and listen again.

So far, so good.

Taking the kitchen shears from the block on the counter, Sophie padded out of the kitchen and back up the stairs.

24

"YOU'RE A FRIGGING idiot." Two hours after leaving Austin, Sawyer was still awake, tangled up in twisted sheets with a boner the size of a redwood.

He'd never claimed to be a monk. When you never knew where you were going to be from one day to the next, or whether you'd even survive another day, getting serious about a woman was the one risk he'd never been willing to take. He'd gone to bed with lots of women, some of whom had been Special Forces groupies whose lack of desire for any sort of commitment beyond a single night had suited him just fine. There were others he could have probably made a good life with. The problem was, he'd always broken those affairs off after a few weeks for the simple reason that they hadn't been Austin.

It was stupid to spend your entire life carrying a torch for a single woman, especially when their timing never seemed to be in sync. A New Age astrologer he'd spent a memorable few nights with when he'd been back in California for training probably would have told him that his and Austin's stars or planets or moons, whatever, simply weren't aligned. And never would be.

The problem was, Sawyer hadn't believed that then.

And he damn well didn't believe it now.

The thing to do, he thought as he crawled out of bed, was to think of their situation as a yet another mission. Separate from the kids, even though taking care of Sophie and Jack was what was keeping them together.

After all, a failure to plan was a plan for failure. And, like with the Jack and Sophie mission, failure was not an option. Which were only two of the platitudes he'd been taught in MARSOC training. The only trouble was, as he'd discovered firsthand, you could plan until the cows came home, as his dad would say, and things could still go all to hell.

He was headed toward the kitchen when there was a knock at the door. The last time he'd had a night visitor, it hadn't been good news. And why the hell did everyone keep showing up when he was butt-assed naked, anyway?

For a fleeting moment Sawyer thought maybe Austin had changed her mind. He looked up at her house, which was dark. It was probably Cooper, come to check on him. Never mind that Sawyer was a bad-assed Marine, Coop would probably be playing the bossy big-brother role when the three of them were toothless and gumming Pablum in the old cowboys' home while checking out the hot young nurses.

Muttering a string of curses as blue as his balls, he marched over to the door and flung it open.

And, aw, shit, saw Austin standing on his porch.

"Uh, hi," she said, quickly dragging her wide eyes from his dick to his chest.

This wasn't good, but damned if he was going to cover up like he had anything to be ashamed of. It wasn't the first penis she'd ever seen. And given that she'd grown up breeding bulls and horses, it sure wasn't the biggest.

"Hi." He stepped aside. "Is there a problem?"

"Apparently so." Her gaze met his, and in her eyes he saw what looked like a wicked sexual humor he'd never associated with her. Austin Merrill had, even in his hottest fantasies, always remained an idealized blond goddess on top of a gleaming white pedestal. Another reason no other woman had ever measured up.

And yeah, even though he knew the vestal virgin idea was sexist, and had possibly come from him having assigned himself her protector at the ripe old age of seven, self-realization, which had never been his strong suit, struck like a lightning bolt.

He might have been afraid of ruining their friendship, but the risk he hadn't wanted to take was finding out that his goddess was, in fact, a flesh-and-blood woman. Which he'd gotten a taste of when she'd practically inhaled his tongue outside that Salem hospital.

"If I'm interrupting something, I can leave," she said.

Okay. That was a joke. Being a big, bad, Marine Special Ops Ranger, Sawyer wasn't used to women laughing at him in what hopefully was going to turn out to be a foreplay situation. But this was Austin. Who seemed to have suddenly developed a sexy, bad-girl twin.

"No." He must've swallowed his tongue because he was having trouble getting any words out. "Just let me . . ." He waved his arm in the direction of the bedroom. "Go get some . . ."

Maybe he was having a stroke. His grandfather had suffered a TIA a few years ago when Sawyer had been home for Christmas, and the old man's thoughts and speech had been messed up for a couple days.

"Underwear?" she asked with a wickedly arched brow. Hot damn, it looked as if he actually was finally going to get lucky with the woman of his dreams. Which was both amazing and terrifying at the same time. *Do. Not. Screw. This. Up.*

"Yeah. I'll, uh, be right back." Geez, wasn't he about as smooth as Scott Eastwood? "Uh, you want to come in?"

"Thanks." She gave him an *I know you want me* smile that had his soldier standing up to salute again.

Growing up, Sawyer had gone skinny-dipping with his brothers and pals in the river and lake. He'd played sports and could snap towels in the locker room with the best of them in high school. He'd been in the Marines and had hot bunked on aircraft carriers. He'd never given a thought about being naked around another man or, for that matter, any female he was involved with. Until now.

He probably set a world speed record for the amount of time it took him to yank on some jeans, pull a gray T-shirt over his head, and return to the living room, where she was standing there, looking good enough to lick in a pair of jeans and a snug, strawberry-pink T-shirt that read *Boots, class, and a little sass. That's what cowgirls are made of.*

"I'm sorry if I got you up," she said.

"I already was." Okay, maybe that was an inappropriate response. He definitely needed to work on his social skills. Open mouth, insert boot. "I was about to get a beer. You want something?"

"You probably don't have any wine."

"Sorry." And why hadn't he or his brothers thought of that while shopping? He'd bet his best trophy buckle that Cooper had kept it on hand when he was going out with Rachel.

"That's okay. I wouldn't turn down a beer."

She followed him into the kitchen.

"Jenna and Layla did an amazing job with this place," she said. "And just in time, because if everything goes well, the kids could be moving in by next week."

"Into the ranch house," he clarified. He was really digging her shirt. Especially since the walk over from the house must've been really chilly.

"True. But I'll bet they'll be wanting sleepovers with you. Especially Jack. Sophie may be a bit of a problem, being how she's crushing badly on you."

"Really?"

"Really." She sighed as she took the bottle he handed her. "For a really smart man, Sawyer Murphy, you can sometimes be a bit dense when it comes to the female of the species."

He tilted his bottle toward her. "You'll be getting no argument from me on that one. As hard as it'll probably be for them to be uprooted yet again, getting settled into a permanent home will be a good thing."

"It will," she agreed. She took another drink of the beer, and just looking at her pink lips on the long neck of the brown bottle had Sawyer thinking things that weren't going to be conducive to having a conversation considering whatever blood was left in his head was rapidly racing south. "I belong to a book club."

"Okay." He didn't get where she was going with that comment, but wasn't going to overthink anything that had her sitting here perched on a stool in his cabin. Even better would be if she were in his bed. On the floor. Against the wall. And that was just for starters.

"We had our last meeting at the Bar M. When we were

talking about Heather's anniversary trip, she and Rachel were laughing about kids being the ultimate birth control."

"I imagine that's probably true."

"So." She put her bottle on the counter, slid off the stool, went over to him, lifted her arms, and linked her fingers together around his neck. "I was thinking, with Lexi flying in tomorrow from Vegas, then the funeral, then Jack and Sophie moving into the ranch house, that this may be one of the few nights we're going to have a chance to be alone for a while."

"It could be."

"And I know we agreed that the wisest plan would be to take things slow—"

"That was pretty much *your* idea." He'd been all for that hot, sweaty sex suggestion.

"True. Because I was trying not to be impulsive. Which hasn't worked out real well for me in the past."

This time, instead of retreating as he had on her back porch, Sawyer stayed right where he was. His hands moved to her waist and drew her even closer.

"Did you come over here to seduce me, Austin Merrill?"

"If you have to ask, I must not be doing it right." Color flooded into her cheeks as she tried to pull away. "I'm sorry, this was a mistake."

Sawyer was not about to let her get away. Not this time. "It's not a mistake. And, for the record, it's also not impulsive. We've known each other all our lives," he reminded her. "There's even a photo in Gram's family album of the two of us, naked as newborn jaybirds, being bathed together in the Bar M's farm kitchen sink."

"That photo would get you put in Facebook jail if you

tried to post it these days," she said with a soft laugh.

"Probably. But you know, I wouldn't mind recreating it. Especially since I can't remember it."

"What were we? Six months old?"

"Probably thereabouts." He could feel her heart beating. Felt his own quicken to match its pace.

"So, of course you wouldn't. Remember, that is."

"All the more reason to create a new memory."

"We wouldn't fit in the sink."

"No. But I *do* have a racy red claw-footed tub."

"Brody found that when he updated the cabin a few years ago to add an extra bedroom for Jim and Janet's youngest. It's a true original he unearthed in a Jacksonville Victorian that was being demolished to make way for some movie star's stupid idea of a log cabin mansion."

"Hooray for Hollywood."

"Dad accused us of having eaten locoweed. But Janet loved it."

His hands slid down and cupped her very fine butt. Another cool thing about cowgirls—riding those thousand-pound horses gave them terrific muscle tone. "I'll bet Jim did, too."

He nipped at her earlobe. "The same way I like a cowgirl with sass." Damn if she didn't smell like a piña colada, which brought up tumbling her not in a hayloft but in the surf on some moon-spangled beach. And since it was his fantasy, there were no worries about getting sand in uncomfortable places.

His hand slid beneath the pink T-shirt, over her silky-smooth skin to cup her bare breast. She was soft. Sweet, and far from safe. But Sawyer was fed up with being safe where this woman was concerned.

"I want you," he said, lifting her up so her legs wrapped around his waist. "So much it aches. But not here. And not fast. I've been waiting more than half my life to have you, Austin Merrill, and I'm damn well going to take my time."

She wiggled against his groin in a way that had him worried he might have exaggerated his staying power. "What if I want you fast and hard?"

"Next time," he said, tormenting them both by rubbing her even harder against him. After making it down the hall without a premature blastoff, he tossed her down on the bed, where she bounced. Twice.

"Ooh," she said, long legs splayed as she looked up at him. "That's definitely hot, sexy Alpha male behavior." She went up on her knees and slipped her hands beneath his rumpled gray T-shirt. "You know that book club I told you about?"

"Yeah." He sucked in a breath as her fingers slid beneath the waist of his Wranglers. Seriously? She was going to talk about a frigging book club *now*?

"Jenna put together a collection of novels for me to read."

"Okay."

"Here's the thing." With a dexterity that allowed her to tie a rope and mend a bridle, she unfastened the metal button at his waist and got busy on his zipper. "They were erotic romance novels."

One more centimeter and he'd lose it. He grabbed her hands and pulled them away from both their bodies to keep them out of trouble. "So, you're into gazillionaires with handcuffs?"

Maybe this wasn't going to be as straightforward as

he'd thought. And maybe he should've read one of those damn books when nearly every guy in his unit was passing them around. When you were deployed in strictly religious countries that banned *Penthouse*, a guy had to get his porn where he could find it.

"No." She bit her bottom lip as she appeared to be thinking that over. "I think a billionaire's hands would be too soft. And anyone can get buff in some fancy city gym."

Her speculative gaze moved over him, from the top of his head down to his thighs, where the rest of her view was blocked by the mattress. "My fantasies run more toward muscles earned the old-fashioned way. By hard, manly work. A cowboy with big guns who knows how to use his rough, calloused hands."

Austin had always been as sweet as pie. And surprisingly innocent for a girl who grew up in breeding barns. In all his years of imagining this moment, he'd been gentle, tender, needing to be careful and make their first time together memorable.

But now, thanks to River's Bend's bookseller, he decided to change directions.

"New plan."

"Oh? And what would that be?" Her voice was breathless and vibrating with anticipation.

He let go of her long enough to yank his shirt over his head and shuck the jeans. "You, Austin Merrill, cowgirl with sass, are going to save a horse." When she lifted her arms, he knew she expected him to pull her shirt over her head.

Which was why he grabbed hold of the V-neck and ripped it down the front, exposing pert, rosy-tipped breasts. "And ride yourself a cowboy."

"Oh, yes," she said. Then, hot damn, licked her lips.

With every atom in his body screaming for release, her jeans went next, which took more time because, as tight as they were, it involved a lot of yanking on his part and wiggling on hers to get them down her legs to where they—damn—got stopped by her red Tony Lamas.

Betting that Mr. Grey guy had never run into this road-block, Sawyer put her foot between his legs, risking a future generation of Murphys, and pulled first one boot off, then the other, leaving her clad only in a pair of pink-and-red caterpillar stripped socks. Which, since he found them strangely hot, he decided to leave on. For a while.

"Okay." The mattress sighed as he knelt over her, his knees on either side of her long, smooth thighs. "Here's what we're going to do. I'm going to touch you."

"Mmm." She closed her eyes and arched her back like a sleek cat waiting to be stroked.

"But you're going to tell me where."

"What?" Her eyes flew open. He might be willing to play along with her big, bad controlling alpha male fantasy, but his fantasy involved full participation on both their parts.

"This is our first time." He skimmed a hand down her side. "I need to know what you want." The other side, his knuckles just brushing against her breast. "What you enjoy."

"I can't." She tossed her head. "I've never . . . Do you always talk while you're having sex?"

"Not as a rule. But this is different. Because you're different." He circled the rosy areola with the tip of a fingernail. "Special." She was making that low humming sound again. "Do you like that?"

"You know I do."

"There you go." He moved to the other breast. "Now, open your eyes and look at me. I want to watch you while I touch you."

Her eyes, heavy-lidded now, were becoming unfocused, but she did as instructed. "Now, tell me what needs attention next."

She clasped his wrist and tried to move his hand. But while years of training and riding thousand-pound horses had made her strong, he was stronger. "Tell me."

He had to tighten his thighs and struggle for control as she licked her lips. "I want you to touch my nipple, dammit."

"Anything to oblige a lady." His smile was as slow as his hands as he did exactly that. Brushing them with a fingertip at first, then pinching them just enough to draw a slight gasp from between those moist lips.

"And now, I'm going to taste you. And because I want to for my own selfish pleasure as much as yours, I'm not even going to make you beg."

"As if you could," she managed as he lowered his head and closed his lips around a taut pink bud.

"You've always had spunk," he said, his words reverberating against that silky piña colada flesh. "It's one of the things I've always loved about you."

His teeth closed down, just enough to draw another of those soft and sexy gasps. She arched her back again as he moved back to the other. Then, when she was going limp beneath him, he lay down beside her and began moving his hand down her body, tracing figure eights over her torso. Which, he noted, had abs a Marine boot camp drill sergeant would be proud of.

"Lower," she moaned. Her long, lean, gorgeously buff body was practically doing a horizontal tango on the sheets.

When she reached again for his hands, again he caught hers, lifted them over her head, and closed her fingers around the bars of the headboard.

"Like I said, I'm going to touch you. Everywhere you ask. Like right now I'm going lower." His fingers danced down to her stomach, which she sucked in at his touch. He paused again. "We agreed to take things slow, so that's exactly what we're going to do. We're going to spend a long time with you telling me everywhere you want to be touched. Stroked. Licked." His tongue made a wet swath over her mound while she actually purred. "Every bit . . . Not too hard. Not too soft." He demonstrated. "Tell me if that's just right?"

"Yes." Her hands stayed where he'd instructed, but her legs fell open, offering more. Offering whatever he wanted. But more importantly, Sawyer reminded himself, what *she* wanted.

"And then, when I've touched and done everything you tell me to, we're going to change places and you're going to touch me wherever I want."

"Oh, goodie."

"Did I mention that sometimes cowgirls with sassy mouths can earn a spanking?" He flipped her over and gave her two light swats on her firm butt and had her practically levitating off the bed. Then kissed the pink spots darkening her pale skin.

"But that's not all," he said as he planted a trail of wet kisses down the back of her leg. "Since we've got nowhere to be and all night to get there, I'm going to explore every sweet inch of your body and find erogenous spots you didn't even know you had."

She actually cried out when he nipped at the back of her knee. Which wasn't a surprise since he'd suspected that there was more than one reason Austin Merrill enjoyed riding horses.

He turned her onto her back again, caught her chin in his fingers, and held her gaze to his. Her pupils had grown so large they were turning her blue eyes to nearly purple. "You up for all that?"

Her smile was slow and hot enough that if they'd been the first man and woman on the planet, and she'd offered him that forbidden apple, he wouldn't have lasted a day in the Garden of Eden.

"Absolutely," she said.

25

"I WISH YOU could stay," Sawyer said the next morning.

"Me, too." The sun was just beginning to rise, casting the snow-clad mountaintop in a pink glow. Although the hour wasn't early for a rancher, if she had her druthers, Austin would stay in Sawyer's bed for the next week. Of course, the red tub had proven to have its own appeal. Especially when they'd gotten sidetracked this morning with the attached handheld shower spray. There were parts of her still tingling that, until last night, had forgotten they *could* tingle.

She began buttoning one of his shirts, which fell to mid-thigh over her jeans. "But I have to drive to Medford to pick Lexi up at the airport."

"Since Dad's guys are taking care of both our stock, I'll go over and have breakfast with the kids."

"They'd love that." She went over to him, framed his handsome face between her palms, and kissed him. She was pleased and relieved that her earlier concerns about whether he'd want to be involved with Jack and Sophie appeared not to have been necessary. "Perhaps you can bring them back here."

"Will do. Maybe we'll wander down to the river and drown some worms."

"I'm not sure Sophie likes fishing anymore," she warned him.

Truthfully, Austin was walking on eggshells where the girl was concerned. The one thing she didn't want to have to worry about was having Heather's daughter run away again.

He shrugged. "Then we'll improvise. Marines are known for their ability to improvise, adapt, overcome."

"And a lot more that probably isn't G-rated enough to become a Corps motto."

"There is that." He flashed that same wicked grin he'd given her just before he'd proven that he could make her scream. In the very best way. He played with the button between her breasts. "I'm sorry I ruined your shirt."

"I'm not." Although there'd been quite a bit of clothes ripping in those books Jenna had given her, none of those fictional heroes could hold a candle to Sawyer Murphy. In any way. "I thought it was thrilling."

After having finally shared her feelings, Austin was surprised how easy it was to tell him everything. Just the way she had when they'd been growing up. She'd suspected that the sex between them would be good. Better than good, off the charts. But she'd never expected that it could crash through those emotional barriers they'd begun building that hot summer day when she'd caught him looking at her bra strap. Adolescence had brought more than physical changes; it had altered their relationship, making them all too aware of the differences in their genders.

Now, having celebrated that difference, they were back

to being best friends. With benefits.

"What?" His question had her realizing she'd been grinning like a fool. Probably a blushing fool.

"I was just thinking that, as horrible and sad as this time is, being with you has given my heart something to be happy about."

He skimmed a finger down her nose. "Back atcha, babe."

They still had so much to deal with. Including how they were going to co-parent, because, although they hadn't gotten into the nuts and bolts about how all this was going to work, they were talking about a minimum of eleven years of hands-on parenthood. Not that family responsibilities ended when a child became eighteen. Look at her. Thirty-one years old and still living with her father. And wasn't that just too pitiful for words?

"I want to walk you back to the house, but I'm guessing that would be a no."

"I'd rather not have Dad and Dan's hands witness my walk of shame," she said lightly.

"No." His tone was strong and firm. Like it had been occasionally during their long night together. But on those occasions, she'd known he'd been playing a role. This, on the other hand, was totally real. Totally him. "There's not an ounce of shame involved in what we did last night."

She laid a hand on his arm and felt the muscle tense. "It's just a saying, Sawyer. A joke."

"Not entirely. If you don't want anyone to see us."

She sighed. They were back to complications again. "It's just that there's already so much going on, and you know as well as I do that, as wonderful as River's Bend is, there aren't any secrets. At least not for long."

She crossed her hands over her heart. Then did the same over his. "I'd like to keep this just to ourselves for a while. I'm not ready for people to start dissecting our relationship."

"Ah. There's that *R* word again."

"We do have one." Damn. Did her voice actually go up on the end of that declaration? She'd sworn to herself, sometime between when he'd carried her to bed last night and the shower sex this morning, that she was *not* going to bring up what kind of future he was thinking of.

"We absolutely do."

"But we're about to be scrutinized by some social worker who could make the argument that beginning a sexual relationship while taking on the care of two orphaned children could create stresses that wouldn't be beneficial to their well-being."

"We'll be sure they're not hurt. But I suppose you do have a point about not risking complicating the custodial process. It would probably also be inappropriate for us to go around town grinning like jackasses when our best friends have just died."

"My heart's still broken about that," she said.

"Mine, too."

"But there's a part that's so filled with happiness that I think it's going to heal the broken part."

"Which is exactly what Tom and Heather would want," Sawyer said. "Not just for their kids, who need for us to have full hearts right now, but for you and me. Because they never would've wanted us to go through life aching. Or ravaged by survivor guilt."

She tilted her head. His tone had changed. Deepened, not in a sexy way but heavy with emotion. She imagined he might know more than a little about survivor guilt. She also knew that this was not the time for an in-depth conversation and that Sawyer would tell her when the moment was right.

"Gotta go," she said. "I'll see you in a few hours."

"Absolutely." He kissed her again, this time just a quick peck on the lips. "Have a safe trip."

"I will."

As she walked back toward the house she'd grown up in, it crossed Austin's mind that, just days ago, neither of them would've given a thought about a trip along the lake and over the mountains, which they'd done all their lives, possibly being unsafe.

Which was when she realized that from here on in, her life would consist of *before the accident* and *after*.

She'd just reached the house when a familiar truck with a *Be Nice, I Could Be Your Nurse Someday* sticker on the back bumper pulled into the drive.

"Hey." Layla Longstreet jumped out of the driver's seat. "I like your outfit. Boyfriend shirts are in these days, I hear."

"Busted." Austin had realized she and Sawyer wouldn't be able to keep their relationship a secret for long, but this had to be an all-time record. Even for River's Bend.

"Don't worry." Layla shoved a wild mass of auburn hair back from her face. Ryan's nurse practitioner partner was, hands down, the most beautiful woman in River's Bend. Probably in Oregon. She was also one of the nicest. "I didn't tell anyone about that hospital kiss. We nurses know how to keep secrets. All I'll say is that I'm really happy you guys finally got together, and I fully intend to grill you for details later because the only sex I'm getting these days is through those books I keep buying from Jenna and living vicariously through my friends. Who are mostly engaged or married. Like Rachel and—" She rubbed her temples. "Damn."

"I know," Austin said. "I spent all day yesterday taking care of funeral stuff and it still hasn't entirely sunk in. The first thing I wanted to do this morning was text Heather and tell her that we'd finally done it."

Layla lifted a tawny, perfectly arched brow. "And? Was the long wait worth it?"

"Way worth it."

"Well, then, there you go. I brought your dad something." A wheelchair had been hitched to the back of the truck bed.

"Ryan and I have tried that idea. And he refuses."

"That's because you weren't me. I'm a nurse. We have superpowers that get people to do whatever we want."

Austin suspected a male would have to have flat lined to be immune to this woman. But Buck Merrill was old-school western cowboy to the bone. As he'd proven, to her distress, he'd rather stay in his self-imposed house arrest than let anyone see him as less than the strong man he'd been only a short time ago.

"You have no idea how much I'm hoping you're right," she said. "Let me help."

"No, that's the cool thing," Layla said. "Not only is it foldable, it's really light. But extremely durable. And it can take a man even heavier than Buck, which not all light-weight ones do." She set it up with a few quick movements and wheeled it up to the front door.

Buck was in the kitchen, leaning on a cane, pouring coffee into the travel mug Austin had bought him after balance problems had caused him to drop regular mugs. This one was specially made not to spill even if it was turned upside down.

"Hey, handsome," Layla greeted him with her Julia Roberts wide smile. "I brought you a present."

He glowered down at the wheelchair. "Not interested."

"You haven't even let me show off the features," she said. "Look, a rechargeable battery that'll go fifteen miles. Double that if you want to get a second battery. Which I got you because they can be charged off board."

"I'm fine right here. I don't need to go traipsing all over the countryside."

"Yeah. Why go anywhere when you can sit in that ratty old La-Z-Boy all day and watch bull riding and fishing?" Layla agreed. "Sounds like a damn near perfect life to me."

He thrust out his gray-stubbled chin. "I get out. I was just out at the corral with Dan helping Jack Campbell learn how to rope that dummy steer the Murphy boy made back in high school."

"Well, good for you." Another smile, even brighter and more enthusiastic than the first. Most men, Austin thought, would have little hearts circling around their heads by now. But her father wasn't most men. "I had the joystick put on the left, because you're left-handed. But it'll go both ways. And look, the armrests can be raised so you can just slide onto it by the side. Easy peasy." She demonstrated. "And did I mention the back rest reclines in five positions? Just in case you decide you'd like to take a little nap while you're out sitting under a tree checking out your stock."

"I don't take naps." It was a bald-faced lie, and everyone in the room, including Winema, who'd shown up during the demonstration, knew it. "And what part of I do

not need a damn cripple's wheelchair do you not understand?"

"Okay." Layla stood up, squared her shoulders, and
pushed her hair back with both hands, which anyone who
knew her recognized as a sign that she was majorly ticked
off and about to get serious. "Here's the deal, Buck. First
of all, it's not a 'damn cripple's wheelchair.' It's a personal
mobility aid.

"Second, Tuesday, we're all going to be doing the sad-
dest thing anyone can do. We're going to be burying
friends. A good man and woman who were part of this
community and had never done anything wrong to have a
goddamn boulder come crashing down on their minivan.
In Our Lady of the Lake Church will be two young
children you know well. And undoubtedly like."

"Of course I do." His tone was strong, but Austin
could sense that he was getting the idea that Layla, who
was standing there, hands on her hips, looking like Wonder
Woman, might just be a force to be reckoned with.

"Of course you do." She smiled as if awarding him a
gold star for the right answer. "Which is why I know you
wouldn't want to do anything to make their already terrible,
horrible day any worse."

"I wouldn't."

"You wouldn't mean to." Austin had always thought
Layla Longstreet was beautiful enough to have become a
movie star if she'd decided to take off to California instead
of remaining in River's Bend, where she'd grown up best
friends with Ellen Buchanan, Cooper's first wife. Now she
realized that if Layla had become an actress, she would've
probably won every award out there because the way she
could switch moods was amazing.

She'd started out unrelentingly cheerful, then, without batting one of those long and impossibly thick lashes, turned into a force of nature. Then, she'd pulled out a more neutral tone, describing the upcoming day none of them wanted to have happen. Now, she was Buck's warm and empathetic best friend. Appealing to his best angels, assuring him that she knew he'd never do anything to hurt two innocent orphans.

"But here's the deal, Buck." She folded her arms. "You crashing onto the caskets while trying to make your way down the aisle, or worse yet, falling into a grave at the cemetery, is going to make that a day everyone, including those two darling children, remembers. And not in a good way."

"I wouldn't do that." He'd folded *his* arms in a gesture Austin knew well. This was usually his final word stance.

Not this time.

"Like you wouldn't fall outside Ryan's and my office?"

Thunderclouds moved across his face, which had reddened to the hue of a roasted beet. "That was a damn accident. There was a crack in the curb."

"Of course it was an accident," she said, swinging back to the good nurse/best friend. She did not, Austin noted, state that everyone knew that there wasn't a crack in the curb. "But, as Heather's and Tom's deaths proves so tragically, accidents do happen.

"You've had a raw deal. It's not fair, and I'm sorry as hell about it. But you're no longer stable on those canes." She told him what Austin suspected he knew himself but hadn't yet accepted. "This chair will not only be more comfortable for you, it'll prevent you from creating a spectacle."

Austin could see that sinking in.

"There's another thing," Layla said, jumping in with yet another argument while the wheels in the stubborn rancher's head were turning. "It'll get you out and about meeting with folks again instead of acting like a hermit."

"I'll look like a damn cripple," he muttered.

"Buck Merrill." Layla's hands were back on her hips. "I am not going to let you wallow in some self-indulgent pity party. You know Dalton Osborne, don't you?"

"Sure. He worked some roundups for me during high school. Before he went off to West Point. He was a good kid. Even lasted seven seconds on Desperado, which is more than most guys ever did."

"Well, he's not a kid anymore. He's a grown man who returned from Iraq with two legs and half an arm blown off from an IED."

"I know that." The chin jutted out again. "I used to see him down at the VFW all the time."

"*He's* still there. You're the one who quit dropping in. And for your information, Dalton has a chair just like this one. Do you think when he drops in for a beer the guys think of him as a cripple? For that matter, is that how you'd define him?"

"Hell, no. He's a hometown hero."

"Who went back to Modoc Community College for a degree in computer programing, got married, has a couple of kids, one whom I just happen to have delivered myself at their home six months ago. Thanks to the G.I. bill paying for his education, he's making a nice living creating websites for businesses all around Oregon. He's even branched out into Northern California and Idaho. And if you ask him, he'd be the first to tell you that he doesn't think of himself as a hero. Just a regular guy.

"But although life gave him a hell of a blow, he picked himself up, dusted himself off, same as he did when he'd fall off those bulls he was crazy enough to ride when he was young and foolish, and has moved on with his life."

"He's young. He's got a lot more life to get on with."

"Like you're so old." Austin checked her watch and decided she had five more minutes, tops, before she had to leave for Medford. "You've got a lot of good years ahead of you, Dad. Years filled with things like walking me down the aisle—"

"Wheeling you down the damn aisle, you mean."

"Better than not being there at all because you can't safely make it on your own two legs," she shot back. "And then hopefully there will be grandchildren. Do you want to be stuck in here while they're out learning to ride and rope? When you could be teaching them the way you did me?"

"That Murphy boy going to be their daddy?"

"I don't know," Austin said. Then decided that not being honest with her feelings had gotten her into fixes in the past, so went for the truth. "I hope so," she said. "I want that, and I think he does, too. But right now we have to concentrate on being there for Jack and Sophie. And since I don't have a clue how to be a parent, I really, really need you to help me."

She didn't know if it was Layla's very sound arguments and persuasion, the idea of future Merrills growing up on this ranch, or the tears she felt over-brimming her eyes, but Buck suddenly folded like a cheap tent.

"I guess it wouldn't hurt to try it out," he mumbled.

Layla had already locked the wheels, but as soon as he'd sat down, she unlocked them, put his hand on the joystick, and said, "Go for it."

Austin and Layla exchanged a look as he took a spin around the room. "It's not bad," he said when he came to a stop again.

"It's the Cadillac of personal mobility cruisers," Layla said.

"Which brings up another thing." He might be down, but he wasn't out. "What does it cost and how am I going to pay for it? In case you haven't heard, we had to let the stock business go."

"Don't you worry that handsome head about a thing. It's all taken care of."

"I'm not taking charity."

"I wouldn't expect you to. Haven't you seen all those commercials on cable TV for various stuff Medicare pays for? It's like that."

"I think it's wonderful," Winema entered the conversation. "And now, when you go out, you'll be able to be sociable again because people will be able to talk to you."

"They haven't talked to me because they feel sorry for me and don't know what to say."

"Wrong. They haven't talked with you because you're so busy looking down at the ground, trying not to trip, they don't want to come up and distract you." She waved a hand toward the chair. "Now no one will have to worry about that. And with that basket on the back, you can even come grocery shopping with me."

"Or I could just be drug behind a wild horse."

"Think of it as hunting. You go out into the wilds of the mercantile, bag your meal, and bring it back here, where, may I point out, you don't even have to cook it."

"Well, this has been exciting," Austin said as the two

began arguing about male and female roles. "I've got to run upstairs for a sec before I head off to the airport. Layla, can you come up for a minute? I have something to ask you. About the kids."

"Sure."

"Okay," Austin said, as soon as she was in her room, grabbing a shirt off a hanger. "No way is that covered by Medicare."

"I didn't say it was. I said it was 'like that.' Don't worry, Ryan and I had a good winter, what with the sudden population explosion. We decided we'd rather spend a little bit of the profits to help a patient than buy new couches for the waiting room. Especially since, I swear, every kid who comes into the place has sticky hands. The vinyl we've got now is more practical, anyway."

Damn. As she pulled on the shirt, her fingers fumbling as she buttoned it, Austin could feel the tears welling up again. She'd sworn she wasn't going to cry during all this, but what with the accident and the deaths and the kids and that incredible night with Sawyer and now this, her emotions felt as if they were on a Tilt-a-Whirl.

"Thank you." She hugged the woman who'd once been Ellen's bestie and had become a close friend to her.

"Just go pick up Lexi," Layla said. "I'm dying to see what color hair she has these days."

26

BEFORE GOING TO Cooper and Rachel's, Sawyer dropped by the Campbells' house, where he found Brody installing a quartz countertop.

"Looks great," he said.

"Thanks." Brody took off his hat. "I'm feeling guilty about it, though."

"Why? It's perfect."

"Yeah. It is. And carefree. Because it's a composite, it doesn't need to be sealed like granite or marble. But here's the thing . . . Heather didn't pick it out. She wanted butcher block. But to keep to the sub schedule, I decided to go with this, because I called a real estate agent I know, who agreed that because quartz is tougher than wood, and everyone's asking for it these days, it'd be better for resale."

"Then you made the right decision. Because Heather would want her kids to get top dollar."

"Yeah." Brody picked up a rag and ran it over the top of the hunter-green countertop. "She was going to buy a new dining set on craigslist and paint it this color. So, I figured she wouldn't mind it for the countertop. She was going for country cozy, and the realtor said this would be a good fit."

"It works for me."

Brody shook his head and dragged a hand down his face. "This is turning out to be harder than I'd thought."

"Yeah." And didn't Sawyer know that all too well?

"But hell, here I am complaining about remodeling a house, and you're about to be a surrogate dad. How does that feel?"

"Terrifying. But Austin's got more of the responsibility, and being a woman, she probably knows more about kids."

"Maybe." Brody looked doubtful.

"You don't think so?"

"I haven't a clue about kids, either. But I do remember stuff my dad did. The same way you remember yours growing up. But Austin's mom took off when she was pretty young. And Buck, as great a guy as he is, in his own way, isn't exactly the nurturing type."

And wasn't that the overstatement of the decade?

"Coincidentally, Buck is who I came by to talk about."

"Is something wrong with him?"

"He seems the same. But I was talking with Ryan, who said that exercise is tough for his muscles."

"Yeah. It wears them out."

"But he also said swimming is good because there isn't any pressure."

"Makes sense. My grandmother takes pool aerobics at her seniors' community."

"That's what I was thinking."

Brody looked at him as if he'd suggested they both take Desperado out for a Sunday ride. "You're going to suggest Buck Merrill, River's Bend's own John Wayne, move into senior housing?"

"No. I'm thinking he take up swimming."

"We're at nearly a mile high here. The lake's cold enough to send a guy's balls up into his throat in July."

"I was thinking of having you build an indoor pool."

"Ah." Brody took off the cap again, scratched his head. "That could work. There's room to extend the family room into the backyard. You'd lose some of the porch, but it could be done."

"Good." That settled, Sawyer decided he'd better pick up the kids. "Work up a price, let me know, and we'll get started."

"Sure. Uh, did you happen to talk with either Buck or Austin about this?"

"Nope."

"O-kay. I'm not going to get shot, am I?"

"Nah. I'm going to use the kids as an excuse. They'll need a diversion their first summer without their folks."

"That could work," Brody decided. "The average size of an indoor pool is about eight by fifteen. I built one a while back for some Hollywood director that topped a hundred thou, but if you're looking utilitarian—"

"I am." Since he wasn't married and the military had taken care of most of his expenses over the years, he'd saved up a pretty hefty nest egg.

"If I were doing it for a client, it'd probably come in around twenty. But I'll do it for cost, which should cut it significantly. Your major expense is going to be expanding the room, but I figure we can round up a lot of volunteers to do framing and other stuff."

"Like Coop said everyone did for Rachel after the New Chance had to be gutted because of the fire."

"Exactly like that. Buck's an institution around here, and there's not a family in the basin the Merrills haven't helped out at one time or another. That's not going to be a problem."

"Great. Gotta go pick up the kids."

"Good luck with that," Brody said. He did not sound encouraging.

"Thanks." As he left the house only to see Sophie walking up the sidewalk, Sawyer figured he was going to need all the help he could get.

"Hey, Sophie," he said with what he hoped would sound like a casual tone. "What are you doing here?" And what the hell had happened to her hair?

"I never got to say good-bye to my house." A challenging defensiveness surrounded her like an electric barbed-wire fence.

"We should have thought of that," he admitted. "Maybe Austin thought it would be better if we waited until the remodel was done."

"Then it wouldn't be *my* house," she said. "It'd be someone else's."

"Good point." He put an arm around her shoulder, encouraged when she didn't pull away until he remembered what Austin said about her crushing on him. Which, since he must seem really old to her, he doubted was possible, but just in case, he eased away a bit.

"Hey, Sophie," Brody said as she made a beeline for the kitchen. "It's good to see you. I'm really sorry about your mom and dad."

"Yeah. So am I," she said with acid teen sarcasm. Not that she was a teen yet. Sawyer wondered if all the horror stories he'd heard married guys on deployment talking about were even halfway true. She ran a hand over the countertop, just as Brody had done. "You didn't do the butcher block."

Sawyer saw fear in the look Brody shot him. "Uh, no. But—"

"This is the color Mom wanted for the table."

"Yeah. That's why I picked it."

"I have this friend. Madison. Her mom wants to redo their kitchen, and she has all these Pinterest inspiration pictures. She says quartz is really trending."

"So I was told," Brody said carefully. "Which is why I thought it might be a good idea."

She pulled open a cabinet drawer beneath the hunter-green counter. Let go of it and watched it slide closed again. "Because we have to sell the house."

"Because you're going to be living with Austin at the ranch," Sawyer reminded her.

"Why can't she move in here with us when it's done?"

"I guess because she has to take care of her dad. And the stock."

"Maybe." She didn't sound convinced. Or at all happy. "I'm going to go upstairs."

"Take your time," Sawyer said. He decided she probably didn't want his company. Damn, this was one of those cases where he knew a woman would be better suited to handle it. Speaking of women, a thought belatedly occurred to him. "Does Rachel know you're here?"

Before she could answer, his phone rang. With Rachel's photo on the screen.

"Hey, Rach," he said as Sophie made a quick exit toward the stairs.

"Have you seen Sophie? I called Austin, but she's on the way to Medford to pick up Lexi."

"She's here. At the house. Her old house," he qualified.

"Thank God. I was worried sick. I don't know how she sneaked out without me seeing her. It must have been when Jack broke the window."

"He broke a window?"

"Well, cracked it. He and Scott were playing catch with a baseball in the backyard. For a skinny little guy, he's got a really strong arm. Unfortunately, he needs to work on his control."

Thinking back on the boy getting stuck in the apple tree, Sawyer concurred. "Don't worry about her," he said. "I'll drop by, pick up Jack, and take the kids to the ranch. See if we can work off some of that energy."

"Good luck with that."

Rachel had no sooner ended the call than Sophie returned to the room with a pink backpack filled with stuff that Austin must have missed. "I'm done."

"Okay. So, the plan is that we'll pick up your brother, then go out to the ranch. I was thinking maybe we'd drown some worms."

"I hate fishing. It's cruel to animals." She shot him a glare that told him that, in her mind, he'd just suggested drowning kittens.

"Fine. You got a book in that bag?"

"Yeah. So?"

"So you can read it while Jack and I fish." He paused a moment, wondering if he'd get in trouble for what had just flashed into his mind, then decided to go for it. "Unless you'd rather bait the hooks. I figured we'd pick up a box of night crawlers at the bait shop."

"Ewww."

"I take it that would be a no." He opened the passenger door to the pickup. "Hop in and we'll go get your brother."

"I can't go to the ranch. My friend is coming over to help me figure out what to wear to the funeral."

Sawyer might not have had sisters, but he realized that this was a big effing deal, and once again he wished Austin were here to handle it. "Why don't you text her to come over to the ranch instead," he suggested. "Maybe she'd like to go riding after you figure out the dress thing. And Austin will be there with Lexi, who, I remember, is a real fashion expert. She works with showgirls in Vegas now."

"Really?"

"Really." He was tempted to suggest that hopefully Lexi would also be able to do something with Sophie's hair, which, and he couldn't lie, looked pretty much as if it'd been attacked by a chain saw.

27

L EXI O'HALLORAN SWEPT through the revolving arrivals door, wearing skinny black jeans, a cheetah-print silk shirt, a wide belt that emphasized her curves, and stiletto pumps so high Austin figured she'd have less chance of breaking her ankle by falling off a horse than trying to walk three steps in those shoes. Over her shoulder was a red purse the size of a small suitcase.

"You look amazing!" Austin hugged her friend careful-ly. Wouldn't tipping Lexi over into that young mother passing by with a toddler in a flimsy-looking folding stroller just add to an already wretched week?

"Thanks. Other than a dress I found hidden in the back of my closet left over from a misguided attempt to please a former boyfriend's ultraconservative Palm Springs mother, this is the only dark outfit I own. Black isn't that popular a color in the desert. Damn." She shook her head, sending sleek, ombre-tinted hair that went from a deep purple at the roots down to light violet at the tips, swinging across her shoulders. "Would you listen to Shallow Girl, bitching about clothes at a time like this?"

"Heather would approve," Austin said. "The two of you had different styles, but you were both always light-years ahead of River's Bend. I've been worried that she's going to be looking down asking, 'Why the hell is Austin wearing *that* to my funeral?'"

Lexi laughed as they began making their way to the baggage carousel. "Don't worry. I'll make sure you pass muster."

"I was depending on that."

"You aren't afraid you'll come off looking like a Vegas showgirl?"

"Not at all," Austin said honestly. "I overcame that fear when you didn't make me look like one of the Kardashians at Heather and Tom's wedding."

"That was a fun time. Everyone was so happy. And Heather glowed like one of those paintings of the Madonna." Lexi blew out a breath and dabbed at her emerald-green eyes. "I should've come home more often. I don't even know her poor orphaned kids."

"You'll like them. Sophie's going to be a beauty like her mother, and Jack, well, he's a pistol. As for not having come home, you've been busy. From what I've seen, things run at a lot faster pace in Vegas."

"Yeah. Including marriages, which, I only wish you'd thought to call me before you staggered into that wedding chapel. I would've stood up at that question about objections."

"If I could've hit the buttons on my phone, I wouldn't have *been* in that chapel in the first place."

"If there was ever a case for drunk dialing, that was it," Lexi said. "That's it," she said, pointing toward a lipstick-red case the color of her purse that was rumbling toward them. She'd leaned forward when a man wearing jeans, a snap-front plaid shirt, a bolo tie, boots, and a tan Resistol reached in and grabbed it as it passed by.

"Here you go, ma'am," he said, placing it between them. "Would you like some help taking it out to your vehicle?"

"Why, aren't you sweet?" Lexi batted her lashes. "But it's not that far, and these four wheels make it easy as pie to roll."

Although his handsome face fell, he didn't argue. "Well, good." He nodded and tipped the brim of his hat. "You ladies have yourselves a nice day."

Although Austin might be in love with Sawyer, that didn't stop her from appreciating watching him walk away, his own duffle thrown over his shoulder. On a scale of one to ten, Sawyer topped the list with a gold-star ten. But this cowboy came in at a close eight. Maybe an eight and a half.

"I'd forgotten how good a cowboy can make a girl feel." Lexi waved her hand in front of her face. "They don't make them like that in the desert. At least not my part of it. And speaking of cowboys, how are you and Sawyer?"

"It's a long story. I'll tell you about it on the drive back to River's Bend."

"That bad? Or that good?"

Despite the reason for Lexi's trip home, Austin felt the smile lifting her lips. "Better," she said. Maybe a woman shouldn't kiss and tell, but she'd been dying to tell Heather about Sawyer. Lexi wasn't her BFF, but there'd been a time, when Buck used to call them the Three Amigas, that she'd come in a close second.

"About time," Lexi said.

ॐ

"SO," RACHEL ASKED while Sophie took her book bag of things she'd taken from the house upstairs to the guest room, "how are you holding up?"

"I've had weeks at an FOB outpost easier than this," he admitted. "I nearly freaked out when I saw her hair."

"It's radical," Rachel allowed. "But not surprising, I suppose. If she's going to cut something, better it be her hair than some other part of her body."

"Jesus." Sawyer was so in over his head here. What he knew about teenage girls went back to his own high school days, which he didn't want to even think about, since Tom and Heather's daughter wasn't that far away from the age of the girls he'd tried, with occasional success, to coax into the back of his pickup bed down by the river. "Girls do that?"

"Too often, unfortunately. I read an article that suggested close to twenty-five percent of girls self-injure. And not necessarily because they're depressed, which I have a hard time believing Sophie isn't, but also because they're trying to find a sense of self. Something that most of us struggle with during those formative years."

Sawyer had a hard time believing Rachel had ever struggled with anything. Then again, she'd been widowed at a young age, lost everything, and after paying off her late husband's considerable debts, driven her young son all the way across the country to begin a new life, only to arrive to find the café that she'd hoped would be the cornerstone of that new life smoldering from a kitchen fire.

"I guess the counselor will talk with her about that?"

"I'm sure she will. Cooper says she's very good. She's done wonders with some of the local kids who were hovering on the brink of going down some dangerous, dead-end paths."

Something that, although it wasn't talked about all that much, was just as easy for country kids as those in the big city. Especially when kids were pretty much on their own when it came to entertainment.

Which, looking back on it, was probably why his dad let him off the hook when it came to ranch chores in order to rodeo. He definitely hadn't been an angel, but when he was roping and bull riding, he wasn't out doing stupid stuff like drinking and driving, blowing up mailboxes with fireworks, and shooting up stop signs.

"That's good to hear," he said. "There's something else I was wondering."

"Okay."

"If you were a woman . . . well, of course, you are . . . but if you weren't getting married to my brother and going out with a guy and he was going to make you dinner, would you like a steak and potato? Or is that too much of a man food thing?"

"In this part of the country, I'd guess the woman would pretty much expect something like that."

"Okay. Thanks." Well, that part of his mission plan might not be as difficult as he'd feared.

"Of course, women do tend to like green food, too," she said.

"You're talking vegetables."

"Or a nice salad."

"You can get everything you need in one of those bags at the mercantile." He hadn't bought any, but he'd seen the woman in front of him checking out with three different kinds.

"You can." Her tone suggested she wouldn't recommend it.

"Something wrong with that?"

"Nothing at all. But it wouldn't be that hard to trick it out a bit. Make it more personal. And show her you went to some extra effort."

"Like how?" he asked just as Jack came crashing down the stairs, Sophie following behind him looking as if she were on the way to the gallows.

"I'll email you a few suggestions," she said. "Nothing difficult, I promise. But it'll make your evening more special. And I know Austin would appreciate you going to the trouble for her." She lowered her voice as the kids argued about something as they passed by on their way out to the truck. "Her husband never treated her with any consideration. So, a few mushrooms and tomatoes, a nice bit of cheese, green onions, an easy vinaigrette, along with a decent cab or merlot from Lombardi Vineyards, which I've finally convinced the mercantile to carry, would definitely score you points."

"You're a gem." He leaned over and kissed her on the cheek.

She patted his. "I'm happy to help. It's heartwarming, not to mention inspiring, to see some happiness during this very sad time."

He wasn't going to deny his and Austin's relationship to his brother's fiancée. "We want to keep it low-key for now. Especially since it might seem inappropriate."

"Love's never inappropriate. But, in this case, I can appreciate your feelings. And your secret's safe with me."

"Thanks." He glanced out at the truck. "I'd better get going before Jack decides to drive to the ranch himself."

Rachel smiled. "You and Austin are going to have your

hands full with that one," she said. "But fortunately, you won't be alone."

Alone. That thought ricocheted around in Sawyer's mind as he drove back to the ranch. That was exactly what he'd thought he'd wanted when he'd returned home. But that was then. Now, he found himself anticipating arriving at the ranch to find Austin waiting.

28

MADISON'S OLDER BROTHER, who dropped out of OIT to tend bar at the Shady Lady, had already dropped the girl off at the ranch house when Sawyer arrived with the kids.

"Your friend's upstairs," Winema told Sophie. "Jack, why don't you go out to the corral with Buck? He's got a new rig he'd probably like to show off."

"We're going to drown worms," Jack said.

"Then I'll change the menu to fried fish for dinner." She made a waving motion with her hand. "Meanwhile, scoot."

As the boy raced out the back door, Winema shook her head. "If he were yours, I'd say you were getting what you deserved," she told Sawyer. "Because he sure does remind me of you at that age."

"I was a perfect young gentleman."

"You were perfect," she allowed. "More like a perfect terror." Then her expression softened. "Except with Austin."

Austin had always been Sawyer's exception. At seven. Twelve. And all the years since.

"You think Austin can do anything with Sophie's hair?"

"Unless it can grow six or eight inches by the funeral, I'd say no." And didn't that send his stomach through the heart-of-pine floor? "But I'll bet my great-grandmother's cast iron chicken frying skillet that hasn't seen soap and water in four generations on Lexi Ann being able to put the girl together."

Lexi O'Halloran had always been ahead of the fashion curve. Sawyer remembered more than one occasion when she'd been sent home from school after an admonition from the principal that "River's Bend isn't ready for that." Although he didn't know two hoots about fashion, he'd often thought that if Sexy Lexi, as the guys had referred to her back in the day, had been eight inches taller than her own five-foot two and had had bones where her curves were, she could've gone to New York City or even Paris and become one of those supermodels.

Sawyer was out at the corral with Buck and wild Jack when the women arrived back from Medford. And yep, as she jumped out of the truck and wildly waved at him, Lexi still looked as if she'd just flown in on a private jet from the South of France, where she'd been tooling around with movie stars.

"Is Sophie upstairs?" Austin asked Winema, who met them at the door.

"In that room we fixed up for her," the older woman said. "Did anyone warn you?"

"About her hair? Yes, both Rachel and Sawyer called while we were on the road." She glanced up the stairs. "How bad is it?"

"Kinda like it was gnawed by a crazed beaver."

Austin briefly closed her eyes. "How much stuff do you have in that bag?" she asked Lexi.

"Don't worry. You've no idea how many just-broke-up-with-my-boyfriend hair disasters I've had to deal with. I don't suppose this cow town has a salon that might at least have some clip-on extensions."

"No salon. And while Rachel's had the mercantile improving their food and wine departments, I doubt you'd find any extensions next to the plastic barrettes and banana clips."

"You're kidding about the banana clips."

"I wish I were."

They found the girls in what had been designated as Sophie's room. Sophie was wearing a sleeveless purple minidress. Her friend was dressed in a bright orange crop top, a pair of Daisy Duke shorts, and tasseled boots. Multi-hued beaded earrings hung from her pierced ears nearly to her shoulders.

"Hey Sophie," Austin greeted her, determinedly not flinching at the hair. Winema had gotten it wrong. It didn't look as if it had been gnawed by a crazed beaver. It looked worse. Much, much worse. "This is my friend Lexi. She's from Las Vegas now, but she grew up right here in River's Bend."

"Really?" Sophie's skeptical gaze swept over the sprayed on jeans, the blousy jungle top, the high, high heels, and the bag that Austin figured had probably cost as much as a month of hay.

"Really." Lexi tilted her head, studying Sophie. Assessing the hair. "That's a darling pixie. It reminds me of the one Zendaya wore to the Grammys."

"That was a wig," the other girl said. "I'm Madison. Sophie's BFF."

Madison Graham, Austin remembered, was the girl

whose sleepover Heather hadn't let Sophie attend. Looking at her outfit, jewelry, sparkly blue eyeliner, and about a bucket of mascara, Austin understood why. Tom may have joked about Sophie being twelve going on thirty-five, but this girl was definitely riding a supertrain to adulthood on an even faster track.

"Hi, Madison. Nice to meet you. And you're right, it was a wig. But she looked really cute and sassy. And believe me, very few of the girls you see on TV or in the movies or music videos are wearing their own hair. Take it from someone who's done a lot of them."

"Really?" Sophie asked. "In Las Vegas?"

"That's my day job. But not only have I done a lot of freelance videos, stars all the time fly me out to do their red carpet hair." She grinned. "Have flat iron, will travel. That's my motto. I have some wild stories I'll tell you later."

"About famous people?" Madison asked eagerly.

"No point in telling stories about people no one ever heard of."

"I like your hair color," Sophie said shyly.

For the first time since they'd broken the horrible news, Austin felt a glimmer of hope.

"Me, too." Lexi's grin faded. "I was worried that it might be too much for a funeral, and here's where I say I'm so sorry about what happened to your folks."

"I am, too," Sophie said.

"Of course you are. It's a terrible thing, but we're all here for you, so if there's anything you need, you just need to speak up, because as brilliant as Austin and I are, we're not mind readers. And even though I haven't seen you since you were the cutest ever toddler, I can see so much of your mother in you that I know we're going to be good friends."

"I don't look like my mother."

"Not yet. But I knew her when she was your age, and believe me, you're going to be a beauty, just like her. Anyway, like I was saying, I didn't have time to change out the ombre, so I just told myself that your mom would like it. After all, she had me put blue streaks in hers for graduation."

"Really?" Sophie's widened eyes looked even larger in her small face without any softening frame of hair. "Mom had blue hair?"

"Well, she wasn't a mom yet, and they were just streaks, but I kid you not. What are you wearing to the funeral?"

"I'm not sure. I'm not good about clothes like Mom was. I took this test in *Seventeen* that said I was a summer, which means I'm supposed to wear pastels, so I don't have anything black. But Madison brought over this dress she thought would be perfect."

"I'm an autumn," Madison volunteered. "So I can't wear it. I sent my grandmother the chart of my colors, but she still totally ignored it and bought me this dress for my birthday. Which has just been sitting in the closet because no way am I going to be seen in public in it. Bad enough I had to put it on for the picture my mother took to send to Grandmother. I was going to remind Gram in the thank you note I had to write to check the color chart next time, but Mom said that would be rude."

"I'm sure your grandmother meant well," Austin said evenly. "And it *is* a lovely color purple."

"It's plum," Madison corrected in a know-it-all tone that grated on Austin's last nerve. "That's between purple and magenta."

"How very clever of you to know that," Lexi said with a smile. "Are you going to be a fashion designer when you grow up?"

"I might be. But I'd really rather have a Disney show like Zendaya and be a big star. I'm a VIP member of her fan club. Which is how I knew about the wig."

"Well, isn't that special?" Lexi's response had Austin biting her lip to hold back a laugh. "That dress will be lovely. As you undoubtedly can figure out from my hair, I personally adore any shade of purple. And if your mother's looking down on you, it'll make her smile because her entire freshman year of high school, shades of purple, from lavender to plum, were all she wore."

"I'd forgotten that," Austin said. "She was all the time having your grandma take her to Klamath Falls or Medford to buy fabric." A memory flashed back. "I brought her back three yards of white cotton with purple polka dots I found in a quilt shop in Idaho while Dad and I were there for the Snake River Stampede. She used it to make a retro halter sundress."

"She has a picture wearing that," Sophie said, seeming actually excited about something for the first time since they'd had to break the news of her parents' deaths. "It's in her and dad's bedroom."

"We'll make sure it gets here during the move," Austin assured her. "She wore it to a barbecue at the Bar M the night your dad asked her to go steady." She smiled and ran a hand over the girl's raggedly cropped hair.

"I knew that. But she never told me she only wore purple that year!"

"I suppose there are lots of things kids don't know

about their parents," Lexi said with a shrug. "I certainly couldn't tell you much about my mom when she was in high school, other than she was in the theater club and played the Ann Margaret role in *Bye Bye Birdie*. Sometimes she'd dance all around the kitchen and reenact the part where Ann sings good-bye to Birdie, who's been drafted into the Army.

"Anyway," she said, shaking off the memory that had brought a smile to her eyes, "Madison's right. This plum will look wonderful with your hazel eyes. Which, by the way, look even larger with that cut. Have you thought about putting some wax on your hair? To give it a bit more definition?"

"No. But I only cut it last night, so I didn't have any."

It was Lexi's turn to widen *her* eyes. "You cut that? By yourself?"

Sophie lifted a hand to the hair in question. "Yeah." She looked as if she were bracing herself for criticism.

"Wow. You're talented. I tried to give myself a bob for my first day in high school and ended up looking like I was wearing a mop on my head."

In reality, the bob had looked as if Vidal Sassoon had done it with his own talented shears, but Sophie didn't need to know that. Watching the girl physically relax had Austin loving Lexi O'Halloran even more than she had when she'd called her friend in a panic the morning after her and Jace's wedding.

Lexi had shown up at the off-the-strip motel and, while Jace was still sleeping off a night of drinking, dragged her down to the Golden Gate Casino. Over a sky-high stack of pancakes that she swore were locals' cure for soaking up a hangover, she'd told Austin to cut her losses and bail.

Now.

Advice Austin should've taken, but as crazy as it had been to get drunk married, it had been even more difficult to think straight with maniacs pounding sledgehammers in your head, running power drills behind your eyes, and your mouth feeling as if you'd swallowed up all the miles of desert surrounding the city.

Tossing the suitcase she'd brought upstairs with her onto Sophie's bed, Lexi opened it, pulled out the tool box that Austin remembered from the pre-wedding makeover, and retrieved a pair of scissors.

"Let's go into the bathroom, sweetie," she suggested. "And get to work."

29

SAWYER DIDN'T KNOW anything about women's hair, but he could tell that Lexi had managed to make Sophie's look as if the short style was intended. And he wasn't sure, but he thought he saw a bit of purple showing through on her bangs. She was also wearing makeup. Nothing too extreme, just a bit of pink on her lips and some mascara that highlighted her wide eyes even more and made her look older.

Which wasn't reassuring. Especially given her friend, who didn't look like the most wholesome influence. Then again, he considered, Sophie had had a good upbringing. As long as whacking off her hair was the worst thing they had to worry about, they'd be okay.

Austin and Lexi took the kids back to Rachel and Cooper's, where they were going to have dinner together. Which, damn, blew his plans for a quiet dinner with Austin. Saying he had some ranch accounting to do, Sawyer begged off. Fifteen minutes later, he was at the mercantile, filling up a cart with the items on the list Rachel had sent him. Tonight's plan might have been shot to hell, but he wanted to be prepared to take advantage of any opportunity that might arise.

He'd been back at the ranch a mere ten minutes when he saw a car driving past the ranch house. It stopped in front of his cabin, and a woman, somewhere between forty and fifty, climbed out. She was carrying a saddle-brown leather purse and a clipboard.

Returning the beer he'd just taken out back to the fridge, he went and opened the door.

"Mr. Murphy?"

"I'm Sawyer Murphy."

"I'm Martha Grimsley. Social Services. I've been assigned to Sophie and Jack Campbell."

"It's good to meet you." Sawyer stepped aside, letting her into the cabin. "I didn't realize you people worked on Sundays."

"We work when there's work to do," she said in an officious tone that had him beginning to worry. "We don't want to keep the children in limbo any longer than necessary."

Sawyer didn't think staying with his brother and Rachel could be categorized as limbo but, having dealt with his share of bureaucracy in the Marines, wasn't going to argue that point. "And both the sheriff and Colton Kane called, asking if we could expedite matters. So." She pulled out a pen and opened her clipboard. "Here I am."

"You do know that I'm not applying for custodial guardianship, right?" Sawyer asked.

"I do. I also know that you were close friends with the deceased and that you live on the property where the children may be staying."

"In the ranch house," Sawyer pointed out.

"Yet they may be frequent visitors. Even, perhaps, spending the night here?"

"That's true." Sawyer belatedly remembered his manners. "Why don't you sit down? Can I get you anything to drink?"

"I'm fine, thank you." She glanced around. "This is quite a nice cabin."

"I like it. It used to belong to the foreman and his family."

"So I was told in the paperwork Mr. Kane emailed me. Would you mind giving me a tour of the rest of the rooms?"

"Sure." Breathing a sigh of relief that the women had seen this coming, he showed his bedroom, where, thanks to the Marine training drilled into him, he'd actually made his bed. The attached bath. "The kids' rooms are across the hall."

She glanced around both rooms, making notes on the clipboard pad. "Is this furniture from the previous family?"

"No. It was bought for Sophie and Jack."

"I see." More note taking. "How did you have time to do all this? Considering you and Austin Merrill have been making funeral arrangements and preparing for her petition to the court."

"Our friends did it for us," he said, wondering if that were some type of trick question. "There are a lot of people who were close to Tom and Heather Campbell. People who care about their children. And want to help ease them over this tough time. And help raise them."

"It takes a village?"

Was that a touch of snark in her tone? "You could put it that way," he said evenly. "Austin was Jack's age when her mother left to go back to Sweden. I was Sophie's age when my mother, who'd been like a surrogate mom to

Austin, died after a long battle with cancer. In both our cases, there were a bunch of adults who stepped in to become part of an extended family, so to speak. Austin and I didn't ever feel alone. Nor will Sophie and Jack."

"Well." She blew out a breath. Wrote some more. "Now I'd like to see your refrigerator."

"My fridge?" What the hell was next? Was she going to go back into his bedroom and find the condoms he'd stashed away in the bedside table?

"It's been my experience that bachelors don't have the best eating habits."

For one fleeting moment, Sawyer was certain that Co-op and Ryan were punking him. Surely she couldn't be serious? As he watched her open not only his fridge but the cupboards, he decided he owed Rachel a huge thank you.

"Once again you surprise me, Mr. Murphy."

"How's that?"

"There's the expected beer, of course. And frozen dinners. But you actually have fresh vegetables."

"I'm a big fan of the food pyramid."

She gave him a long look. He suspected she wasn't buying that. But the mixed greens, spinach, fresh fruit, and other stuff on Rachel's list backed up his claim.

"I'm meeting with Ms. Merrill tomorrow morning. If that goes well, so long as the judge rules in her favor, which, given her high standing in the community, I can't see any reason why he won't, you can expect the children to be moving into the ranch house next week."

"That'll be good for them," he said. "Getting settled somewhere permanent."

"Yes." She was headed back to the door when she turned. "One last thing. I'm told you were one of those

Special Forces soldiers sent to Afghanistan. And that your unit took heavy losses."

Sawyer wondered how the hell she knew that, then realized that since he'd been wounded and gotten those medals, it had probably made the local paper.

"That's true."

"Do you have any lingering problems from that?"

Sawyer had two choices. He could tell the truth to a woman who wouldn't begin to understand what he and his unit had been through. Who might not realize that no one could experience war on any level and not return home changed in some way. Or have nightmares. Which he figured the majority of civilians occasionally suffered and he'd never heard of them having to defend themselves.

Or he could lie. Not for himself but for Jack and Sophie. And Austin, whom he didn't want to be forced to handle this guardianship deal on her own.

He folded his arms. Met the social worker's stern gaze. "None at all."

She nodded. "Fine. I believe we're done here. Thank you, Mr. Murphy. Have a good rest of your Sunday."

"You, too, Ms. Grimsley." He shook the hand she'd extended, then stood in the doorway, watching her climb into a car as gray as her personality and drive away.

Then he went back into the kitchen, popped the top on that beer she'd interrupted, turned on the TV, and channel surfed until he landed on a Giants home baseball game just as Williamson splashed a homer into McCovey Cove with the bases loaded in the bottom of the eighth. Which, short of a miracle, pretty much put the already-five-runs-behind Braves out of the game.

"Now what?"

He could go over to Rachel and Coop's. But the truth was that he was exhausted from the past two days. He'd humped his butt all over some of the most dangerous, godforsaken places on earth. He'd gone as many as thirty-six hours without sleep, many times needing to stay alert enough to fight off the bad guys. During SERE (Survival, Evasion, Resistance, Escape) training, he'd suffered six long winter days in the wettest, darkest, location on the continent: Washington's Olympic National Park rainforest.

Maybe he wasn't cut out for this parent gig, he thought, not for the first time, as he went and got another beer from the fridge and grabbed the cardboard six-pack to save walking back and forth. Fortunately, he and Austin hadn't discussed marriage. Which, under any other circumstances, would probably be a given. But as much as he wanted her, and he did, with every atom of his being, neither did he want to screw this up.

So, for now, until he discovered whether he could live up to what would be required of him—not just short term, like this damned depressing funeral gig, but forever—as he unscrewed another beer top and began channel-surfing again, Sawyer decided it'd be better for everyone involved if they just took things one day at a time.

30

AS MUCH AS she would've liked to be with Sawyer, Austin couldn't deny that having Lexi back in River's Bend lifted her spirits. It was like being back in high school, where they stayed up all night and talked about boys. The only difference was that this time the boys were men, and although Austin didn't want to be judgmental, she thought Sawyer topped Lexi's lounge singer by a mile on the hot boyfriend scale. She had to admit, after listening to the mix tape, that he had a nice voice, though she'd bet he didn't look nearly as good in a pair of Wranglers.

Not that she was superficial enough to judge a male solely by his body. But when a man had a body like Sawyer Murphy's, well . . .

She'd gotten the call from a Ms. Grimsley at precisely eight this morning. The only reason she knew the exact time was that the county social worker had told her that she'd be at the ranch at "precisely" ten. Despite both Tom and Heather listing her as Jack and Sophie's guardian in their wills, despite Colton Kane's recommendation to the court, despite her long relationship with the children, and her reputation for being a good and honest person who'd never even gotten a jaywalking ticket (not that Cooper would ever ticket anyone for that), as she watched the hands of the kitchen rooster clock slowly tick off the minutes, her nerves became more and more tangled.

"Go over to Sawyer's cabin," Lexi said finally. "Work off some of that energy before you drive us all crazy."

"Lexi!" She tilted her head toward the marble slab part of the counter, where Winema was rolling out dough for bread. The house was run on a schedule, and Mondays had always been bread baking day.

"Don't mind me," the housekeeper said. "Just because I'm old doesn't mean I don't remember having sex. And I vote for a roll in the hay." She punched the ball of dough down with her fist. "So to speak. Truth be told, hay is a lot pricklier than it's portrayed to be in all those cowboy romance novels Jenna sells at her store."

"Damn. There goes one item off my bucket list," Lexi said.

"I may go over there," Austin said. "But to hear how his visit with Ms. Grimsley went." When the woman had mentioned visiting him yesterday evening, Austin had thought it strange that he hadn't called, or at least texted her about it.

"Go," Lexi said. "Don't worry about me. If you don't think Buck would mind me borrowing his truck, I'll drive into town and see what's changed."

"He'd be fine with that." Thanks to Layla, her father was practicing riding around the place in his new cruiser, which was as good off-road as advertised. Watching him out the window, she wouldn't have been surprised to see him doing donuts in the corral soon. "Would you mind running an errand for me?" An idea had occurred to Austin during the night. One she thought Sophie would enjoy.

"Sure."

When she heard what the errand entailed, she grinned. "That is so cool. She'll love it."

Austin certainly hoped so. One thing she didn't want to do was give the girl another reason to cry on what would have to be the worst day of Sophie's young life.

⌘

WHAT THE HELL was it with people showing up all the time? The pounding on the door echoed that in his head as Sawyer pushed himself off the couch and staggered to his feet. The TV was still on, some perky blond's voice stabbing like an ice pick into his brain.

"Coming." He dragged himself over to the door, and *damn*. Feeling like he'd stumbled into Groundhog's Day, there was Austin on his porch, looking pert and pretty and smelling like those piña coladas again.

"Hey." The morning sun had turned into a blazing fireball that was scorching his eyes. He blinked and felt sandpaper behind his lids.

The smile on her face turned upside down as she gave him a hard look he wasn't used to seeing from her. "You look like death warmed over."

"Now there's a coincidence," he drawled, bracing one hand against the doorframe. "Because that's pretty much how I feel."

"I can't believe you'd do this, Sawyer Murphy." Energy, and not the good kind, radiated from her as she pushed past him into the cabin as if she owned the place. Which, matter of fact, she did. She took in the bag of chips, the empty beer bottles, and when had he gotten that Jack Daniels out, anyway? "Not now. Not today of all days."

He dragged a hand over his hair. Ran his fuzzy tongue inside his mouth, which felt as if it had sucked up algae from a hundred-gallon stock tank. "I haven't done anything today." Not even peed. Or showered, which he really needed to do because even he could smell the alcohol oozing out of his pores.

"Why don't you, uh, you know . . . sit down . . . and I'll, uh, be back in a few." And with that brilliant display of intelligence, after nearly tipping over when he waved an arm toward one of the leather chairs, he staggered—okay, escaped—out of the room.

Putting his hands on the edge of the counter, he leaned over the sink, squinting against the light at his face in the mirror. His eyes were as red-veined as a Modoc County roadmap and his face was the color of cement.

After taking care of ridding his body of some of the beer and whiskey he'd drunk last night and scrubbing the fuzz off his teeth and tongue, he ran some water into his hands and swallowed three vitamin Ms, which was military-speak for Motrin.

Next he took off his shirt, then, biting back a moan as his head threatened to explode, bent down and shoved his jeans down his legs. Fortunately, sometime between the baseball game and the chatty morning TV blond, he'd taken off his boots. Next he gingerly lowered himself to the closed lid of the commode, managed to pull off his socks with only the faintest of groans, then turned on the water, which—thank you God and Brody Ames for installing the on-demand water heater—took seconds to warm up to steaming.

Climbing into that tall lion-footed red tub was a lot trickier than it had been with Austin, but thankfully he managed the maneuver without breaking his neck. Turning the hand shower spray to pulsing massage to hopefully beat the toxins out of his aching body, he couldn't help wondering if Austin would even be there when he came back out. Which might not be a good thing since he wasn't sure he was in good enough shape to walk into a human hornets' nest.

After deciding that trying to shave might risk slitting his throat, he braved leaving the bathroom. The bottles and chip bag were gone from the table, the couch cushions straightened. Following the rich aroma of coffee coming from the kitchen, he found Austin standing at the stove, a frying pan in her hand.

"You don't have to cook me breakfast," he said as his stomach roiled at the thought of food.

"Don't flatter yourself thinking I'm doing it for you." She pulled out a carton of eggs and some butter from the fridge. He thought she might have arched a brow at the salad stuff, but his vision was still a bit blurry and he couldn't be certain. "I need you in good shape for the children today. The eggs are full of amino acid that will prevent liver damage and help with that headache. Fortunately, you have spinach, which is, by the way, a big surprise, which provides potassium, which will help restore your electrolytes, and some toast will raise your blood sugar."

She ran a glass of water from the tap. "Drink this to start rehydrating. Then you can have your coffee."

He gulped the water like a guy who'd been crawling across some Middle East desert for a month, then curled his fingers around the mug she held out to him and breathed in the fragrant steam. "I think," he decided, "I just may live."

"You don't have any choice." She waved a spatula she'd found somewhere in a drawer at him. "You have responsibilities."

The coffee scorched whatever fuzz might be left on his tongue, but as he felt the caffeine hit his dehydrated brain, Sawyer didn't care. "Anyone ever tell you that you can be a little bossy from time to time?" He took another drink.

"They have. And I'm proud of it. Now sit down and tell me about this Ms. Grimsley. I'm meeting with her for a home inspection at precisely ten this morning, and I need to know everything." She suddenly paled. "Please tell me you weren't drunk when she showed up last evening."

"I swear." He lifted his right hand. "I hadn't had a thing to drink." He didn't see any point in adding that if the social worker had arrived three minutes later, he would've been caught with a beer in hand. But since prohibition had been repealed a very long time ago, that wouldn't have been a crime.

"Okay." She began whipping the eggs in a bowl while throwing some spinach leaves into the pan. Where they immediately began to shrivel up, but since she seemed to know what she was doing, he just drank his coffee and watched the show. "So, what's she like?"

"Like a Dickens character."

She glanced over her shoulder at him after putting the bread in the toaster. "Dickens wrote a lot of characters. Which one?"

"I'm talking about the name thing. She's well named because she's really grim."

"Oh, dandy." She poured the eggs onto the spinach. "What did she do?"

"She checked out all the rooms. She seemed surprised the bedrooms had been set up for the kids."

"Surprised in a good way?"

"Well, as good as she could show, I guess. She asked if I'd bought the stuff, and I said that, no, we'd had help. Then she made a crack about it taking a village. Which kind of pissed me off, so I told her, politely, that you and I had lost our mothers, but we'd had a lot of support from people, so we'd never felt deprived or alone."

"That's a good comeback."

"Thank you." He was relieved to have done something right and hoped that meant that she might let him off the hook when it came to the drinking thing.

"Then she checked out the fridge and cupboards."

"Seriously?"

"Yep. I actually seemed to get a point for having veggies."

"You do with me, too," she admitted. "What else?"

"It looked like she was all done. She doesn't give any real feedback for what she keeps writing on that damn clipboard of hers, so don't let it make you nervous. I think it's partly a power play on her part." Sawyer had dealt with enough officers who got off on control games that he'd recognized the behavior right off.

"You said it looked like she was done." She put the spinach eggs on a plate, spread butter on the toast, and put it with a fork and napkin in front of him. "But she wasn't?"

"No." He began shoveling it down. Hot damn, it was good. "She acted like she thought of something on the way out, but I'm pretty sure she's just streamed too many old episodes of *Columbo* because it sure seemed like a setup to me."

"What did she ask?"

"About my war stuff." He talked around the bite of buttered toast he'd just taken. "And whether I had any PTSD issues."

She'd paused in wiping crumbs off the counter. From the way her shoulders had tensed, he knew she'd caught the significance of that question, too. "And?" she asked with what he could tell was forced casualness. "What did you tell her?"

"I told her no."

"Which isn't exactly the truth."

"No," he admitted. He polished off the veggie eggs, then put down the coffee and went over and drew her into his arms. "You, your dad, and my family know I have issues. Hell, everyone who comes home has to have some problems. But I swear, I won't let them get in the way of the kids' happiness."

"But last night—"

"Was an anomaly. It won't happen again."

She pulled away from his light embrace. Sat down at the table. Knowing they were going to have to talk about it, he decided to move the venue.

"Would you mind if we went out on the porch?" He needed some fresh air and wide-open spaces for this conversation. And no way did he want to return to the scene of last night's crime.

"Sure." He noticed her starting to glance at her watch and decide not to. Knowing she was willing to risk being late for Ms. Grim, he found that encouraging.

The foreman's cabin didn't have a swing like the main house, but it did have two rockers side by side. He waited until she sat down in one, then chose the other.

"It's been a rough few days."

"For everyone," she pointed out.

"True. But it kicked in some memories that I'd stuffed down. Ones I've been trying to ignore."

"I imagine war brings a lot of bad memories."

"True. But except for nightmares, which everyone has, for some reason, I was mostly able to deal with that stuff. Which doesn't have anything to do with strength of character, or personality. Maybe it's just the way our different brains are wired. I mean, look at doctors who cut into people's bodies. Or Tom, who'd have to put down animals. They can do their jobs and not have it haunt them or they wouldn't make it through med school in the first place. Or they'd quit when it got too tough.

"Or cops, like Coop. You know he had to deal with stuff when he was working those mean streets in Portland, and hell, he was leading the search team that found Ellen's body. But somehow he managed to deal with all that, while most people wouldn't be able to handle it without stress having them crack."

"I get your point. So, are you saying you're not haunted by battle flashbacks?"

"Well, sure. But, like I said, they're not that big a deal. I can shake them off, and some days it's even like those things didn't happen to me. That they're more like some movie I've seen."

"Yet something bothered you last night." She reached out and took his hand, linking their fingers together.

"It's the funeral stuff." He drew in a deep breath. Blew it out. "You knew that my last mission turned into a blood bath."

She nodded. "The one where you got injured. And

were given those medals for."

God, he got sick of hearing about those damn medals. "Yeah. That one."

He told her some of it, leaving out the worst details because there was no way he wanted anyone, least of all her, to have those images in her head.

"I'm so sorry." She was holding his hand so tight she'd probably cut off his circulation, but Sawyer didn't really care.

"It was bad. But, like I was trying to explain, I sort of got past it. For the most part. Maybe the same fog of war fogs memories or emotional connections for me. I don't know." He shrugged. "But then, after I got out, I visited all the families of all the guys who didn't make it home."

"How many?"

"Six."

"Why?"

"They were my team," he said simply. "I owed it to them to let the families know that their last thoughts were with them. And that as bad as it had admittedly been, there'd been a moment of peace."

She tilted her head. Studied him. "Was that true?"

"With some."

"But not all."

"No." He could still hear the screams and sobs. And not only when he was sleeping. "Not all."

"That was your way of honoring them, wasn't it?"

"I guess." Another shrug. "To be perfectly honest, I hadn't thought through the reasons. All I knew was that since they hadn't come home, at least alive, I couldn't come home until I met their families and visited their graves."

"Oh, wow." He saw her taking all that in and realized

that she was probably one of the few civilians who could, in some small way, understand what he'd ended up going through. "That's a lot of raw emotion you were taking on."

"The Marines have a notification officer who informs the family of a death," he said. "And unlike the other branches of the military, stays with them through the burials, and longer, if needed. Those guys take on a lot and tend to burn out. But as good as they are, and as much as they care, they didn't know the Marines personally."

"Not like you did."

"No. Not like I did."

A long silence stretched out. Then, finally, she said, "Okay."

"Okay? That's it?" Surprised to get off that easily, Sawyer stood up and looked down at her.

"Any time you want to talk about it more, or about the men you lost, I'm always here. But I get why the past few days had to trigger some really painful emotions, and I'm certainly not one to preach about trying to ease pain by turning a flamethrower of alcohol onto a lake of gasoline. It's not effective, has the totally opposite result that you're hoping for, and it leaves you messed up. However, in a way, I suppose it can be cathartic. So."

She stood, as well, went up on her toes, linked her fingers around his neck, and kissed him. "I'm going to go have myself a good cry about all this, then get myself together for Ms. Grimsley."

He put his hands on her hips. "What are you going to do afterwards?"

"I have to pick up the kids. We decided they'd be spending the night here and going with us to the church for the funeral."

"Good plan. I do have one question." He played with her braid, brushing the silky loose hairs below the elastic band holding it together against her throat.

"What's that?"

"Do you think you could pencil in a quickie before leaving to pick up the kids?"

"Just like a man," she said on an exaggerated sigh. "How soon your people give up the effort of a slow seduction after getting the woman to give it up."

"I'm up for a slow seduction any time you want. But don't judge until you've experienced my quickie."

"Nothing wrong with your ego, is there, Sawyer Murphy?"

He bent and kissed her again, slow and long and deep, thinking he could easily spend the rest of his life doing nothing but making love to this tropical-smelling, sweet-tasting cowgirl.

"It's you," he said, releasing her when what he wanted to do was drag her, caveman style, off to his bed "You're my inspiration." He ran a hand over her shoulder, down her arm, linked their fingers together, and lifted her hand to his lips. "My everything."

"Well." She took a deep breath. "You've convinced me. I'll be back, hopefully before noon. Be ready."

31

SAWYER HAD BEEN right about Ms. Grimsley being every bit as grim as her name. Austin became more and more nervous as she was subjected to an hour-and-a-half-long interrogation that had her expecting the woman to go out to that gray sedan and pull some bright lights and rubber hoses out of the trunk.

Still, she did her best to answer calmly and truthfully. Even when it came to Sawyer.

"We've been best friends most of our lives," she said when asked about their relationship. "His mother stepped in after my mother left."

"To return to Sweden."

"Yes." Sawyer had also been right about the note-taking.

She glanced up at Austin over the rim of her cheaters. "That must have been difficult."

"It wasn't easy. But I suspect growing up with a chronically unhappy mother would have been more difficult," she said mildly. "And I had a great deal of support. As I said, Sawyer's mom was wonderful, as was Winema, our housekeeper. And there were teachers and so many others who made certain I never felt abandoned." That might have been fudging the truth a bit, but she couldn't see that part of her life was any of Ms. Grim's business.

"Yes, Mr. Murphy mentioned all that," she said. "How close were you and he when you were married?"

"Excuse me?"

"To be more to the point, did your friendship with Sawyer Murphy have anything to do with your divorce?"

Austin felt the color flooding into her cheeks. She wasn't embarrassed but angry. Folding her hands together so tightly she could feel the nails biting into her skin, she lifted her chin and looked the officious, annoying woman straight in the eye. "No," she said. "He did not. I wasn't in contact with him during my marriage."

"I find that strange." More damn writing. "Given that you'd been so close all your lives until then."

"Why would you find it strange? Given that Sawyer was deployed and I spent so much time traveling with the ranch's stock business. Our lives were on different paths. I also fail to see where our relationship during that time has anything to do with whether I'd be a good custodial parent to Jack and Sophie Campbell," she said with a great deal more poise than she was feeling.

For the first time, Austin was actually grateful that Lexi had sneakily entered her in the Modoc County Miss Teen Rodeo competition the summer after eighth grade. Although she'd intended to back out, when Lexi pointed out that no way would Sawyer not want to date a rodeo queen, Austin had gone ahead with the pageant.

Being the youngest girl in the competition that had contestants to the age of eighteen, she hadn't even placed in the top ten, which was a huge relief, because no way would she have wanted to travel all over the state representing Oregon rodeo. However, the interview competition and the mock TV interview had proven good training for today's interrogation.

"Yet you're back together now," the woman pressed on.

"Sawyer is leasing property and living on the ranch. In the foreman's cabin," she pointed out.

"Yes. I was there last evening."

"So I heard."

"Do you have an intimate relationship?"

"Again, I don't see what that has to do with the issue at hand."

"These are young, impressionable children we're talking about, Ms. Merrill."

"I'm well aware of that, Ms. Grimsley." Austin couldn't help putting a bit more stress on that first syllable. "And if you're worried that Mr. Murphy and I plan to be having wild orgies in front of Jack and Sophie, you can rest assured that will not be happening."

"But you can't dismiss the possibility of sexual intimacy."

Seriously? Did she ask this of married applicants? Surely she didn't expect people to take an oath of celibacy to win guardianship?

"No. I can also not dismiss the possibility of lightning striking the barn. Or a boulder falling on the roof of my truck while I'm driving into town." Austin stood up. "If we're done here, I really need to pick up the children."

The social services caseworker stood, as well. "I have one last question. Have you seen Mr. Murphy exhibit any evidence of post-traumatic stress disorder? And do you think the children would be safe in his company?"

"No to your first question," Austin said. Which was true. "And absolutely, positively yes to the second."

Grimsley nodded. Closed her clipboard. "Thank you."

"Thank you," Austin said, changing to a more conciliatory tone. It wouldn't help to have the woman leave in a huff. "I realize that the county only has the children's welfare in mind, and I know Tom and Heather would appreciate your thoroughness. As do I."

She walked the woman all the way out to the car, waved goodbye, then breathed a huge sigh of relief.

Feeling as if she'd been rode hard and put away wet, Austin turned and headed toward the foreman's cabin.

❧

SAWYER OPENED THE door even before she knocked, suggesting he'd been watching for her. And didn't that cause a little kick of anticipation?

"What took you so long?" Without giving her a chance to answer, he scooped her into his arms and his mouth claimed hers, and he was kissing her as if they'd been apart for days, months, years.

And wow, his kisses! World-class didn't even begin to describe them, she thought, her head spinning dizzily as he carried her down the hall to the bed where she'd been so thoroughly ravished two nights ago. If kissing were an Olympic event, he'd win the gold medal. Hands down. Along with the silver and bronze.

He only broke the bone-melting contact long enough to put her on the bed and cover her body with his gloriously muscled one, then resumed kissing her, slow and deep, as if they had all the time in the world.

"So much for the quickie," she managed to say as he

caught her bottom lip between his teeth and lightly tugged, setting off little explosions inside her.

"Oh, we'll get to that." His lips skimmed up her face, warming her cheek before lingering at her temple. His breath warmed her skin when he lightly blew at a strand of hair that had escaped her braid, then nipped at her ear, drawing a moan when his tongue took a long lick down her neck. When his open mouth paused at the hollow in her throat, Austin knew he could feel her wildly beating heart.

A heart that had only ever truly beat for him.

"This is just a warm-up." She could feel his smile against her lips as his mouth returned to hers. And—oh, yes!—he began moving his body against hers.

"I like warm-ups."

Which was a misnomer, because the friction between their bodies was creating such heat they could well be in danger. She could see the headline in the *River's Bend Register* now: *War Hero and Former Miss Teen Rodeo Queen Die from Spontaneous Combustion. Nothing Left but Ashes.*

"Good." Rolling over to lie beside her, he began unbuttoning her blouse with an intense fascination that made it seem as if it were the first time he'd ever been exposed to a woman's bare flesh. "You're wearing a bra." His fingers slipped beneath the cup, trailing sparks over her breast.

"I came straight from the meeting with Grim," she managed breathlessly. The last time she'd had less air in her lungs was when she'd fallen off Blue.

"You were in a hurry."

She could only nod as he bent his head and licked the crest of her breasts. "For this?"

Another nod as his fingers poised on the front clasp of the bra.

"I like this." His knuckles brushed over the cups. "I wonder how many men in River's Bend know that you wear girly pink-and-white polka dots beneath those practical cowgirl working shirts?"

Austin decided he didn't need to know that the bra, which she'd never worn before, was yet another outlet mall purchase Heather had talked her into. "I don't exactly go around town flashing all the males I see."

"I'm glad to hear that." One flick of his wrist and his palms were on her breasts, which she could have sworn were growing to a full B cup beneath his touch. "We can keep it our secret." When he took a nipple between his lips and tugged, as if pulled by an invisible cord, her back arched off the mattress in a silent plea for more.

But instead, he lifted his head and looked down at her for what seemed like forever. The teasing smile had left his lips and his eyes turned sober. Not wounded sober, the way they'd been when he'd told her about the deaths and visiting his dead teammates' families, but serious.

She'd seen him look that way before, she realized with a flash of memory. The day she'd walked into their classroom late. The day she'd learned that her mother had gone away for good. They were the eyes of a boy back then, but they'd been both caring and careful. As if he'd been afraid of saying or doing the wrong thing.

"I don't want you to think I'm just in this for the sex."

"I don't." If he'd only been interested in sex, they probably shared around fifteen years of backstory when he could have had it. As much and as often as he'd wanted.

"So, okay. Now that we've got that clarified, you up for the quickie part now?"

The laugh that exploded out of her surprised Austin.

And from the grin that had replaced his grave expression, she knew it had him, as well.

She rolled over on top of him, shoved her hands beneath his Jaspar Lepak *Music in the Mountains* festival shirt, and spread her fingers across his magnificently cut chest. "Giddy up, cowboy."

∾

"DO YOU THINK this is all too easy?" Austin asked a few minutes later as she re-buttoned her shirt.

"Is what too easy?" Sawyer asked, causing a tinge of remorse as he zipped up his jeans.

"You. Me." She waved a hand toward the bed. "This."

"Would you prefer for it to be difficult and complicated?"

"No, of course not. But with all that's happening—"

"All the better that something in our life is going smoothly." He ran his knuckles down the side of her face in the way he might do to gentle a nervous mare. "If it feels easy, it's because it's right. It's what's been missing for me with any other woman."

"Me, too," she admitted, covering his hand with hers. "With other men. Including my ex." Especially Jace. "They were never you."

"Well, then, we've nothing to worry about."

And didn't she wish that were true? But Austin had lived in volcano/earthquake country all of her life and knew that there were always faults and fissures lying beneath the most seemingly tranquil landscape.

"I keep forgetting to tell you that I love that way you smell," Sawyer said.

"It's body soap, lotion, and shampoo," she sat down

on the bed and pulled her boots back on. "Lexi made it last winter when seemingly everything in my life was falling apart and I couldn't afford the time or money to escape to some tropical island. So she said this would bring the island to me."

"I'll have to thank her for that. Although if I ever start belting out the piña colada song while making love to you, it's on her."

Austin laughed again, amazed she could find any humor in anything this week. "You really do make me happy."

"Good." His smile was slow and warm, wrapping around her like one of Heather's quilts. "Because that's all I've ever wanted to do. So, now that we've taken the edge off, so to speak, how was your meeting with the lemon-sucking Ms. Grim?"

"I'm not entirely sure. I couldn't get a read on her."

"Yeah. Like I said, that's her power/control thing."

"She did ask about us."

"What about us?"

"It was a strange conversation, but mainly, I think she wanted to know if we were going to have mad, ripping-clothes-off sex in front of the children."

"Did you tell her we'd never do that?"

"Yes. And that it wasn't any of her business."

"Good for you."

"She also did the same thing to me she did with you. Her last question was whether or not I'd witnessed you exhibit any signs of PTSD. And whether I thought Jack and Sophie would be safe with you."

His smile, which had broadened across his handsome face when she'd told him how she'd stood up to Ms.

Grim's sex interrogation, faded. "And what did you say?"

"No." She stood up and wrapped her arms around his neck. "And positively, absolutely yes."

"Thanks for the vote of confidence." He pulled her closer. Then gave her another of those devastating kisses that threatened to have her melting into a puddle of lust onto the heart-of-pine floor.

"I have to leave," she murmured.

"I know." He cupped her jaw in his fingers, tilting her head, fitting his mouth even more perfectly onto hers. "Just one more minute."

"Just one," she said as their breaths mingled and she could feel his erection against her. Denim, she was discovering, was no insulator against heat.

The kiss was slow. Sweet. Warm.

Someone whimpered. And someone's hand—it must be hers, but she couldn't remember it moving—was cupping the back of his neck. "Maybe two minutes."

The second kiss was long and lingering, and this time as she seemed to float off the floor, the sound she swore she heard was that of angels singing.

The thought of those angels was all it took to have her come plummeting down to earth with a crash.

Knowing her well, Sawyer sensed the change immediately.

"It's okay to be happy," he reminded her.

"It's hard," she admitted.

He smoothed a hand down her back. "I know."

And he did. Worlds more than she ever would.

"I've really got to go."

"And I've got some stuff to do."

"Ranch stuff?"

"Sort of. I had an idea about the rest of the day and evening."

"Oh?" They'd agreed against having any funeral home visitation because it would be one more event Jack and Sophie would have to be put through.

"How about we just treat the rest of today like a holiday?"

"A holiday?" She looked at him as if he'd suggested they both strip off all their clothes and go streaking down Front Street at high noon.

"Not a celebration-type thing," he assured her. "But a family thing. Have a nice, slow afternoon centered around the kids enjoying themselves. Maybe go pick out those trees Father Cassidy talked about at The Plant Place, take a ride along the river, play some games, get a few people— you, me, the kids, Winema and Buck, Rachel, Cooper, and Scott, Ryan and Layla, my folks and grandparents, and Lexi—together for a barbecue. I already bought a couple steaks I was planning to grill for a romantic dinner with you—"

"Wait." She held up a hand. "You were going to cook? For me?"

"Yeah. That's what the green stuff in the fridge is. Rachel gave me some recipes she figured even I could pull off. But we can do that anytime. I figured while you're picking up the kids, I'd go raid the Bar M meat locker for some ribs and steaks and burgers, and maybe a hot dog or two if Jack would rather have those than a burger. You and Sophie might want to make a pie or cookies or something, and we manly men will, of course, take care of the grilling."

"I can grill," she said. "Despite all the male-oriented marketing campaigns that suggest otherwise, it doesn't take testosterone to char a mountain of red meat."

"I've not a single doubt you could do anything you put your mind to," he said easily. "But a little male bonding will be good for Jack. And Buck."

She hadn't thought of that. "You want to help Dad get his cowboy back on."

"It was just a thought."

"A wonderful one." She went up on her toes and, even knowing she was risking another delay, kissed him. "I'll see you later. Maybe you guys can work with Jack's roping while Winema, Sophie, and I start baking. I'm behind on things for the New Chance anyway. Rachel's been wonderfully patient, but since I'm making pies, I might as well make a bunch."

"If you need a taster, just shout."

"I will." She paused, the words *I love you* on the tip of her tongue. But those three words were too important to say as she was going out the door.

After the funeral, she decided as she drove out to Rachel and Cooper's place. Once they got all this behind them.

32

SAWYER HAD BEEN right. The day, which could have been wretchedly awful, turned out not to be that way at all.

Oh, Austin would've been happier if Sophie hadn't insisted on Madison joining them. The girl had shown up in those same Daisy Dukes, a gauzy, off-the-shoulder ivory top thin enough to show the shadow of the black bra she was wearing beneath it, and another pair of those tasseled boots, this one with, heaven forbid, rhinestones on them.

The girl had resisted when Austin suggested she'd be happier riding in a pair of jeans. Ten minutes of her inner thighs rubbing painfully against the leather saddle, which was exactly what Austin had warned her about, she'd begun to whine. After five minutes of nonstop complaining, Austin, Madison and Sophie were on their way back to the house.

"You could borrow a pair of mine," Sophie suggested.

Madison swept a look over her supposed best friend. "Thanks, but they'd bag like clown pants on me. I wear a juniors size one. You're probably a five. Maybe I'll just go out and work on my tan."

Good idea, Austin thought. Before she said something

she really shouldn't.

"Would you like to go work on your tan with Madison?" she asked Sophie. *Dear Lord, please let her say no!*

"Tanning's boring. And besides, I sunburn too easily." Yes! There was a God!

"You can help me make some pies. I thought I'd make two for dinner, and some more to freeze for Rachel to put on the menu at the New Chance."

"I'd like that," she decided. "Mom really liked those cookies you taught me to make."

"Your mom had quite the sweet tooth. I always was surprised she never baked."

"She told me that she might have talents, but cooking wasn't one of them," she said, following Austin into the kitchen, where Winema was busy making potato, macaroni, and green bean with bacon salads for the cookout. "She set a cabinet on fire once frying chicken."

"I remember that." Austin pulled two aprons out of a drawer and tossed one to Sophie. "It sounds scary, but later it became something we all laughed about. In fact . . ."

"What?" Sophie asked.

Great move. Bringing up Friday night's dinner, when Tom and Heather had been alive and laughing, with so much to look forward to. "She mentioned it recently, that's all."

"That's how the remodeling started," Sophie. Austin breathed a sigh of relief at having dodged that conversational bullet. "Then, once she got started, she just sort of kept on going." Her eyes misted. "She's never going to see it finished."

"I know. I've thought about that, too. But it's going to be a beautiful home for some new family." Austin measured out the flour for the crust. "Are you too disappointed about having to live here?"

"Not really. I guess." Sophie's gaze drifted out the window to the corral, where Buck was feeding the still unnamed colt a carrot. "Could I have a horse?"

"There are quite a few you could ride anytime you'd like."

"No, I mean, like, my very own. Like you can ride any of them, but Blue is your special one."

"That's a good idea," Austin said. "We'll have to have you try out several." She thought a bit about that as she cut in the chilled butter. "There's a sweet mare who's as smart as a whip. I've been considering working with her on barrels."

"Could you teach me to do that? Mom said you've won a lot of championships."

"In my day." Austin had given up rodeoing herself once she'd ended up having to fill in so much of her father's jobs as he'd become more and more weakened from the PPS. "But, I have to tell you, it's not easy. It takes a lot of hard work and practice."

"I'd like that," Sophie said. "And I don't mind hard work. I want to become a vet like my dad. He sometimes took me out on calls with him. I got to help deliver a calf once."

"Oh, that must have been special."

"It was. Dad was afraid I'd faint or get sick, but I loved it. Maybe I could help around here when your horses are born."

"There's nothing I'd like more." Austin held her breath, waiting for the reason for Sophie's parents having been out on Duck Pond Road Friday night to come up, but apparently she hadn't made that connection. "So, would you like to start peeling those apples?" she said as a diversion.

The day stayed low-key as Sawyer had suggested. Giving a nod to the younger generation, Thomas Rhett, Chris Young, and Jake Owens sang for the gathering from the outdoor speakers. Taylor Young was added at Sophie's direct request, which was fine with Austin, who was also a fan. Unsurprisingly, Madison, who thankfully would not be spending the night, complained about the "shit-kicker crap."

The aroma of roasting meat drifted from the grills. Rachel and Cooper had brought over Scott's mini-trampoline. Sawyer had set the roping dummy on the corner of the yard for Scott and Jack to practice on, though they seemed to be pretending to ride it a lot more than roping. Which was fine with him, because the sound of Jack laughing was music to Sawyer's ears.

That scantily dressed, way-too-old-for-her-years friend of Sophie's was flirting outrageously with him, which, while seeming to entertain his big brothers, made him as nervous as a cat in a thunderstorm. It also did not escape Tom and Heather's daughter's notice.

"Madison's really pretty, isn't she?" she asked him as she wandered over to where he was basting the ribs.

"She's nice enough looking," he said carefully, wondering where the hell Austin was when he needed her? "But I'd guess a lot of boys around here prefer a girl who looks like she'd be comfortable on a ranch. Or a horse," he couldn't resist tacking on.

Austin had already filled him in on the argument about going riding in those shorts. Sawyer wondered what kind of parents allowed their preteen girl to actually wear skintight shorts that barely covered her butt cheeks and worried, not for the first time, about his ability to pull off this co-parenting gig.

"Do you really think so?"

"Absolutely." He ruffled the short hair he was getting used to. "You remind me of your mom, and if I were a boy, I'd be looking for a girl just like you."

"You're just saying that to make me feel better because my parents died."

No beating around the bush with this one. "No. I'm saying that because it's true." Then decided since they were all going to be together in this for the duration, he'd better let her know what she could expect from him. "I'm guessing you won't always like everything I say. Some of it might piss you off. Or embarrass you." He remembered Buck having done just that to Austin a time or two. "But one thing you can always count on is that I mean whatever I say."

"Okay. Then here's a question."

And didn't that cause the same churning in his gut that sitting in the chute atop Desperado had caused? "Ask away," he said with fake bravado.

"Are you going to marry Austin?"

"Oops." Sawyer was saved by a sudden flare-up on the steak side of the grill. Grabbing a bottle of water, he was spraying the flames when Austin showed up.

"Hey, Sophie," she said. "Would you mind giving Rachel and me a hand with putting the side dishes on the table?"

"Okay," she said. "Just so you two know that I know what you're doing. Mom and Dad did the same thing when they didn't want to talk about something."

That said, she tossed Sawyer a look. "Later."

Austin and Sawyer watched as she headed off toward where Rachel had begun carrying the bowls of salads, baked beans, grilled corn, and macaroni and cheese over to the long tables covered in red-and-white-checked plastic tablecloths clamped down at the corners.

"Thanks for the save," he said.

"You looked as if you'd just drawn Bodacious. I figured someone had to come to your rescue."

Referred to as both "the greatest bull to ever buck," and "the most dangerous bull in the world," Bodacious had been infamous for lowering his head and bringing his rear up, which would force a rider to shift his weight forward. Then he'd lift his huge head up full force, head-butting the rider and smashing his face. After two particularly dangerous incidences, one of which shattered every bone in a rider's face and required six hours of painful surgical reconstruction, he'd been forced into early retirement. But was later inducted into the Pro Rodeo Hall of Fame.

"You know how we thought Jack was going to be the problem?" he asked.

"I believe you thought that. I, however, having been a teenage girl, suspect otherwise."

"I bow to your superior knowledge and wisdom." Which he did, with an exaggerated sweeping gesture with the hand holding a pair of barbecue tongs.

"I hope she wasn't flirting too badly."

"No. I think you may be right about the crush, but she's nothing like her friend."

"Who, in my opinion, is no friend at all but a mean girl. So, what was the problem?"

"She wanted to know if we were going to get married."

"Oh. Well. I'm going to have a little talk with her tonight. About her mom. I have a gift I want to give her before tomorrow. But if she asks me, I'll simply tell her that we haven't even discussed the possibility."

"Okay." He began taking the T-bones and rib eyes off the grill to rest.

As he watched her walk over to help Rachel and Sophie, Sawyer assured himself that the fact that she'd so easily brushed the topic of marriage off was a good thing. Still, he found himself wishing that she hadn't been so damn quick about it.

33

THE HOUSE WAS quiet. Proving herself to be the best friend in the world, Lexi had driven Madison home, Winema had gone home, and Buck had retired to his bedroom. Jack had conked out, proving that even dynamos could eventually wear down, and Sophie had hidden herself away in her room.

Seeing the light still on beneath the door, Austin knocked lightly.

"Come in," Sophie said.

She was lying in bed, reading a paperback book featuring a teenage girl standing in the middle of what looked to be the rubble of a city, surrounded by flame and smoke. Wondering if dystopian fiction was the best thing to be reading the night before your mother's funeral, Austin wished she'd thought to have Jenna suggest some YA romances.

"I'm just dropping in for a minute," Austin said. "I don't want to keep you up."

"Like I'm going to be able to sleep the night before we stick my parents in the ground."

"That's what I wanted to talk with you about." Austin took the white box from behind her back. "I brought you something."

"A funeral present?" Unsurprisingly, she didn't sound all that thrilled at the idea.

"No. More of a legacy." She handed Sophie the box. "From your mom."

Sophie lifted the lid. Lying on a bed of ivory satin that had once been white was a pearl necklace and earrings. "My mom wore these for her wedding."

"I know. They were the same ones her mother wore. And I happen to know that she hoped that someday, when you got married, you wouldn't think they were too old-fashioned."

"Mom said Jackie Kennedy said that pearls were always appropriate."

"I'd guess that Jackie would've known better than most women. Being such a fashionable first lady."

"Mom said that she was an icon." Sophie picked up the necklace and ran her hands over the gleaming pearls.

"I thought you might want to wear them tomorrow. In memory of Heather."

Her young face fell. "My ears aren't pierced. Mom said I had to wait until I was thirteen."

"No problem." Austin lifted them from the silk. "Lexi got the posts taken off for now and replaced with these magnetic clips. You place one on the back, then put the earring on, and voilà. Let me get you a mirror."

She went over to the small dressing table that had belonged to her mother, which she'd kept in her own bedroom for years after Britta's departure. The matching silver brush and mirror set had been a wedding present from one of her wealthy Swedish friends. Sophie had always wondered if she'd left it behind because she didn't want any memories of her marriage. Whatever the reason, every night, until she'd entered high school, Austin had brushed her hair with that brush and felt a little closer to the mother whose face she could no longer remember.

"Oh." Sophie breathed out a little breath as she took in her reflection. "They're beautiful."

"Just like your mom. And you."

"I wish I hadn't cut off my hair."

She wasn't alone there. "It'll grow back," Austin assured her. "And that short pixie cut Lexi gave you really shows off the earrings. And your long neck, which accentuates the pearls."

"Madison calls it my heron neck."

Madison is a mean girl who'll grow up to be a mean bitch. "It's a ballerina's neck," Austin corrected mildly. "Madison's probably just envious because she's so much shorter than you."

"That's what Mom called it when I told her what Madison had said." She ran her fingers over the pearls, which just rested on her collarbone. "That I have a ballerina's neck."

"See? I told you that your mom and I think alike. Great minds. And you look so beautiful. I know she's looking down and feeling so proud."

Apparently that was the wrong thing to say, because Sophie broke into deep, gulping, gut-wrenching tears. Austin sat down on the bed, wrapped her arms around Heather's daughter as she had in the truck by the river, and stayed with her until she'd cried herself out.

After putting the necklace and earrings back in the box and leaving the box on the bedside table in case Sophie would want to look at them again during the night, Austin kissed the top of her head and, trying to walk on silent cat feet, left the room. She paused in the doorway and looked back. Sophie had already fallen asleep.

SOPHIE WAS DREAMING of riding a dragon across the skies, like Princess Cimorene, youngest daughter of the king of Linderwall from The Enchanted Forest series her mother had bought her for her twelfth birthday.

She was off to fight evil wizards who had stolen her magic pearls and planned to use them to claim the dragons' Caves of Fire and Night, when she heard someone saying her name.

"Go away." She had a world to save. She couldn't be bothered with younger brothers.

"I *need* you." Jack had taken her arm and shook her so hard she fell off her dragon, landing with a crash onto her mattress.

"What do you want?" she snapped, still caught up in avenging-princess mode.

"You have to help me."

His plaintive cry for help cut through the dream fog. Sophie pushed herself up. "Are you lonely? Do you want to sleep with me?"

"N-n-no." He was stuttering. Through tears, she realized. "I w-w-wet the bed." Looking at his carrot top hung in shame and embarrassment caused Sophie's heart to melt on the spot. Just like the way evil wizards in her dream had melted when she'd dumped soapsuds on them.

"Don't worry." She gathered him to her and hugged him. Hard. "Let's go back into your room and get you some dry pajamas. And I'll change the sheets."

Austin had shown her the linen closet at the end of the hall when she'd first arrived, in case she or Jack might want any more pillows or towels.

She was in the laundry room, hoping to get the sheets washed and dried before Winema arrived in the morning, when Austin walked in. "Jack had an accident," she said. "But you don't have to worry. I changed him and the bed, and now I'll just wash these—"

"You go back to bed," Austin cut her off. "I'll start the wash, and Winema can toss the sheets in the dryer in the morning. Is Jack all right?"

"He's upset. I told him I wouldn't tell anyone."

"Then it'll be our secret for now. But if it becomes a habit, I will need to know. Not because I'm worried about the bed but because the books I've read the past few nights say it's a typical sign of stress in a boy his age. So, we'll want to get him help."

Sophie breathed a sigh of relief. She still wished her parents hadn't died. And she was still mad at God, or fate, or whoever had dropped that stupid boulder on them. But at least she wouldn't have to take care of Jack on her own. And that, she decided, as she didn't pull away from Austin's hug, was something.

34

SOPHIE HADN'T THOUGHT she'd be able to sleep the night before her parents' funeral. Especially after Jack had gotten into her bed with her, crawling beneath the covers, snuggling so tight against her she hadn't been able to move so much as a toe. But when she woke up, she realized the sun was slipping in through the gaps in the wooden blinds. And she was all alone.

Worried about her brother, she got out of bed and went over to the door, which hadn't been open after she'd gone back to bed after the bed-wetting incident, and could hear Jack's voice drifting up from the kitchen. He was, as he always did, bombarding everyone with questions.

And didn't she have a bunch of her own? All about why her parents had to die. Questions she suspected she'd never get any answers for. It was the suddenness that made things so much worse. She remembered a girl, Amber Cunningham, who'd been in her Brownies troop back in second grade, whose mother had died after a long illness. It had been a long time ago, and Sophie had forgotten what had been wrong with her, if she'd ever even known, but she vaguely remembered Amber missing a lot of meetings to spend time with her mother at the hospital.

At the time, she'd thought it sad and had, like the other girls in the troop, made sympathy cards after the mom had finally died, but the enormousness of it hadn't sunk in. Because how could it? Because she'd been like Jack, unable to fully appreciate how Amber's life had so horribly changed. But, although she got it now, at least she thought, Amber had had time to adjust to the idea of losing her mother. It hadn't come out of the blue, like, literally, a boulder falling from the sky.

Amber's dad had moved the family back to Vancouver, Washington, shortly after that, and eventually Sophie forgot about her. Now she wondered how Amber was doing. Did she have a new mom? Stepsisters or stepbrothers? Were they just one big happy family like the Brady Bunch?

At least, she thought, Austin didn't have any kids she'd have to try to get along with. Sophie supposed that was something. But if Austin married Sawyer, they'd probably have kids of their own. Then she and Jack could end up the extras. She knew Austin would try to treat the kids all the same, but wouldn't she secretly prefer her own to those she got from her friends' will? Like some stupid random prize in a Cracker Jack box?

Thoughts continued to circle around and around in her head as she got through the morning in a brain blur. It was like those near-death movies, where the person was floating above their body watching things happen. She was aware of people talking to her, and she guessed she was answering them back okay, but none of it seemed real.

Austin had helped her get dressed, and Lexi had put some stuff in her hair that she said would "give it definition," and brushed some mascara on her lashes, blush on her cheeks, and some stuff on her lips that tasted like cherries and was more gloss than real lipstick. But, as she stood in front of the full-length mirror in the corner of the room, she decided that she didn't look as dead as she felt inside.

"You look beautiful," the wonderfully familiar voice assured her. The voice she'd kept hearing in her head as she'd rerun seemingly every conversation she could ever remember having with her mother. Even the bad ones. Especially those. "And so grown up."

She spun around, blinking furiously at her mother, standing beside the bed, dressed in the wedding gown Austin had taken to the funeral home.

"Mom? Is that really you? Are you really here?"

Her mother held up a hand and studied it. Her plain gold wedding band flashed in the sunlight. "It appears I am." Then she smiled, that slow, beautiful smile that always made Sophie feel like the most special girl in the whole U.S.A. Even the entire world. "We didn't get a chance to talk before . . . well, you know," she said. "What happened to your dad and me. So I was hoping that I'd be able to come here today. Just to let you know how much your dad and I love you, and how I know that you're going to have a wonderful life."

"You do? How?"

"I've seen it."

"You've seen my future?"

"Of course."

"What happens?"

"Oh, I can't tell you," she said. "Knowing could change things. I think." Her brow furrowed. "I'm not yet sure how everything works. This is all very new."

"You mean heaven?"

Her mom tilted her head in that way she had when she was considering things. Like when she'd decided against the sleepover at Madison's. "I suppose. I'm not sure it has an actual name, the way we think of it."

"Oh." That made sense. After all, there were all kinds of people in the world, all who had their own languages. And, Sophie decided, thinking of her friend Willow, whose mother was Wiccan, their own beliefs. "Is it nice there?"

Her beaming smile was like the brightest sun warming an icy winter's day. "Very nice. I'm not sure there's a word strong enough to describe it."

"Is it like in the Bible stories? Are there angels with wings strumming harps? Are Grandma and Grandpa there?" And although she worried it was going to sound ridiculous, she had to ask. At least for Jack. "And Marmalade and Riley?"

Her mother's brow furrowed. "Do you know, I can't remember. Isn't that strange? I wonder why that is." She touched a finger to her lips. "I suppose so those of us lucky enough to come back for a short time won't give away the secrets."

She nodded, seemingly satisfied with that idea. "That must be it. But what's important is that you know that your life is going to be beautiful and happy. I wanted a chance to tell you that, wherever you go, I'll always be there. Loving you. And being so proud and happy for you."

"So, you'll be able to come back a lot?" Sophie had never heard of such a thing, even on those Hallmark Channel movies, but she never would have thought she'd be standing in a bedroom at Austin's ranch house, talking with her dead mother.

"No. I'm pretty sure this is a one-time thing." She smiled again, that special smile that touched the very center of Sophie's broken heart. "Though when you feel the air stirring, or when you're sad and feel as if someone's arms are wrapped around you, know that it'll be your mother."

She crossed the floor. Not really walking, but she didn't exactly transport herself, either. It was sort of floating, with the white tulle of her wedding dress sweeping across the wood floor. She stopped in front of Sophie. "That's a very good color on you. It brings out the green in your hazel eyes."

"Austin and Lexi told me it's your favorite color. That you wore it for a whole year."

"I did. Do you want to know why?"

"Yes." Sophie wanted to know everything.

Her mother's eyes twinkled with amusement. "We had to fill out this personality test in homeroom our first week of high school. I don't remember why. But I did find out that your father's favorite color was purple. So, since I really, really wanted him to ask me out, I decided to make sure he noticed me."

"You never told me that."

"I never told anyone but Austin . . . You're wearing my mother's pearls."

Sophie touched a hand to the necklace. "Austin gave them to me last night."

"They look perfect on you. And you're turning into such a young lady." The air stirred as her mother's hand brushed over them. "It won't be that long until you'll be wearing them at your own wedding."

Someone began tapping lightly on the door. "Sophie?" Austin asked. "Are you ready?"

"No. Not yet," Sophie said, desperate for this moment, or visitation, or whatever it was not to end.

"You have to go," her mother said gently. "Your brother needs you. And I've already overstayed my allotted time."

Sophie wondered how wonderful heaven could be if people were put on time clocks, the same as they were down here on earth. Then felt guilty for not being grateful that she was being given this special gift, which she was certain she wasn't imagining, but was truly real.

"I don't want you to leave."

"I know." The smile faded for an instant, and she thought she saw moisture in her mother's gentle brown eyes. "But I promise, I'll always be watching over you." The smile was back. On her lips and in her eyes. "And won't you be easier to watch over than your brother?"

Sophie felt her own lips curving at the idea of her mother watching wild Jack from heaven. Then something occurred to her. "Is he going to be okay, too? And happy?"

She ran a hand over the top of Sophie's head. It was odd, like when she'd touched the pearls. It wasn't as if her hands were actually touching, but Sophie could feel them, like a bit of air. "Of course. Both my precious babies are going to have very special lives. And do amazing things."

There was another tap on the door. "Sophie? Are you all right?" She could sense the concern in Austin's voice as she heard her talking to someone else. Someone with a deep, male voice. Sawyer.

"Close your eyes," her mother said gently.

Unable not to, Sophie did as instructed. And felt a touch, like the faintest flutter of butterfly wings, on each cheek, then her temples, then her lips.

A soft breeze warmed her face.

And then, when she opened her eyes, she was standing there. All alone.

But, she thought as she drew in a deep breath, then blew it out before opening the bedroom door, maybe not as alone as she'd feared.

35

THE DUAL FUNERALS were not as horrible and sad as Austin had feared. Nearly Jack's entire class had shown up with their parents (who sat at the back of the church classroom, while their children sat on pillows up front) to watch Jack and Sophie put the notes they'd written to their parents into two boxes. A small flowered china one Tom had bought Heather for Sophie's birth, and a cherrywood one Heather had asked Cooper, who was a woodworker, to make for Tom last Christmas for his paperclips that kept getting caught up in the vacuum. Earl Earle had promised to put the boxes into the appropriate caskets before burial.

Rachel had brought a book that a friend had given to Scott when his father had died. Beautifully illustrated, *Lifetimes* explained life and death in a sensitive, caring way to children suffering a loss, explaining that everything, plants, animals, birds, fish, and people, had their own special lifetime. That there's always a beginning. And always an ending.

"And the in between," she read quietly to the avidly attentive children who'd grown hushed as she'd turned the pages, "is living."

Sophie, who was only there for Jack, had chosen not to speak. But Jack had insisted that he'd wanted to say something.

"I had the best mom and dad ever," he said. "Mom gave me this string when I was a little kid." He pulled it out of the pocket of his dress jeans. It was four wool threads: blue, red, yellow, and green woven together. "She said that it repa . . . repr . . ."

"Represented," Sophie said from where she was standing against the wall with Austin, who was wearing a Lexi-approved basic black dress she'd bought to wear to last year's Cattleman's Association banquet. Standing with them, Sawyer was in a dark suit borrowed from Cooper and dress boots that appeared to be the same ones he'd worn to the couple's wedding.

"Yeah. Represented," Jack said with a decisive nod of his red head. "That's it. It means that it's like us. Mom, Dad, Sophie, and me. And that as long as I keep it, we'll all be together. No matter what."

Austin felt the tears stinging against the backs of her lids again. So much for swearing not to cry until they'd gotten through all this. "Did you know about that?" she quietly asked Sophie.

"Yeah. She gave me one, too. I use it as a bookmark in my diary."

The diary Austin had stuck into the suitcase at the last moment. She'd seen the woven threads, never knowing their significance. "That's very special."

"Yeah."

"So," Jack said. "Because Mom and Dad's special life-time ended, we're going to bury them, like we did Riley. Though not at Austin's ranch," he tacked on, looking over at Sophie as if worried she'd yell at him again for getting it wrong. "But in a special place Sawyer and Austin found for them in the cemetery, where Sawyer's mom is, too. But they won't really be gone, because they're always going to be watching over us, and we'll always be connected. Because of this string."

He blew out a breath. "And I guess that's all I wanted to say."

He sat down as the children clapped, the same way they had when Rachel had finished reading the book. In the back of the room, Rachel was passing the box of tissues to the parents, many of whom were openly sniffling, while others dabbed at wet eyes.

The children seemed less affected, some even raising their hands to ask questions about life and death to a deacon who ran the youth programs. Rather than a sad occasion, it seemed more a celebration of Tom's and Heather Campbell's lives, as Austin had told the children funerals should be. And when Kasey Montgomery, who headed up the choir, stood up to sing Jack's choice of "Circle of Life" from *The Lion King*, every boy and girl, who'd all probably watched the DVD a dozen times, at least, jumped up to joyfully sing along. While in the back of the room, another tissue box was brought out and passed around.

They'd been blessed with a bright, warm, and sunny day, so the children were able to go outside into the church courtyard and send iridescent soap bubbles floating into the blue sky while Sawyer and Cooper helped Sophie and Jack plant the two elm trees they'd bought yesterday in memory of their parents.

After that emotional twenty minutes, Austin was glad

that neither she nor Sawyer had opted to say anything personal during the adult service. She knew she wouldn't have made it through the funeral mass without bursting into tears. Which she nearly ended up doing as the caskets had been carried out to "Amazing Grace" being played on a set of bagpipes by a member of the volunteer fire department wearing the Clan Campbell tartan.

And finally, as they'd stood there while Father Cassidy concluded the funeral service, looking past the caskets toward the reflection of the puffy white clouds in the clear blue waters of Glass Lake, Austin understood about Sawyer's dad's bench beneath the tree. It was a perfect place. A calm place. One she thought the couple, who'd spent so many happy family times on that very lake, would have approved of.

She'd seen the Carpenters sitting in the back of the church, which had been filled to standing-room only, as she'd filed out with the family behind the caskets. Her eyes had met theirs for a moment, and she'd wanted to let them know in some way that they were not to blame. But they quickly looked away. The devastation of the events had shown on their faces, and she could only hope that they'd found some comfort in the service. The fact that they hadn't come to the interment suggested acceptance might be a long way off.

She'd just made a mental note to ask the priest, Cooper, or maybe even Ryan if there was anything that could be done to ease the couple's minds and hearts when Kira Taylor, Sophie's honors science teacher, came over to her.

"I was glad to see Sophie looking well," she told Austin after introducing herself. "We've been worried about her."

"It's been difficult, but she has a lot of love and support."

"I knew she would, which is why I haven't wanted to disturb whatever stage of grief you all are in right now," she said, a bit of the soft, magnolia South in her voice. "I was going to email you, but decided that was too impersonal. Do you have any idea when Sophie will be coming back to school?"

"Probably in another day or so," Austin said. "We're sort of playing everything by ear."

"Totally understandable. We weren't sure, being so close to the end of the year, that she'd be back at all. We were hoping she'd at least be able to make graduation."

Graduation? How could she have forgotten about that? Heather had gotten Sophie a certificate for a mother-daughter mani-pedi. And planned to surprise her with an appointment to have her ears pierced while they were at the spa, which Sophie had been asking for since fourth grade.

"I expect so."

"I'm glad. She's achieved some special awards, and I'd hate to have her miss receiving the recognition she deserves. So, we'll be looking forward to seeing you next Saturday."

"Absolutely," Austin said as her mind spun. "I'm sorry, things have been so hectic. What time was that again?"

"Five thirty. We wanted to leave time for parents to take their graduates out to dinner."

Another note to self: Ask Rachel for a reservation for four. No, she amended, glancing over at her father, who was sitting in his cruiser, talking with Fred Wiley and Cal Potter. Make that five.

36

THE OTHERS TOOK the children back to the ranch while Sawyer and Austin spent thirty minutes at the funeral luncheon, listening to stories of how Heather and Tom had impacted so many lives. After leaving the others still sharing memories, they drove to Colton's law office for the official reading of the will. They weren't the only people in the room. Although the couple hadn't had a great deal of money, they'd always been generous, which had continued beyond their death.

They'd given bequests to the Modoc County and River's Bend Food Banks; Our Table, a local nonprofit focusing on providing the community with locally grown, accessible, and affordable food; and Project Linus, a national nonprofit that provided homemade blankets for children in need. There was also a gift to the volunteer fire department to aid in the search and funding for a full-time professional fire chief.

While the others were not a surprise, given the couple's long-held advocacy to fight hunger and Heather having woven countless blankets for Project Linus, Austin had to wonder if one reason for the fire department being included stemmed from that fried chicken grease fire.

The rest of their estate, as Colton had already told them, had been put in a trust for Sophie and Jack, with Austin as guardian.

"Whew," she said as she and Sawyer drove out of town. "I'm really glad you had that idea to make yesterday a quiet one. Because this has been one of the longest days of my life."

"It's partly the pressure to make everything turn out well. Not just for Tom and Heather's memories but for the kids."

"Exactly." She thought back over the day. "Did Sophie seem different to you?"

"Other than looking too grown up for comfort?"

"It was more than that," Austin mused. "She seemed to be really at peace for the first time since all this happened."

"That'd be great if it's true. But it seems awfully fast."

"I know. But just for today, I'm going to be optimistic." She told him about the graduation. "Her teacher says she's going to get some awards."

"I'm not surprised. She's smart as a whip and super responsible."

"That undoubtedly comes from being older."

"Yeah. She'll probably grow up to be just like Coop. Playing big sister to Jack even when they're in their eighties."

"Probably. She didn't seem overly upset that Madison didn't show up." Austin would be eternally grateful for the mean girl's absence.

"Maybe she's wising up. That girl is trouble."

Yet another thing they agreed on.

WHEN THEY ARRIVED at Green Springs, Jack was out with Cooper, Buck, and Scott playing horseshoes.

"Good thing for the windows the horseshoe pit is far from the house," Rachel commented dryly as Jack's horseshoe went sailing over the post.

"The kid could end up with one helluva sports career," Sawyer said. A second horseshoe landed even farther than the first, a good three feet left of the target. "Though we'll have to work on control."

Sophie, who'd gone directly to her room after arriving home, came downstairs dressed in jeans and a pink T-shirt with a silk-screened rainbow and unicorn on the front. *Always be yourself*, it read. *Unless you can be a unicorn. Then be a unicorn.*

"Did you mean what you said about me having my own horse?" she asked Austin.

"Of course."

"Then can we go look at the horses now?"

There was nothing the girl could have asked for today that Austin wouldn't have moved heaven and earth to try to give her. This, fortunately, was easy. "I think that's a great idea. Let's go steal some carrots from the refrigerator."

Carrots in hand, after stopping to get a halter and a lead rope, they went out to the pasture where the horses were grazing beneath the spreading arms of a tree growing next to the natural springs that had given the ranch its name.

"Which one is mine?" Sophie asked.

"Let's call her and see," Austin said. Then cupped her hands together and called out, "Misty!"

A copper-red mare immediately lifted her head, whinnied, then came trotting toward them.

"I guessed it'd be the gray horse," Sophie said. "Is she named after *Misty of Chincoteague*?" The series of books about the wild ponies had been Austin's favorites, and she'd loved sharing them with Sophie over the years.

"No." The sorrel came up to the fence and nickered. "She was born on a morning the fog was rolling in from the river, like ghosts floating in the air, so thick you could hardly see your hand in front of your face." As soon as she'd said the ghost reference, Austin wished she could pull the word back. "Here." She handed Sophie a carrot in hopes of distracting her. "She loves carrots even more than sugar cubes. Hand her one."

Sophie held out the carrot. She'd been around horses enough at Green Springs that she had a healthy caution but no fear. "Hi, Misty. I'm Sophie. And we're going to be very best friends."

The horse had always been mild-tempered, affectionate in a way not every horse was, and easy to train. When she lowered her head after finishing off the carrot, Austin knew for a fact that Misty and Sophie would be well suited.

"She likes you. And wants you to touch her."

"Good Misty. You're so beautiful." She ran her hand down the flaxen mane that matched the mare's tail. "I thought this was going to be the worst day of my life," she told Austin as she rubbed the horse's forehead. "But it turned out to be really good. I saw my mother and now I have my very own horse."

"You saw your mother?" The revelation was stated so casually Austin wasn't certain she'd heard right.

"She visited me right before the funeral," Sophie said as Misty nudged her. "Can I give her another carrot?"

"Sure . . . Before the funeral?"

"That's why I didn't open the door right away. Because she was telling me about my life and Jack's, how our futures were going to be amazing, and that she'd always be with me."

"That's very special."

Sophie turned away from the mare just long enough to smile. "Isn't it? She couldn't remember what heaven's like, but that's okay because she told me it's wonderful."

The girl had always had an active imagination, but Austin had the feeling that she wasn't making this up. "If there's anyone who could pull off a visit like that, it'd be your mom," she said. "Did she visit Jack, too?"

"No. He's too young to understand. And maybe she was afraid she'd freak him out."

"But you weren't afraid?" Austin wanted to be ready for any possible nightmares.

"Not at all. Oh, she told me why she wore purple all year."

"Oh?" This was getting curiouser and curiouser.

"Because it was Dad's favorite color and she wanted him to notice her."

"I told her at the time that he'd notice her without that," Austin said, even as goose bumps rose on her arms. How else could Sophie know what Heather had only shared with her? "But she was very determined."

"Mom's that way," Sophie said easily. "I'll bet that's why she got to come down to visit. Because she can talk anyone into anything once she puts her mind to it."

Austin laughed. "That's definitely true." And didn't she have the tacky girl-in-the-country-song outlet mall outfit hanging in her closet to prove it?

ᕰ

AFTER STAYING HOME for two days, which she'd mostly spent grooming Misty and riding her around the corral, and then with Austin and Sawyer on the river trail, Sophie worried about going back to school. Would everyone stare at her, like she was some kind of freak? Or worse yet, would kids keep coming up to her to tell her how sorry they were and she'd have to keep telling everyone that she was doing okay?

Which she sort of was, which was a major surprise. Maybe because, although it might be her imagination, she could still feel her mom. Not in some weird stalker way, watching every single thing Sophie did or listening to her thoughts, but more like she was somewhere out there— wherever *there* was—in case Sophie needed her.

Ms. Taylor welcomed her back to her honors science class and an extra helping of warmth in her pretty Southern accent, but not a lot of fuss. She'd treated her as if she'd just been out with the flu or something. Which Sophie was grateful for. She hadn't seen Madison yet, because Madison wasn't in honors. Not because she wasn't smart enough, because she probably was, but because, as she'd told Sophie, who'd been excited about being accepted, all that extra studying required would take time away from fun things. Like boys.

Sophie had never minded the extra work her honors English and science classes entailed because except for sort of crushing on Parker Long—who could actually make constellations sound interesting—she wasn't all that interested in boys. Although Parker wanted to be an astrophysicist when he grew up, and maybe an astronaut, he'd still told her, during their biology section, which was her favorite part, that it was way cool that she was planning to be a large-animal vet, like her dad.

She usually passed Madison in the hall on her way to civics, but today she didn't see her until lunch. She was sitting at their usual table with their crowd when Sophie came in carrying the lunch Winema had packed for her. Because, seriously, who'd want to eat the carb-heavy junk the cafeteria served?

"Sophie!" Madison screeched, jumped up from the bench, and gave her a huge hug as if it'd been years instead of days since they'd been together. Sophie figured they'd probably heard her over in the high school a block away. "We were just talking about you! How *are* you?"

"Okay, I guess. For someone who just buried her parents."

"Yeah. Like I told you when we texted, that sucks. Sorry about missing the funeral."

"No problem." Sophie shrugged as if it hadn't bothered her. Which, actually, it had. A lot. If Madison's mom and dad had died, she would've been there for her. "We were kind of busy, anyway."

"And it *was* a school day," Madison pointed out.

"Which you ditched to go out to the lake with the gang," Shelly Denny said with a giggle.

"You went to the lake?" Okay. Now Sophie was getting majorly mad.

"No one goes to class the last couple weeks of school," Madison said defensively with a toss of her hair. "And it was such a great day."

"My brother took a bunch of us out on our family's boat," Shelly said.

Her smirky smile suggested she was enjoying this. She and Sophie had never been friends. Madison was all they'd had in common. Madison also once confided that Mark Denny, who was three years older, had sexted her a picture of his penis and wanted her to Snapchat one of her bare boobs back to him. She'd denied doing it, but now Sophie wondered.

All the insults Madison had ever thrown her way came flashing back, most recently making fun of her dress size, which was, by the way, not a fat size at all, and that heron neck thing. She'd also said Sophie was too old to like horses, because, like, Madison had given up reading those lame kind of books back in sixth grade after she'd discovered the *Twilight* ones. Which Sophie had never been able to get into, but she loved the Enchanted Forest series and had read every Harry Potter book as soon as it had come out. Another thing her supposed BFF had ragged her about. Because geek girls were so uncool.

And getting back to horses, excuse me, Sophie thought, Austin was super cool and she had a lot of horses. Plus, she even bred them and trained them and had promised to let Sophie help deliver the next baby that was born.

"You know what?"

"What?" Madison asked.

"You." She jabbed a finger toward Madison, then turned to Shelly. "And *you*. Both of you are irrelevant." In Sophie's tween world, there was no worse insult. Okay, maybe *slore*, which was a blend of slut and whore. But she never would've said that. Especially in front of the entire class that now seemed to be watching.

She spun around to walk away, belatedly realizing she didn't have a clue where she was going. She could just march out and head home, but the teacher monitoring the door might catch her and stop her from leaving. Next time she did some big drama thing, she'd have to think it through better ahead of time.

"Sophie!" She heard someone calling her name behind her and saw Becca Thomas, a girl from her science class, coming toward her. "I'm sorry about your mom and dad," Becca said, her brown eyes looking genuinely sad behind her black-framed glasses.

"Thanks."

"You want to come sit with us?"

Sophie might be one of the school's smart kids, but eating lunch at the nerd table? Seriously? *Kill me now.*

Then she saw Parker Long. OMG! Smiling at her!

"Yeah. That'd be cool. Thanks."

Maybe her mom was right, Sophie thought as she almost floated across the black-and-white tile floor. She had her own horse, who had the same name as her most favorite fictional horse ever. And Parker Long, a possible future astronaut from River's Bend and the cutest boy in school, had just smiled at her.

Not the kind of smile he'd shared when she'd helped him with the chapter assignment comparing and contrasting genetic engineering with selective breeding, which, to be honest, her dad had helped her with the night before. But like she'd seen boys smile at girls when they really, really liked them.

Maybe, she thought as she shyly smiled back at Parker and felt her heart floating up to the rafters like one of those bubbles Jack and his friends had blown into the sky, her life really *was* going to be amazing.

37

THEY'D GOTTEN PAST the funeral, and the kids were back in school, seemingly doing well, especially Sophie, who seemed to have not one but two new best friends: Becca Thomas, whose single mom turned out to be the manager Rachel had hired for the New Chance, and Parker Long, whose parents were both teachers at Eaglecrest High. They'd been coming over after school to do homework together and learn to ride with Sophie.

Becca was darling and sweet and, after some initial nervousness, had taken well to Ginger, one of the older trail horses who'd retired from herding work. Parker was not only impossibly cute, something Sophie had obviously noticed for herself, but he was also a natural-born athlete. Which, she thought, would probably come in handy if he were to stick to the goal of achieving Ryan Murphy's initial plan of becoming the town's first astronaut.

When Jack had learned that Scott was going to go to summer day camp, he'd announced that he didn't want to play T-ball this year but wanted to attend camp, too.

"Look at it this way," Sawyer had said, when Austin dithered over what Heather and Tom would have wanted, "we just escaped being *those people*."

"What people?"

"Those poor parents who live in kids' sports chauffeur hell."

She'd laughed. "Good point." Then signed the permission slip.

With life seeming to become more normal again, at least a new normal, Austin and Sawyer began acting like the teenage lovers they'd never dared be. They kissed nearly all night long on the porch swing after everyone was asleep. They enjoyed sometimes hot and fast, sometimes slow and sweet nooners on the bed in his cabin, and once, in a moment of pure lust when he'd been grooming Duke and she'd been brushing Blue, they'd climbed into the hayloft and learned that Winema had been right about the fantasy versus the reality.

"Not that it was bad," Sawyer said, brushing straw off his bare butt. Being a gentleman, he'd willingly taken the bottom position.

"It couldn't ever be bad," Austin said as she pulled her shirt over the new lacy bra she'd ordered online. "But I have to admit that I was a bit worried at first about mice."

"That's what those fat barn cats are for," he said. "You didn't seem too concerned."

She leaned up and touched her reddened, kiss-swollen lips to his. "That's because you're so good at distracting me."

"*You're* the distraction," he said. Then pulled her into his arms for a deeper, longer, definitely Olympic gold medal kiss.

To make room for all the family and friends, Mountain

View Middle School's graduation was held in the high school gym. A temporary stage had been set up for the students, who were sitting in metal folding chairs on the basketball court. The immediate families sat behind them, while other friends and well-wishers took to the bleachers.

The Murphys and Merrills took up the entire first row. The Murphys were represented by Sawyer, Ryan, Rachel, Cooper, Scott, Dan, Mitzi, and the Murphy brothers' grandparents, Betty and Mike. The Merrill contingent consisted of Austin, Jack, Buck, and Winema, who'd scored a family ticket without a word of complaint from the PTA volunteers who'd organized the event.

"Kira Taylor wasn't kidding when she said Sophie was going to win some awards," Austin murmured to Sawyer the third time the girl, clad in a burgundy cap and gown, climbed the stairs to the stage.

"She's one smart cookie," Sawyer said. "And so far, after an understandably bumpy start, pretty easy." He flashed Sophie two thumbs up as she caught his eye on the way back to her seat in the honors section between Becca and Parker. "And have you noticed that we haven't heard a certain former BFF's name called once?"

"I noticed," Austin murmured. "And I'm not sure it's seemly for adults to gloat about a child's lack of achievement."

"She stood Sophie up at her parents' funeral," he reminded her. "To go out on the lake with boys." Who, he'd learned from Cooper, had gotten a citation for speeding the ski boat too close to the little kids' shorefront wading zone.

"Good point," she decided. "I'm giving myself permission to gloat."

He took her hand in his and laced their fingers together

in that easy, familiar way he had. "We'll keep it to ourselves," he promised.

Afterwards, in the New Chance's private dining rooms that Brody had finished just in time for the celebration, they talked about what to do about the most surprising award Sophie had received. A week's scholarship to Sea Camp on the coast in Shelter Bay.

"I thought you wanted to grow up and take care of horses like Dad," Jack said.

"I do," Sophie said. "But this is the coolest biology camp, where I'd get to go out on boats and study whales and puffins and tide pools and all sorts of coastal environment. The seas and the land and sky are all connected. We need healthy land, like the Murphys and Merrills are doing with their ranches, to have healthy seas, and we need healthy seas to protect our land. Parker said his older brother went a couple years ago and it's really, really cool. But I never expected to win it! I didn't even know Ms. Taylor had nominated me."

"That's so exciting, and we're all really proud of you, sweetie," Austin said. "But your birthday comes during those two weeks. What about your party?"

"I honestly never wanted that tea thing, anyway," she admitted. "Not that it wouldn't be fun, I guess. But I really was doing it for Mom." There was a momentary sheen in her eyes she blinked away. "But Mom told me I'd do amazing things, and this is really, really amazing."

"It is," Sawyer agreed. "I knew a kid in my ranch management class who'd gone to it in high school. By the time we graduated, he'd switched majors and is now working studying orcas up in Puget Sound."

"That would be so cool," Sophie said. "Except I'm

going to be a vet."

"You've plenty of time to decide," Austin said, trying not to feel guilty for the flood of relief that she'd escape the tea-hat-making challenge.

"It's best to leave your options open," Ryan said. "If I'd stuck with my first goal, I wouldn't have ended up back here doing what I love."

"This is an exciting time for you, Sophie," Cooper added. "And a terrific experience."

"Though we'll miss you," Austin admitted.

"It's only two weeks," Sophie assured her. "And maybe we can have a barbecue party at the ranch when I get back."

"Absolutely," Austin said. "For family and friends."

"I'd like that." Then the girl's face suddenly fell. "But what about Misty?"

"Don't worry, we'll take care of her," Sawyer and Austin said together.

"Aren't you going to come home every night?" Jack asked.

"No." She didn't tack on "idiot child," but the tone was back, making Austin smile. She shared a look with Sawyer and knew yet again they were on the same wavelength. Sophie Campbell was getting her spunk back. "It's too far away. That's why it's called a *sleep-away* camp."

"I'm going to camp, too," Jack piped up, not wanting to be left out of the conversation. "It's not a sleep-away. But it's still going to be cool. We're going to study beaver dams and swim and row boats and do crafts with bark and stuff and even go up to the top of Modoc Mountain."

"You're going to climb a mountain?" Sophie challenged.

"Well, not exactly climb," he admitted. "But even better, we're going to ride the ski chairlift."

"But not all the way to the top," Winema entered the conversation. "Because that's reserved for my people."

"Really?" His freckled brow furrowed. "Why?"

"Because it's holy land. Like a church. Or a shrine. We believe our ancestors' spirits live among the clouds around the top of the mountain. So, we go there to collect herbs for ceremonies. And to talk, and pray to our ancestors."

"Really?" Jack's eyes widened.

"Really," she said. "For thousands of years it's where the spirits dwell in harmony with nature and man." She glanced over at Sophie. "It's all very interconnected, as you pointed out with your sea and land analogy."

"Do you pray to *your* ancestors?" Jack asked.

"Every year on the summer solstice," she said. "And other times. Just when I need to talk to them."

"You're really lucky," Jack said, "that you can talk to them whenever you want."

Winema smiled. "I am," she agreed.

Austin glanced over at Sophie, whose expression revealed that she was remembering that special conversation with her mother before the funeral. Then the conversation moved on, to the plans for the Fourth of July rodeo and August's Gold Dust Days, celebrating the commemoration of River's Bend's founding by Malachy Murphy.

To which Jack vowed that this year he was going to find the "biggest gold nugget ever!" Which was actually fool's gold seeded along the river bank so everyone panning could find some, but not a person in the room was about to share the ploy.

As the sheet cake decorated with a mortarboard, *Con-*

gratulations, and Sophie's name created with royal icing Austin had made for the occasion was brought out from the kitchen, Austin looked around the table and realized how all these people, with so many interwoven connections, had, in a very special way, created the big family she'd always dreamed of.

38

"IT SEEMS STRANGE without Sophie here," Austin said as she and Sawyer worked out in the corral with the colt. She appreciated his help since, although the colt was accustomed to her, it was good to get him used to being around strangers. Especially since the Flying Goose still took their cows up into the mountains for the summer, moved them around up there, then brought them back down, which involved a lot of different people and horses.

Being adaptable was especially important in this case, since the rancher planned to have the colt ridden by a swing rider, a cowboy who rides along the main body of the herd, keeping them bunched together and moving. Personally, Austin thought the Bar M's and Sawyer's way of just moving pastures was a great deal easier, especially since it had been proven better for the cattle, but she wasn't one to tell others how to run their businesses. Unless it involved mistreating her horses.

"It's also quiet during the day without Jack," he said. "I saw Buck driving out when I came back from town."

"He's off to the VFW. He's got it in his head that the ranch needs a new website, now that we're out of the stock business. It's long overdue," she admitted. "But I've been so busy. So, he's going to see if Dalton Osborne would be willing to take on the job."

"He updated the Bar M's last fall."

"So Dan told Dad. I guess he's also done Fred Wiley's Feed and Seed and the New Chance."

"Rachel says he's better than the guy she hired to do the one for her catering business back east."

"Well, I'm just glad Dad's finally getting out of the house. Thanks to Layla."

She glanced over at the house, which was partly covered with plastic now that Brody had started in on the remodeling for the pool. She'd feared her dad would balk at what he'd think of as charity, but all it had taken was to suggest that it would be a great surprise belated birthday gift from the community for Sophie, and he'd been all in.

It was funny, she thought. Although he'd always been loving but gruff with her, over the past weeks, Tom and Heather's kids had managed to wrap him around their little fingers.

"I guess Brody took off for lunch."

"Yeah. He said he had to drive over to K. Falls to pick up some stuff."

"And Winema's babysitting grandkids over at her daughter's place. So," she said. "It's just us."

"Just us. All alone," Sawyer agreed.

"It seems, being two intelligent people, we should be able to think of something to do to fill the time," she mused.

"I've got a suggestion."

She tilted her head and looked up at the devils dancing in his eyes. "Great minds."

AT FIRST JACK was unhappy that Scott had chipped a tooth and had to go to the dentist on the very day that the campers were going to go up the mountain. He liked the other kids okay, but Scott was almost like a brother. Not old enough to be bossy, but it was good to have a guy to talk to about stuff. Like about his mom and dad dying. It was weird. There were times when he'd close his eyes and not even remember what they looked like. Which Scott had told him was normal, so his stomach had mostly stopped aching whenever it happened.

Scott had also told him how Cooper had taken him and his mom on the outlaw train ride, and how cool it had been, so Jack had asked Sawyer, who'd told him that he should've thought of that, and he and Austin would take him this very weekend.

Which was another thing. Before she'd gone off to that sea camp, Sophie had told him she thought Austin and Sawyer might get married. Which he thought would be really neat because then he'd have a new mom and dad. But she'd said that they might have other kids and what if they liked those kids better?

Jack didn't think that would happen, because Scott was all the time saying that he really hoped his new dad and mom would have a baby brother or sister after they got married, and he said that Sophie was just being dramatic, like girls sometimes were.

It was all really confusing. Which was why Jack had come up with his secret plan.

"YOU KNOW," AUSTIN said after they'd let the colt run

back to his herd in the pasture and put the tack away. "I just realized that you've never seen my bathroom. Brody remodeled it a couple years ago."

"It's a little hard to come up with a reason to go up to your room when your dad's in the house. And I'm a little too old to be climbing up a tree to sneak in your window."

"Yeah." She swept a look over the snug blue *Bikini Kill* T-shirt clinging to his hot, sweaty, ripped torso. "I can tell how ancient you are. And have you noticed that all your shirts just happen to be girl bands?"

He grinned. Shrugged. "What can I say? I like women." He took his time checking her out the same way she had him. "One particular woman especially. One who, unless my lying eyes deceive me, isn't wearing anything under that shirt."

Hers was a boring plain navy and felt as wet as his looked. The temperature had been building all day, feeling like an evening thunderstorm was brewing. Meanwhile, a storm of a different type altogether was rising in his eyes.

"That's for me to know and you to find out," she said. She rubbed the back of her neck. "I'm hot, sweaty, and I smell like a horse. What would you say to a shower?"

"You're on."

The shower in question was in the ensuite bathroom off her room. It was a walk-in, with no glass doors to clean, nor curtain to stick to your body on a cold winter's day. The floor was heated, and for pure luxury, which they didn't need today with the temperature climbing into the nineties, two red heat lamps had been installed overhead.

"Wow. There's room for a party in here," he said when he saw it.

"That was exactly the idea," she said, pulling off her

shirt.

There was a time, when she'd been younger and all the girls had been flashing their boobs, lifted up and pushed together by those silly water bras, at Sawyer Murphy that she'd been afraid if they ever did make love, he'd be totally turned off by her AA cups. Even the first time they'd made love, although she'd matured into a full A, she'd still wished that she could wave a magic wand and have Katy Perry's or Scarlett Johansson's breasts suddenly show up on her chest.

But amazingly, he'd loved them. Just as he made her lack of curves everywhere else seem sexy, running his hands and mouth all over the body that had been, like his, built by hard, physical work.

"God, I love your body," he said, as he had so many times over the past days.

She'd already pulled her boots off before coming into the house. Now she shimmied out of her jeans, showing off the new scarlet, high-cut lacy bikini panties. An affair, she'd discovered, was dangerous to her credit card. "I'm glad to hear that," she purred in a way she'd only ever done with Sawyer. "Since it's all yours."

"Right answer." He yanked the shirt over his head, threw it on the floor next to her clothes, stripped, then reached in and turned on the water. Which, like the foreman's cabin, featured hot water on demand. Then he pulled her into the water, beneath the six sprays that told Sawyer what he'd already figured out for himself. That inside that lean and fit cowgirl body dwelt the heart of a hedonist.

Going down on his knees on the tile floor, he took the low-cut waistband of the sexy-as-sin panties and pulled them down her legs with his teeth.

After she'd stepped out of them, he stood up, grabbed a bottle of body soap—strawberries today—and, working up a lather between his palms, began to smooth it all over her body. "You smell good enough to eat," he growled against her slick, wet stomach.

And as the room steamed up and the warm water streamed over them, Sawyer feasted.

THEY'D JUST MANAGED to stumble out of the shower when Sawyer's phone, still in the pocket of his jeans, began to chime. "It might be one of the kids," he said, digging it out, which wasn't all that easy since they were inside out. "Hey, Coop," he answered when he saw his brother's name on the screen.

"What?" He hit the speaker icon. "Say that again."

"We got a call from the camp director," Cooper Murphy said, once again using his official sheriff's voice. "Jack got away from the group." He paused a heartbeat, during which time Austin couldn't breathe. "On the mountain."

39

As Sawyer broke every speeding law in the state driving to the mountain, Austin seated beside him. The adrenaline racing through her, speeded up even more by the wild beating of her heart, had her head spinning.

"How did he get away?" she asked. Then waved the question away. "Never mind. He's Jack. The mistake was letting him go to that stupid day camp. Even Heather and Tom didn't think he was old enough to play junior Little League."

"Don't play 'if only,'" Sawyer said. "It doesn't do any good. He'll be all right."

"You've grown up hiking and riding on this mountain the same as I have," she argued. "You know how large it is. How many crisscrossing trails. How many creeks and ponds, and oh, God, he could fall or drown or run into a mountain lion or a bear or—"

"We'll find him," Sawyer repeated. "Coop's called in all his deputies."

"Which would be two."

"True. But people are coming from Klamath and Lake Counties. The National Guard offered some copters to patrol the area, and all the ground and air search units are standing by, waiting to be deployed. He's not going to be hiding, Austin. He'll be looking for them at the same time they're looking for him. They'll find him. You'll see."

"Like Cooper found Ellen?" she shot back, her nerves tangling, her gut roiling. She'd no sooner said the words than she wished she could take them back. "I'm sorry. That was cruel."

"But true," he allowed. "And I'd rather have you say it to me than my brother."

"So many people get lost up here every year," she said. Hadn't she gone looking for them herself? And some of those, older and far more experienced than Jack, didn't make it off the mountain alive. *Please, please, please.* The single prayer repeated over and over again in an endless loop.

The command center was already being set up at the Glacier Summit trailhead, where Jack had first been discovered missing, when they arrived. Teams were being organized, sectors assigned. Whenever she'd taken part in a search, she'd always cared for the lost person, but she'd also always been able to keep some emotional distance. Not today.

Rising high to dominate the mountain range on the north end of the basin, Modoc Mountain boasted three glaciers from which numerous creeks and streams flowed, along with beautiful alpine lakes, which could prove deadly to a lost, exhausted, frightened child. A little boy who, having wandered far enough and long enough, might foolishly pause to take a drink, or even wade into the lake to cool off from the late-afternoon heat that was growing more and more oppressive.

The mountain was tall enough to make its own weather, and the thick, black clouds it was gathering around its snow-clad summit were making this situation even more dangerous.

"It's going to storm," Austin said, her blood chilling despite the heat.

One summer, when she'd been riding trail, helping the crew at the Arrowhead spread take a herd up to the high pasture, a thunderstorm had blown in quickly, making the air so electric that all the hair on her arms had stood on end and her ponytail had shot straight up. Seconds later, a jagged bolt of lightning had speared down from a low, rumbling cloud, striking a cow, killing it instantly, and setting off a stampede that had risked lives as the cowboys had scrambled to try to round up the cattle again before they went running over the edge of one of the many canyons.

Sawyer shot a look up at the sky. "We've got awhile," he said. "And yeah, it's scary as hell," he admitted, as if not wanting to dismiss her very real fears. "But the odds are in his, and our, favor. He hasn't been gone all that long, and he's outnumbered. We'll find him."

As a distant rumbling came from the mountaintop and one of the anvil-shaped clouds blocked out the sun, Austin kept praying. *Please. Please. Please.*

JACK WAS BEGINNING to think this might not have been his best ever idea. He thought all he had to do was to just slip away behind those trees, come around again, and follow the trail he and the other campers and his counselors had been on while they continued back down to the ski lift for the ride back down the mountain.

But he hadn't figured there'd be so many trails. And some would stop, so he'd have to cut through the brush and around more trees, until he found it again. Or maybe it was a different one. When he got to where two trails crossed, he couldn't figure out which way to go. Parker, Sophie's boyfriend, had been telling him all about how to navigate by stars, but it wasn't dark yet, so even if he could remember what he'd said, it wasn't any help now.

He did know that the sun rose in the east and went down in the west. That's why his mom was always taking pictures of sunsets, saying Oregon had the most beautiful sunsets of anywhere in the whole wide world. But it was hard to even see the sun through all the trees, and when he did, it didn't look like it was going to be setting right away.

Which was when he realized that knowing east or west, or even north or south, wouldn't help him, because the trail they'd been on didn't go straight up the mountain, it went around. So he didn't know which direction the ski lift or home was.

He stepped over some deer poop scattered on the rocky trail. He'd learned to tell all different kinds of wild animal poop in one of the camp workshops, which he'd really liked, but a lot of the girls had made lots of stupid *eewwww* sounds, and some had even refused to look at it.

Especially the bear poop that had fur in it from some animal it had eaten, though mostly bears liked fruit and berries. He passed some wild blueberry bushes and a tree stump that looked like the picture the counselor had shown him where a bear had torn apart a tree looking for honey. Winnie the Pooh and his honey pot was a pretty good story when he'd been younger. But no way did Jack want to meet up with a bear.

He wasn't on the river, which he knew was big and wide and, his parents and Austin and Sawyer had warned him, dangerous, but he had just come to a creek. Sophie, who was all about saving the planet since she'd gotten accepted at Sea Camp, had told him creeks and streams flowed into rivers, then rivers into bigger rivers, then finally into the ocean. So, if he followed this little creek, he'd eventually get to Black Bear River. Right? And then he could find his way back to Green Springs.

CAL POTTER WAS not only River's Bend's volunteer fire chief and the senior of the department's two deputies, his five-year-old German shepherd, Marley, who usually hung around the fire station, was a trained and certified SAR (search and rescue) dog. Having witnessed him working before, Austin knew that, while some dogs tended to air scent naturally and others preferred ground scenting, Marley would flip between the two, depending on the situation.

Cooper had told Austin that he was calling Cal, so she'd brought along a pair of Jack's Captain America underpants and his Batman pajama top she'd pulled from the hamper.

"Okay, Marley," Cal said, putting the underpants under the dog's ultrasensitive nose. "This is Jack. Okay? Jack. Got it?"

The dog barked and began pulling at his lead. Getting out in the woods, sniffing stuff, finding someone who earned you treats was akin to spending a weekend at Disneyland to Marley.

"Okay," Cal told him. "Let's go find Jack . . . Austin,

Sawyer, you guys come with us. The kid's gonna be wanting you."

Marley took off, headed up the trail, Cal following. Since the clouds that had been gathering fast, racing across what only an hour ago had been a bright blue June sky, had darkened to pewter and had begun to weep rain, Austin dearly hoped the older man's optimism was justified. *Please, please, please,* she prayed as they headed up the mountain to find Heather and Tom's son.

❧

JACK WANTED TO be home. It was dark beneath the trees, and rain was dripping on him as he trudged along, trying not to listen to the sounds of rustling in the needles and leaves underneath his sneakers. He'd been hot earlier, but now he was getting cold and scared. Scared of never being found, scared of dying, like his parents and Riley and Marmalade and his grandparents before he was even born. And scared of getting in really bad trouble when he did get found. He wondered if Sawyer was one of those dads who spanked kids. His dad never did. His mom, either, but he'd known a boy in preschool who'd told stories about being spanked for all sorts of things.

Birds chirped and squirrels had chattered down at him from the treetops when he'd first started out on his quest, like one of the ones in the *How To Train Your Dragon* video game Santa had brought him for Christmas. But now, as the rain started coming down really hard and the wind started blowing, everything had gone quiet. Making the woods really spooky like those trees in *Wizard of Oz*, which his mom voted for a lot when they were choosing movies to watch.

"That's what you need," he muttered as he climbed over a log that had fallen across the trail. "Some magic shoes that you could click and be back home. At the ranch."

Which, for a few minutes, got him thinking that it was funny how, when he thought about being transported home, it was Green Springs, and not his old house, he could see in his mind. He was going to have to ask Scott when he quit thinking of Connecticut as his real home. If he hadn't known better, Jack would've thought Scott had lived in River's Bend all his life.

He heard the sound of water rushing and got excited. Maybe he was finally at the river! Then he turned the corner and found the sound coming not from Black Bear River but from a big waterfall roaring over a cliff into the pool at the very end of the trail.

40

I T WAS THERE Marley found Jack, sound asleep in a grove of conifers, not ten minutes from where he'd taken off. He'd been circling around, and if it hadn't been for Horse Camp Falls, he might have made it back on his own.

"Hey, Jack," Sawyer said as the boy stirred, awakened by Marley's joyous barking as Cal tossed pieces of beef jerky the dog snatched out of the air. "Whatcha doing up here?"

Jack sat up, rubbing his eyes. Tears had left streaks in his muddied face. "I was climbing up to the top to pray to my mom and dad. Like Winema."

"Oh, darling." Austin crouched down beside him. "You can do that anywhere."

"I can?"

"Sure," Sawyer said. "I prayed to my mom just the other day. Climb up and we'll take you home."

"I wanted to talk to Mom," Jack explained as they made their way back to the command center. "I wanted to tell her that you guys are really nice and I was glad you were my new parents and I really like living at Green Springs."

"I'm glad," Austin said.

"And I wanted to ask her if you guys were going to have any other kids besides me and Sophie. And if you'd love them any different from us."

"I'm up for more kids," Sawyer said. "If Austin is. After we get married."

"I've always wanted a large family," Austin said. "And of course we'd love you all the same." Then as Sawyer's words sank in, she stopped in her tracks. "Wait. We're getting married?"

"Well, sure. It's time, don't you think?" Sawyer asked.

"Yes, of course." This was not something she was going to screw up again. But . . . "Did you happen to have any plans to ask me?"

"As a matter of fact, I have two steaks in the fridge, along with two big Klamath bakers, and some more of that green stuff. And a marble cheesecake and raspberry sauce Rachel made up. I figured I'd make that dinner we missed. If it works for you, we can still do it tonight."

They'd been walking one by one in a line, Marley in front, followed by Cal, then Sawyer and Jack with Austin bringing up the rear. Now she stepped off the trail, went around, and kissed him.

"That totally works for me," she said. "I'll want to get married soon. Maybe a double wedding with Rachel and Cooper."

"Sounds great to me," he said. "I'll bet they'll be all for it."

"All right, then. And I'll need a dress. I wonder what flowers Rachel's chosen. She's got such good taste, I know they'll be perfect, and . . ."

As they continued down the mountain, his soon-to-be

adopted son on his back, Austin Merrill busily making plans on starting this new future together, Sawyer thought how he might have taken off on a long and winding road with many detours, but after all these years, he was finally home.

Where he belonged.

With the woman he'd loved all of his life.

Did you miss the first book in the River's Bend series?

Here's an excerpt from *River's Bend.*
(Cooper and Rachel's story.)

"THE BID IS fifteen hundred and sixty dollars. Do we have fifteen-seventy? Seventy-five? Who'll give me fifteen-eighty?"

Rachel Hathaway stood silently at the back of the wainscoted room, her gray eyes resolutely dry as she watched the past fourteen years of her life being sold off piece by piece. The thick cloud of perfume hovering overhead was beginning to give her a headache.

When she was a little girl growing up on an Iowa farm, her parents had encouraged her to believe in fairy tales. An obedient child, Rachel willingly complied. After graduating with an advertising degree from Iowa State University, she went off to New York City, where she got a job working as a copywriter for a prince of a man named Alan Hathaway.

On their first date, she and Alan decided they wanted to have children together. On their second, Alan proposed and Rachel moved into his one-bedroom castle in Brooklyn. As the years went by, Alan's business grew by leaps and bounds, allowing them to move into a larger palace in Connecticut where Scott—heir to the Hathaway Advertising throne—was born.

The only problem with fairy tales, Rachel had discovered, was that they didn't warn you that the prince could die of a perforated ulcer, the creditors could end up with the castle, and it could be back to the ashes for Cinderella.

"Ladies and gentlemen," the dapper auctioneer cajoled winningly, "may I remind you that this table is in excellent condition. Even without the matching chairs, it could be considered a steal at two thousand."

Remembering the years of celebratory dinners shared around the elegant dining room set, Rachel wondered how anyone could put a price on love. She'd worked the floral needlepoint covers for the chairs herself that long-ago winter when she'd been pregnant with Scotty.

Flushed with the glow of impending fatherhood and concerned for her health, Alan had insisted she quit working. Bored nearly out of her mind, she'd taught herself needlework to pass the long hours spent waiting for her husband's return from his Madison Avenue advertising agency.

"Fifteen-seventy-five," the auctioneer conceded when his efforts were met by a stony wall of silence. "Going once, twice, gone to the lady in the red hat. The next item going up for bid is a superb-quality Sheraton revival satinwood bookcase."

"You look as if you could use a break," Janet Morrison murmured as the workmen carried the dining room set from the dais.

"I'm fine," Rachel insisted, her gaze directed toward the bookcase.

She and Alan had discovered it in a little out-of-the-way shop in London the summer Scott had turned two. They'd justified the hefty purchase price by telling each other that the bookcase would become a family heirloom. Something their son would pass on to his children.

"Well, I'm in desperate need of a cigarette," Janet said. "Come keep me company."

Taking Rachel by the arm, she practically dragged her out of the library, down the long terrazzo hallway and out onto the back terrace.

"I thought the doctor warned you to give those things up if you wanted a speedy recovery," Rachel reminded her long-time friend and neighbor.

"I still have a few weeks until surgery." Janet lit the cigarette with a gold monogrammed lighter. "Besides, everyone I know gains at least ten pounds when they quit smoking. I'm attempting to forestall the inevitable as long as possible."

At forty-eight, Janet was fourteen years older than Rachel. Her honeyed complexion was nearly flawless, save for the small network of lines fanning outward from her eyes and the slight bracketing around her russet-tinted lips. Like so many other women in the neighborhood, she was resolutely fit, tanned, and blond.

Cursed with fair skin that refused to tan and rain-straight black hair, Rachel had, on more than one occasion, envied her best friend.

"I still don't understand why you feel you need a face-lift," she said honestly. "I think you look great."

"Easy for you to say," Janet retorted. "Your husband didn't just hire a new secretary who looks as if she should be turning cartwheels and leading cheers for the high school football team." She groaned the moment the words left her mouth. "Oh, damn, honey. I'm sorry. It just slipped out."

Rachel could feel her lips smiling, but inside she remained numb, as she had for the past eighteen months. "Don't worry about it. I'm fine. Really."

It was Janet's turn to submit Rachel to a lengthy examination. "No," she said finally, "you're not. Oh, you've been putting on a good show, but anyone who truly knows you could see that you've just been going through the motions. Although it's no wonder, considering the mess Alan left behind."

Rachel didn't immediately answer. Instead, from her vantage point atop the hill, she looked out over the acres of serene, unspoiled woodland, realizing that this would be the last time she'd be able to enjoy the view. The trees were still a deep, leafy green, but in another few weeks they'd be ablaze in their autumnal coats of red, gold, and bronze, and she'd miss seeing the free-flowing stream cutting through the brilliantly colored forest.

Come winter the stream would freeze solid, but for the moment it tumbled merrily over moss-covered rocks, oblivious of its fate. The same way she'd been before Alan's death.

"Do you remember when I began volunteering one day a week helping people who visited the food bank fill out SNAP applications?" she asked.

"Of course. I didn't really believe that there were any food stamp recipients in Connecticut."

"I know. You asked me to bring a few extra stamps home for pâté and caviar."

"We were having a party that weekend, and every little bit helps. Is this trip down memory lane leading anywhere?"

Rachel dragged her hand through her hair. Her simple

gold wedding band—one of the few pieces of jewelry she hadn't sold—gleamed in the afternoon sun. "I met so many women there, women who'd led lives of convenience and comfort, who were suddenly forced into dire financial straits due to divorce or their husband's death.

"They weren't underprivileged. They were intelligent and well educated. Yet each had made the mistake of allowing her husband to make all the decisions, to handle the money without her knowledge or consent. I felt sorry for them, but inside, I couldn't help feeling a little smug, you know? Because Alan and I always shared everything." She sighed heavily. "At least I thought we did."

"How could you have known the recession had put Alan's business into such a slump? He was only trying to protect you."

That was the same thing Rachel had been telling herself over and over again these past months as she'd struggled to pay off the debts incurred by her late husband. Unfortunately, she hadn't reaped any financial rewards by understanding Alan's motivation.

"I know. I just wish he'd trusted me enough to come to me with his problems."

Janet put her hand on Rachel's arm. "And what could you have done?"

Looking down at her friend's perfectly manicured fingernails, it occurred to Rachel that her own nails were ragged and unpolished.

"The same thing I've done," she answered without hesitation. "Sell the Manhattan apartment, the house, the furniture, the jewelry, take Scotty out of private school, and return to work full time."

"That's not the life Alan wanted for you."

"Well, like it or not, it's the life I ended up with. If he'd only bothered to ask, I would have told him that I'd rather go back to our first apartment than continue living in Connecticut without him."

"He undoubtedly believed he could turn the business around." Rachel exhaled a soft, rippling little sigh. "I know." And he would have. If it hadn't killed him first. Both women remained silent for a time, gazing out over the rolling expanse of lawn. The tennis court needed work. The red clay was badly scuffed and covered with debris. Dead leaves floated on the swimming pool she kept forgetting to cover.

"So, how's Scotty taking the move?"

"I thought he'd be upset about changing schools for the second time in eighteen months and leaving all his friends behind, but all he talks about is moving to the Wild West. In fact, not only have cowboys replaced the Yankees in his nine-year-old hierarchy, I haven't had to listen to a Spiderman or Masters of the Universe plot for six weeks."

"Kids are resilient."

"Isn't that the truth? Although it was tough in the beginning, now you'd never know that his world had been turned upside down." Rachel was grateful for her son's apparent ability to bounce back from what had been a disastrous eighteen months.

"How about you? How are *you* holding up?"

Rachel took her time in answering as a covey of quail bobbed across the lawn. Drawing in a breath, she leaned her head against one of five white wooden posts supporting the slate roof. The post bore the inscription *Alan Loves Rachel*. Her husband had carved the romantic declaration the weekend they'd moved into the house nine years ago.

"I'm fine. Really," she said as her friend gave her a long, judicious look. "You're still too thin, but I think you're beginning to look a little less tense. And either you've discovered some miracle cosmetic cover-up I don't know about, or the circles beneath your eyes are finally beginning to fade."

"I've been sleeping better lately." Ever since she'd made the decision to move to Oregon. "Sometimes all through the night."

"Well, that's something. Did you finally break down and take my advice?"

"Advice?"

"About seeing Larry Newman."

Dr. Lawrence Newman was president of the country club and on the board of directors of several hospitals, as well as being a leading psychiatrist. There were probably very few people in Rachel's circle whom he hadn't seen on a professional basis, causing Alan to have once suggested that if the good doctor ever decided to write his memoirs, the book would probably sell out in Greenwich within minutes.

"I had one appointment."

"Really? How did it go?" Rachel shrugged.

"It didn't. I didn't go back."

"If it's the money, I can lend you Larry's fee."

They both knew it would be useless to offer Rachel the funds outright. While the rest of her life may be in tatters, Rachel's pride had remained formidable. Ignoring legal advice to declare bankruptcy to get out from under the burden of her husband's business responsibilities, she'd insisted on paying off every last dollar, at considerable personal sacrifice.

"It's not the money." Rachel felt her cheeks burn as she remembered the look of pity on the psychiatrist's handsome face. After the pity had come the pass.

"Larry hit on you, didn't he?"

"You don't sound surprised."

"Rachel, practically every woman at the club has had an affair with the guy."

"You're kidding."

"Not at all. Don't tell me you never noticed? Ever since he moved to town, there's been enough hanky-panky to generate a new *Sex in the Suburbs* series that would make *Peyton Place* look tame by comparison."

"I never knew." Rachel wondered if Janet had participated in any of the alleged hanky-panky.

"How could you, since whenever you and Alan showed up at any functions, you couldn't keep your eyes—or your hands—off each other." Janet shook her head. "Didn't anyone ever tell you wide-eyed innocents that lust is supposed to die by the first anniversary?"

"And love? When does that die?"

"By the fifth. At least."

"I never stopped loving Alan."

"Nor he you. That's what made the rest of us jealous as hell." She stubbed the cigarette out on the stone terrace with the toe of her Christian Louboutin pump. "I do wish you'd spend tonight with us instead of staying at some dreary motel."

"It's not dreary." Just not the Four Seasons Alan would have booked. "And I truly appreciate the offer, but I really want to spend our last night in town alone with Scotty. In case he gets depressed about leaving the only home he's ever known and wants to talk about it. Also, because of delays cataloging everything by the auction house, instead of moving last month, as I'd hoped, it's already mid-September. Oregon schools started earlier than here and I don't want him too far behind."

"He's a bright kid. He shouldn't have any trouble catching up," Janet assured her. "Look, I understand why you want to open your own restaurant. You've gone to cooking school, you've catered every party around here for the past five years, even before you took my advice and started charging, and everyone loves your food. But what in the hell made you decide on that Last Chance Café in Oregon? What's wrong with Connecticut? Or even Manhattan?"

"It's the *New Chance*," Rachel corrected. "In the first place, I could never afford to open a restaurant in Manhattan and Connecticut isn't that much less expensive. For what six month's rent would cost here, I was able to buy the café outright. And have enough left over to rent a house."

"Both sight unseen," Janet reminded her.

"There were photos on the internet." The real estate agent had sent the link after Rachel had responded to a classified listing in *Restaurant Magazine*.

"Blurry photos. And what you could see isn't going to win you any Michelin stars." "I'll admit it looks as if it could use a little work. But it's rather . . . unique." In a rustic, Oregon ranching country way.

"Unique." Janet sniffed. "That sounds like real estate jargon for a dump. Along the lines of a 'Honeymoon Special.' Or 'Handyman Fix-up.' For heaven's sake, Rachel, just because Alan died doesn't mean you have to banish yourself to the wilderness."

"I'm not banishing myself," Rachel repeated what she'd been saying since she'd come up with the plan. "I'm starting a new life." In a new town and a new house where every room she went into didn't remind her of her husband, forcing her to face all the years they'd never have together.

"So, start a new life here," Janet insisted. "Expand your catering company or open a small restaurant, begin dating again, enjoy yourself for a change."

"I tried dating, remember?" Her one-time excursion into the singles world, with the agent who'd listed the Manhattan apartment Alan used whenever he stayed in the city, had turned out to be an unqualified disaster.

Janet shrugged. "So, Bernie was a bust. There are a lot more fish in the sea."

"That's probably true enough. But I'm not into angling these days."

"I'm really going to miss you." Janet threw her arms around Rachel.

Moisture stung her eyelids as Rachel returned the hug. "And I'm going to miss you."

"I'll come visit," Janet promised as they parted.

"By next summer I should have the café running well enough to take a few days off," Rachel said. "We'll drive over to the beach. The scenery's supposed to be magnificent, and Chef Madeline Durand has opened a restaurant and cooking school on the coast."

"I'll bet her restaurant's not in a log cabin," Janet said.

"You'd win that bet. But it is in the Shelter Bay farmhouse she grew up in."

"How quaint." Janet shook her head. "Sorry. I really don't mean to sound so negative. I just don't want to lose my BFF. I'll fly out there next summer," she confirmed.

Rachel wished Janet wasn't making it sound as if she were planning a trip on a Conestoga wagon to the wild and wooly western wilderness country.

Her decision hadn't been entirely impulsive. Using due diligence, she had, after all, searched out River's Bend's website and discovered that the town that billed itself as "Oregon's Most Western Town—where spurs have a job to do and cowboy hats aren't a fashion accessory," had a year-round population of three thousand, eight-hundred and thirty-six citizens. The top two industries were ranching and tourism, the second due to its outdoor lifestyle, proliferation of dude ranches, and the number of western movies that had been filmed there.

"It's a date," she said. Both women's smiles were forced. As they walked back into the house, Rachel knew that in spite of all best intentions and promises, their lives, which had been entwined for so many years, were inexorably drifting apart.

To keep up with publication dates, other news, and a chance to win books and other cool stuff, subscribe to the JoAnn Ross newsletter from her website at www. JoAnnRoss.com. Also connect with her on Facebook, Twitter, Instagram, and Pinterest.

Other Books from JoAnn Ross

The Shelter Bay series
The Homecoming
One Summer
On Lavender Lane
Moonshell Beach
Sea Glass Winter
Castaway Cove
You Again
Beyond the Sea (pre-publication title, A Sea Change)
Sunset Point
Christmas in Shelter Bay, November, 2016

The Castlelough series
A Woman's Heart
Fair Haven
Legends Lake
Briarwood Cottage
Beyond the Sea

River's Bend Series
River's Bend (Cooper's story)
Long Road Home (Sawyer's story) Pre-publication was Hot Shot

Orchid Island Series
Sun Kissed

7 BRIDES for 7 Brothers Series
Finn—7 Brides for 7 Brothers (Book 7), December, 2016

About The Author

JoAnn Ross wrote her first novella—a tragic romance about two star-crossed mallard ducks—for a second grade writing assignment.

The paper earned a gold star.

And JoAnn kept writing.

She's now written around one hundred novels (she quit keeping track long ago), has been published in twenty-six countries, and is a member of the Romance Writers of America's Honor Roll of best-selling authors. Two of her titles have been excerpted in *Cosmopolitan* magazine and her books have also been published by the Doubleday, Rhapsody, Literary Guild, and Mystery Guild book clubs.

JoAnn lives with her husband and two fuzzy rescued dogs, who pretty much rule the house, in the Pacific Northwest.

Sign up to receive the latest news from JoAnn
joannross.com/newsletter

Visit JoAnn's Website
www.joannross.com

Like JoAnn on Facebook
facebook.com/JoAnnRossbooks

Follow JoAnn on Twitter
twitter.com/JoAnnRoss

Follow JoAnn on Goodreads
goodreads.com/author/show/31311.JoAnn_Ross

Follow JoAnn on Pinterest
pinterest.com/JoAnnRossBooks

Follow JoAnn on Instagram
instagram.com/joannrossbooks

Made in the USA
Middletown, DE
10 June 2018